I0778354

# Rock and a Hard Place
## VOL. 1, ISSUE 7

### WINTER 2022

| | |
|---|---|
| EDITOR-IN-CHIEF | *Roger Nokes* |
| MANAGING EDITOR | *Jay Butkowski* |
| CONTRIBUTING EDITOR | *Albert Tucher* |
| ASSOCIATE EDITOR | *Paul J. Garth* |
| ASSOCIATE EDITOR | *Libby Cudmore* |
| ASSOCIATE EDITOR | *R.S. Sullivan* |
| GUARDIAN ANGEL | *Jonathan Elliott* |
| COVER ART | *Heather Garth* |

FIND US ON THE WEB: *www.rockandahardplacemag.com*

FOLLOW US ON FACEBOOK: *@RHP.Press*

FOLLOW US ON TWITTER: *@RHP_Press*

EMAIL US: *editors@rockandahardplacemag.com*


ISBN: 979-8-9852904-3-1 (Paperback)

ISBN: 979-8-9852904-4-8 (eBook)



*Rock and a Hard Place Magazine* is a labor of love, produced by a team of volunteer editors to showcase the best in dark fiction, crime, dystopian fiction, and noir. For access to behind-the-scenes content, including audio conversations with the creators and exclusive stories and artwork, and to contribute financially to the cause, join our Patreon at: https://www.patreon.com/join/rhpmag. To make a tax-deductible donation to RHP, visit https://fundraising.fracturedatlas.org/rock-and-a-hard-place-press-llc.

# DEDICATION

Lucky Issue 7 is dedicated to all those people who,
if it wasn't for bad luck, would have no luck at all.

# ACKNOWLEDGMENTS

***Rock and a Hard Place Magazine*** lives and breathes through the creative expression of emotions and ideas contained within. We're eternally grateful to the artists, authors and editors who contribute a small slice of themselves to put on the page. Their commitment to the vision of our publishing house—a vision of subversive empathy, of the importance in highlighting the humanity and emotional conflict inherent in noir—means the world to us.

Thank you to our readers for caring enough to devote your time to these stories, and thank you to our Patreon financial backers for putting your money where our mouths are:

Christopher Witty
Dustin Walker
Jamie Beaty
Mahaley Lozano
Mark Pelletier
Rob Smith
Jay Bechtol
Susan Kuchinskas
Todd Robins
Liz Renner
Susan Jessen
Scott Cumming
Richard Risemberg
Ted Flanagan
Chris Rhatigan
Ryan Citron

# CONTENTS

## VISUAL ART

# FOREWORD:

A mentor of mine once told me that noir is "bad things happening to bad people." He would know, he was a piece of shit who flushed his life and writing career down the toilet for a couple bottles of drugstore rum and the implied promise of grad-student pussy. It's an easy sentiment to reach for. A cheap one even, mired in the mortal fallacy that if you stay behind the line that they've drawn—the cops, your boss, God—you have nothing to worry about.

But what can I say? These are noir times we're living in, through no fault of our own. And there's a comfort, almost, in reaching for noir when life gets grim. Sort of like reading advice columns or relationship advice on Reddit. It puts your life in perspective. At least I'm not locked in a car trunk, as Leo Rosser finds himself in Jason Allison's "The Trunk." I've never found a dead body in a shitty motel bathroom, the way the characters in Rob D Smith's "As Long as You Look Faraway" did. Maybe I can handle another goddamn Zoom meeting. Because we're all good people, right? Okay so maybe we lie every so often. Maybe we go where we shouldn't go. Maybe we do that little thing that our brain tells us not to do, because it's wrong, morally or legally. But who's keeping score, right? Everyone else gets away with it. No reason I shouldn't too.

But if these days have proven anything, it's that we're all a little bad luck away from being the main characters in our own personal noir. You can be doing the right thing—protesting police brutality and violence against people of color—and some smug little shit will walk away clean after putting a bullet in your back. You get laid off. You get sick. You make a bad choice that seems like the only one to make in the moment, because you don't have the gift of foresight. Anxious times. Last-ditch measures.

Noir isn't about bad things happening to bad people. It's about shitty things happening to desperate people.

And we're all desperate sometimes.


Libby Cudmore,

*Associate Editor*

*January 2022*


For the RHP Editorial Board: Roger, Jay, Albert, Libby, and Jonathan

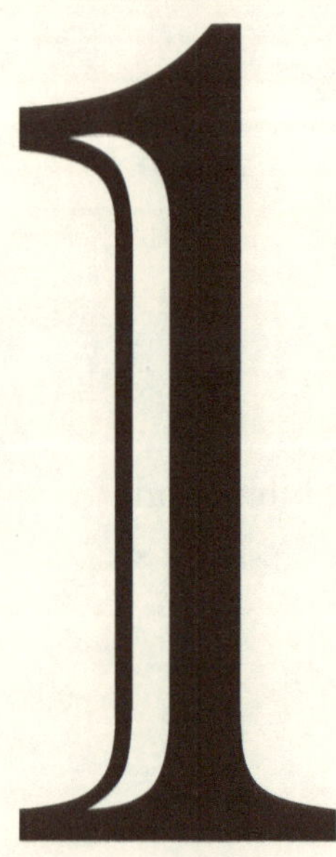

"Leo was alone again. Which wasn't a good thing to be, coming off a serious bender."

# THE TRUNK
### Jason Allison

This wasn't the first time Leo Rosser had been locked in the trunk of a car. It was, however, the first time he'd been locked inside his own car. Two things separated his situation today from the one back in '95. First, Leo was alone, and grateful for the room. The two hours he and Vinny had spent stuffed into Vinny's father's El Dorado had been . . . unpleasant. Second, this time around Leo was the instrument of his own imprisonment.

Meaning he'd locked himself in.

On purpose.

Leo shifted inside his cherry, year-old 1998 Lincoln Mark VIII (in white pearlescent). He'd removed the milk crate filled with Armor All bottles from the trunk, but wondered now if a professional kidnap/robbery team would've done the same before ordering Leo in. At gunpoint. On pain of death. Because that's what happened.

Yes, Officer, that is exactly what happened.

The law, for Leo, wasn't so much expected as planned on. Cops were not, historically speaking, people Leo gravitated to, cops being what they were, and Leo being who he was.

But needs must.

Leo breathed deep, as though that would tell him how much oxygen he had left. Leo's coke-addled brain didn't take concerns like those under consideration. The owner's manual listed the trunk as offering 14.7 cu$^3$ feet of space. It didn't seem that big. Leo dealt every day with dumpsters that measured their contents in cubic yards, but metric/Imperial conversions were difficult when Leo was sober, impossible when he was zooted.

In the end, Leo had just said, "Fuck it," and climbed in.

Now, he had regrets.

"Stupid fuckin' idea," he said to no one.

Most of the ones Leo had while he was high were stupid. As the dopamine receded, worst-case-scenarios raced through Leo's mind at light speed. Through the storm of imagined catastrophes, Leo couldn't see a way out of either his car or his big-picture situation, that is, the coke Leo really, *really* liked.

Which is why Leo was in the trunk.

Leo blinked. All he saw was darkness. Leo kept a heavy, D-cell Maglite in the milk crate, and his coke-addled brain had considered keeping it with him. But what were the chances of a professional kidnap/robbery team leaving Leo with a foot-long aluminum pipe? It wouldn't make sense. And sense was what his brain was trying to make of the world. Which would've been easy had Leo been doing blow exclusively. But he hadn't. He'd ranged deep into the kinds of substances Marie frowned upon. To extricate himself from this potential marriage-ender, Leo's world had become 14.7 carpeted cu$^3$ feet.

What day was it?

Leo thought it was Saturday. There's no way he had spent more than one night at Frankie's crash pad over on Shakespeare.

Right?

Leo brought his wrist close to his eyes and squinted. It was either 4:55 or 11:25. Leo hoped for the former. Time became a bit liquid whenever he got high.

Leo pounded a fist against the deck lid. "Hey! Help! I'm in here!"

Nothing.

Waste Management's trucks started rolling down Ryawa Avenue around five. He hoped a driver would hear him, but their diesels ran loud. Maybe Leo's coke-and-pill-addled brain had picked a bad spot. Then Leo remembered he'd had the presence of mind to park the Lincoln in a WM garage sidewalk cut. Eventually a pissed-off driver would bitch to his foreman, and they'd come out and Leo would pound and scream, and they'd call the cops. Then Leo would explain all about the professional kidnap/robbery team and how they ordered him to three (or was it four?) ATMs before locking Leo in his trunk.

At gunpoint. Did he mention they had guns? Because they had. Big ones.

No, Officer, he couldn't identify them. They were wearing masks, those knit ones you pull over your head, with holes for the eyes and mouth. What were they called?

In his mind Leo saw how this would end. Marie would cry and hold him, and Leo would hug his sons. Two kids and nearly a dozen Christmases binds a family, and Leo wasn't going to let his occasional lapses in judgement tear theirs apart. Leo's smaller lapses in judgement would be easier to conceal if not for Leo's Big Fucking Lapse In Judgement, which had led to his first experience in confined automotive spaces.

Something metal probed the Lincoln. Leo froze. Passenger side. Or was that the driver's side? There was no up or down inside the Mark VIII's pitch black trunk. It was like outer fucking space.

The car rocked side to side. Not a lot, just enough for Leo to feel it. Leo didn't move or speak. The plan, as devised by Leo's booze-and-coke-and-pill-addled brain, was to get someone's attention, have them call the cops and tell them what happened. But Leo's slightly-less-coke-and-pill-addled brain knew this was the Bronx and suspected everyone in it capable of at least a Class C felony.

So he remained quiet. Leo pressed an ear to the sidewall and felt a vibration. The car rocked back toward one corner. Someone was stealing the rims off his cherry Mark VIII.

He kicked hard. "Get me outta here! Hey! I'm in here!"

Leo planted the sole of his Timberlands against his sweet ride's ribcage. He almost felt guilty.

A man yelled out in Spanish. The sounds stopped and the car settled.

"I'm in here!" Leo deployed one-third of his foreign language knowledge. "*Aquí!*"

Leo twisted his neck and pressed the side of his face against what he thought was the back of the trunk. A solid thunk sent waves of pain through his skull.

"Shit!" Leo rubbed his head.

"The fuck you doin' in there?"

The voice was clear and close. Leo imagined him bent low by the license plate.

"I got robbed by two guys wearing baklavas."

"That Greek dessert with the flaky crust?"

"What? No, the masks."

"Damn. I love that stuff."

Leo exhaled through gritted teeth. "Listen, call the cops. I need to get outta here."

The man was quiet for a moment. "How'd you get in there, anyway?"

Was this guy an idiot? "I just told you, I was robbed and—"

"I got that," the man said. "Lotsa people get robbed. But not a lotta people get stuffed in some car's trunk."

"This's *my* trunk, my car."

"You say that like it makes things better."

Leo muttered a curse.

"Point is," the man continued, "I'm out here daily, right? This's my world, and I need the full story before exposin' myself to potential retribution. You get me?"

"No."

"Like, what if you're in deep to the Russians, right? I get you out, then they come lookin' for me. Thinkin' I'm one of yours. Then I'm gettin' hunted down for complicity."

"Russians? What fuckin' Russians?" Leo squeezed his eyes shut tight. This was worse than dealing with Leo Junior. "There's no Russians. Can't you gimme a hand?"

"My man, I'm out here conversatin' with a bumper. That's more than most folks'd do."

Leo silently conceded the point.

"And I got considerations of my own in this negotiation," the man continued. "The cops'll dust whatever phone I call 'em from. Latent fingerprints. You dig? And if the Russians got someone on the inside . . . whoo boy. Then I'm runnin' from *two* organizations bent on my destruction."

The guy was a 9-iron. This was just Leo's luck.

Leo spoke slowly, deliberately. "There aren't any Russians. I swear. If you get me out . . . I can pay you."

The man went quiet. Leo had struck a nerve.

"I thought you had your pockets run?"

"I did. But I got money. I own a scrap metal shop over on East Bay."

Another pause. "You talkin' 'bout RJO?"

"Yeah. I'm the R."

"Ah." The voice drew closer. "You don't do right by your prices, R."

That was a fact. The nebulous world of scrap-metal tended to attract flexible types, and Leo bent till they broke.

"My boy—I won't say his name cause it ain't pertinent—my boy brought you two coils just last week and you offered ten cents on the dollar. In the good book they call that usury."

"I don't think that's what usury means."

"You want out of that trunk or what?"

"All right, all right," Leo said. "But he'd clipped what he brought me. That shit was hot."

"And you took it just the same."

Leo did. Leo did that a lot. The man continued.

"Just cause an item's been reappropriated don't mean you get to fuck over the man facilitatin' the reappropriation. The universe remembers. Maybe that's why you're where you are."

Leo couldn't help himself. "The market sets the price. I'm the one risking my ass even dealin' with you guys." He shouldn't have said that last bit.

The man laughed. "Like the Forty-First is ever gonna lock you up."

Leo needed to focus. "Listen. You get me outta here and I'll take care of you and your boy. I swear."

A truck roared by. Airbrakes hissed as the sound rotated around Leo's world. He pictured a garbage hauler turning into the WM garage.

"You still there?" Leo called out when it had gone.

"Yeah. But these unions boys are eye-fuckin' me somethin' fierce. I gotta jet."

"No, wait!"

"Someone'll be along, R, don't you worry." The voice moved close again. "Maybe in the future you be more considerate to people who don't got many options. You get what I'm sayin'?"

"Yeah, yeah. Hey, before you go, be straight with me?"

"Ask your question."

"You steal my rims?"

"You think I'm some kinda pit crew? Nah man, I didn't take your wheels."

Leo exhaled. The 20-inch BBS set the Lincoln rolled on had cost him nearly two grand.

"But you're gonna need new mirrors."

Leo was alone again. Which wasn't a good thing to be, coming off a serious bender. Leo thought back three years, to Delfini Construction, him and Vinny messing with the scales and four very angry Albanians. After the Nassau County cops had dropped him back home, Marie had made Leo swear she'd always know everything about RJO Scrap. Marie was not to be denied when she got in a mood, and Leo and Vinnie's moronic scheme had put her in a mood like no other. Now Marie took note of every dollar that came in, and, more relevantly, every one that went out. This put a crimp in Leo's binge fund.

Which is why he was in the trunk.

Leo rolled, bit by bit, from lying on his left shoulder to his right. Something hard pressed into his hip. He felt his Armani Exchange jeans and his world exploded with sound.

Startled by his Mark VIII's alarm, Leo jumped and smacked his forehead against the deck lid. The blow plus the pills plus his experiment with the pipe (don't ask. It didn't happen. Except that it did.) meant Leo's skull pulsated like a Saturday night at the Tunnel. Orbs of color lit his world. Leo rubbed his forehead. He hoped first that he wasn't bleeding, then that he was; it would help sell the story. Leo licked his fingers but tasted no iron. The alarm blared on.

"Stupid, fuckin'—"

His car keys were in his pocket. Leo struggled to pull them out, but the limitations imposed by 14.7 cu³ feet of Michigan steel made removing the fob an exercise in gymnastics for which Leo, on his best days, was unsuited. Leo's head throbbed. The alarm continued wailing.

He paused to reassess his situation. The farther Leo got from his coke-and-pill-and-pipe-(Nope. Didn't happen.)-addled brain, the worse an idea the trunk became. Leo twisted his chest left while turning his hips right and worked the keys from his pocket. In the darkness he felt his Yankees key chain, the metal key and the plastic fob. He knew the buttons from memory and killed the alarm. Or did he? The horn pattern continued cycling, but Leo chalked that up to his still-kind-of-fucked-up state. After a few seconds his head cleared, and the alarm faded.

Wait.

What kind of professional kidnap/robbery team would lock Leo in his trunk *with the God damned key?* This was exactly the kind of thing Marie would see clean through. Leo slapped his forehead. It was moist with sweat.

Cops in the Point were relentless ball breakers, and Leo looking like a strung-out guinea from Five Towns meant they'd toss him the second he climbed from the car. Then they'd search the Lincoln proper, seeing as it was a crime scene.

The key had to go.

Another truck rumbled past. Leo thumbed the fob and the trunk cracked open. He peered out and tried to position himself relative to the world. His kind-of-sober brain hoped his coke-and-pills-and-pipe-(so he'd smoked crack. What of it?)-addled brain had parked the Lincoln where he'd intended. The DEP plant was in front of him, its massive chimney belching smoke into the night. But so were the taillights of a Buick Regal, which meant Leo had parked facing the wrong way.

Leo pushed the deck lid up. He leaned out over the sidewalk. The Lincoln's nose was a good four feet into the cut, like he'd planned, but he'd definitely set down on the wrong runway, automotively-speaking. Headlights crawled up Ryawa Avenue and Leo collapsed into the trunk, pulling the lid nearly shut. When they'd passed Leo casually climbed out and shut it, as if the trunk were a totally normal means of egress. In Hunts Point, it almost was.

The sewer on the corner was roped off by orange cones. The grate was sealed, pending replacement. Leo peeped around the corner. Tractor trailers bound for the food market were lined up in the distance. Leo crept along the Waste Management garage, staying tight to the building as he scouted for the best spot to divest himself of his keys. Mid-block he was struck by two realizations:

1)   He probably resembled someone a 911 caller would term "suspicious," and

2)   He might be a bit paranoid, given the sheer volume of substances flowing through his nervous system, and, as a result, might be overthinking the efficiency of an NYPD evidence search.

"Fuck this."

Leo wound up and hurled the fob and key and key ring toward the chain link fence encircling the DEP plant. On the far side was thick undergrowth and a stench that kept all but the most hardcore junkies at bay. The keys floated through the night sky, bounced off a fencepost and clattered to the sidewalk. His Yankee keychain glinted in the glow of a DEP security light.

"You gotta be kiddin' me."

Leo dashed across Ryawa. His not-quite-sober brain failed completely to register the chromed-out Peterbilt rolling his way. Truck drivers in the Point operated on a Horn-First/Brakes-Maybe system. The blast of noise from atop the cab sent Leo stumbling back just in time for the rig, ringed in amber running lights, to pass close enough for Leo to piss on.

Once it was gone, Leo checked both ways for homicidal CDL-holders, crossed the street and lost his keys deep in the DEP plant. He turned to head back to his car and checked the time on his Tag. Sunrise was less than an hour away. Traffic would grow and someone- not the someone who'd stolen his mirrors -would hear Leo's pounding.

Sixty minutes to save his marriage. All he had to do was get back in the trunk and tell the cops what happened. Leo arrived at his Lincoln. The street was empty. He reached out, noticed his Tag Heuer and froze. What kind of professional kidnap/robbery team . . .?

Leo looked back at the thick greenery beyond the DEP fence and sighed.

Ninety seconds and two successful crossings later, Leo was back at his Lincoln, a Swiss watch and American key fob poorer. As a final precaution, Leo patted himself down. All he had now was his wallet, which held only the Chase card he'd used –been *ordered* to use, at gunpoint –at the three (or was it four?) ATMs from which he'd taken money before being forced into his trunk. By those two guys Leo couldn't identify, on account of them wearing baklavas.

He'd come this far. Leo wrapped his fingers under the deck lid and pulled. The coupe rose slightly on its haunches. The trunk didn't budge.

"Shit."

Leo looked down the block, then over both shoulders. He had been de-trunked for a dangerously long time. Though Leo was pretty sure he knew the answer to this question, he slid to the driver's side door and pulled on the handle. Leo winced. It was the Bronx; he always locked his ride.

"Stupid idiot."

He dropped his forehead gently against the Lincoln's roof. Leo Junior, Artie and Marie flashed through his mind. He had to get back in that trunk. Leo peeled himself from his car. Alongside the Waste Management garage were hunks of broken concrete. Leo walked over and bent to grab one about the size of a softball when headlights swept the building.

Leo became one with the earth, wedging himself into a disused loading dock. He felt a growing, tepid wetness; he had landed in a puddle. He remained still as a WM diesel filled the street with noise. When it passed, Leo pressed his palms against the wet pavement and forced himself upright. It wasn't until after Leo had brushed himself off that he registered the distinctive stench of piss coming off his hands.

That had been in the puddle.

That Leo had been crouched in.

Leo shut his eyes. When the blow and pills and pipe went away, Leo didn't care for what remained. In the blackness he saw his life slipping away. The guys in his world talked big about how they kept their women in line. And maybe they did. Maybe they hadn't had to beg—literally, hands and knees, the whole nine—for forgiveness after the Big Fucking Lapse In Judgement. And then again when their wife found a glass vial dusted with white power after a weekend at Harrah's about which Leo remembered little. And again, when Vinnie left a

Ziploc of X in Leo's garage. But Leo had. And if Leo wanted to continue seeing his sons outside the supervision of a court-appointed monitor, he had to stick to the script.

He palmed a rock that had been at his feet. Light started breaking over the Corrections barge that floated off the end of the Point. He'd been inside once, to bail Vinnie out. The thought of spending even a single night in that toilet made him shiver. Leo stepped back a good six feet and hurled the rock as hard as he could at the passenger window.

When it dented the bodywork a half-foot below the glass Leo wasn't surprised at all.

His second effort hit the mark.

And tripped the alarm.

Leo gripped his head with both hands. Hands that were still damp with piss. Someone else's piss. His no-longer-cherry Lincoln was a God damned circus tent. Head- and taillights flashed. The horn blared in short, rhythmic bursts. Then it became a siren. Then a slightly deeper siren. Then a French cop car, then a—Jesus Christ, Leo, pop the fucking trunk!

He opened the glovebox and hit the release. The trunk cracked. Leo dove in, reached up, grabbed the deck lid, and pulled it down as hard and fast as he could manage.

Right onto his hand.

Leo screamed. With his other hand he sealed himself inside, marking the third time in his life—second today—that Leo had been locked in a trunk. The alarm cycled. A Waste Management rig came to a stop alongside the Lincoln. Leo's world was noise and confusion. The two conspired with Leo's strained nervous system to trigger his bladder's release valve. His thighs grew warm and wet. His hand might be broken. His head throbbed.

In the darkness Leo wept.

It was an ugly cry. Strands of spit and phlegm dangled from his mouth and nose. He cried with unrestrained passion, his body convulsing arrhythmically. Leo Rosser, thirty-six, covered in piss from at least two sources and locked in his own trunk in an effort to keep his spiraling life from flaming out entirely, had hit bottom.

Leo sobbed so violently he didn't initially register the rough scraping sound underneath the Lincoln. But when something attached itself to the car with a thunk, Leo blinked tears from his eyes and concentrated. The Lincoln shook as though someone had sat on it.

"Help! I'm in here!"

The Waste Management Cummins nine-liter diesel overpowered everything but Leo kicked and screamed just the same.

The Lincoln's back end rose about a foot.

Leo was getting towed.

"You gotta be kiddin' me."

He pounded and shouted. It did no good.

The big coupe lurched and stopped then started rolling again. The truck's engine faded. A pothole sent Leo bouncing off the deck lid. As the Lincoln was dragged across the Bronx, Leo had what Father Cardozo would call an epiphany.

Leo needed help.

He had just blown over a G on the kind of binge that usually ended in the ER. And it's not like it was his first. If Leo kept going like this, sooner or later he'd catch a bad batch and that would be that. No more kids, no more Marie. No more nothing.

Leo resolved to tell Marie everything. The blow, the pills (not the crack. Let's be reasonable), the cash he'd wasted, his constant struggle, why he was in the trunk. Marie was a good woman, better than he deserved, and she'd forgive him. He hoped.

Leo crossed himself. He hadn't been to Our Blessed Lady of Immaculate Consumption, or whatever it was called, in years. It was time he returned to the flock.

The car slowed, then turned, then climbed. The city pound on 141st Street sat like a fort atop a hill. Leo breathed in sharply. His nose burned. He was almost home. When Leo climbed out of his beat-to-shit Mark VIII, he'd be a new man. A better man.

When it stopped moving, Leo began screaming.

"Who's in there?" a woman asked.

"Me! I got . . . it was . . ." Leo composed himself. "I need to get out of here. Please."

His pleas seemed to generate some discussion.

"We gotta call the cops."

"Fine. Great. Can you just let me out first?"

"Sorry. We got procedures for this sorta thing."

"For a guy locked in a trunk?"

"Yeah we do. This's the Bronx. Gimme ten minutes. Hold tight."

A half-hour later sunlight cracked the darkness. Leo squinted and shaded his eyes with an upturned hand. Two cops stood over him.

"Come on. Slow."

Leo swung one leg out. His other caught the Lincoln and he went down chin-first.

One of the cops snickered. Leo got to all fours, then to his feet. The cops were old-timers. They stood with thumbs hooked into their belts and disbelief fixed to their faces. Their nameplates read O'Leary and Del Vecchio.

"You look like you got one hell of a story," O'Leary said.

Leo did. Tell it. Be honest. Get help.

The cops waited. Del Vecchio spit out his gum.

"Well?" O'Leary said. "We don't got all day."

Leo pinched the bridge of his nose as he drew a deep breath.

"So these two guys with guns busted into my office . . ."

JAYWALKING NOIR

RICHIE NARVAEZ

"He knew she'd been in jail, but not what for, and Stacy preferred to keep it that way. Better for everyone, especially Sylvia, if no one knew about her past."

# BIG DADDY
### Rusty Barnes

*1995, Splitsville PA, Pocono Mountains*

Stacy Rich kept a boxcutter in her uniform pocket because of men just like Big Daddy. The more she learned about him, the more scared she got. Respect. He had it. Big Daddy's meaty fingers kept shoving into everything illegal she tried to do. Even in her new straight job, housekeeping at Buckingham Honeymoon Resorts, Big Daddy's considerable reputation kept her from making a dishonest buck for fear of raising his legendary ire. The last person who'd done so had ended up dead, throat-slit and floating, at the edge of the lake at the Tobyhanna Army Depot. Stacy knew something about the kind of men who did those gigs, saw them in their matching track suits and ordinary-guy clothes. They looked like they had jobs, not like gangbangers or men just out of the joint not even trying to go straight. They dressed nice and normal, but their eyes were off, as dead as a bug's. She'd spent her life around men like them and knew them well.

She'd also heard from her friend Pablo that Big Daddy needed someone trustworthy, someone rock-solid, but hard. Unable to be fucked with. Stacy needed a steady, unflashy source of secondary cash, which, for an ex-con, didn't come easily. Her daughter, Sylvia, was special needs, and even the cheap pre-school she was in cost all the money Stacy made and most of the pittance her baby's father, Alfred, paid in support. This housekeeping gig was the best legal she'd been able to haggle, but it didn't take her long to figure out how shit went down, and she kept her ear to the ground waiting for the right opportunity to present itself.

In the meantime, Stacy smiled and yessired the guests till she felt like her eyes might pop out. Day after day, cleaning the filthy pig s' rooms. Champagne bottles floating in the pool, cum in the saunas, boob prints on the glass of the pool room, puke in the trash cans. Video cameras pointing at the round beds where they all did their honeymoon business. Stacy had seen it all, but even the laundered sheets and towels that came in off the truck every morning in six-foot tall blue plastic bins had the stink of Big Daddy on them. He controlled nearly everything that involved money or illegal trade in the Poconos, from the shores of Lake Wallenpaupack to the streets of East Stroudsburg, to the city and back. She didn't even know what he looked like. He was just *there*, slinking along Route 80 from the city every day like a great goddamned nightmare.

Stacy waited in the laundry area with the other housekeepers plus a houseman per crew, waiting for room assignments. "Stacy, take Chaz and Phyllis and do the Lakeside Chalets. Hustle and you can get to the Sweetheart Towers by noon," Edna, head of housekeeping, said. Chaz, a lanky guy with a little hipster beard, grabbed a vacuum and a box of trash can liners. Phyllis sighed, still hungover from last night's afterwork stint at the Pocono Gardens, the local watering hole frequented by most of the housekeeping and maintenance staff. Stacy grabbed the keys to the number one truck and took off out the door. She didn't like anyone else to drive, not since Chaz had let the truck out of gear and let it ride into the shallows of the lake.

Phyllis leaned over, pressing her boobs into Stacy's shoulder, and laid on the horn as they passed the maintenance building and the men lounging about at the front of the garage. "I got laid last night and I don't give a fuck," Phyllis yelled out the window.

"Christ, you stink," Stacy said.

"I told you I don't give a fuck," Phyllis said. "If I wasn't hammered still, I'd give those guys an eyeful."

"Do it," Chaz said.

"White people are fucking weird," Stacy said, taking the curve toward the Chalets at a high rate of speed, bouncing packets of burgundy towels against the wall of the built-up truck. Chaz nodded as if he knew exactly what Stacy meant. White-ass poser motherfucker. He'd asked Stacy one day if she wanted some cocaine. No big deal. Kept it in his lunch-pail like a cheese sandwich, and together they'd snorted lines off the back of a rose-colored toilet in the Sweetheart Towers and renewed their scrubbing of the whirlpool tub with vigor.

Ever since then, he'd wink at her occasionally like they were part of some secret club of outlaws. He knew she'd been in jail, but not what for, and Stacy preferred to keep it that way. Better for everyone, especially Sylvia, if no one knew about her past.

"Damn right I'm weird," Phyllis said. She leaned out the window again and yelled at a group of ducks waddling across the road to the lake. "Waah! I don't give a fuck!" Stacy shook her head at Chaz, who laughed and drummed his hand against the side of the towel rack to a tune only he could hear.


This particular tub had a ring of grime, and it took all of Stacy's two-handed strength to get it off. "I don't know what these people are doing in here," she said, "but this tub is dog-filthy."

"They're not supposed to have dogs," Phyllis said, sweating freely as she and Chaz changed the round bed with rectangular sheets.

"I don't know what all this is, but it comes off like gravel." Stacy leaned back on her calves from inside the tub.

"Maybe maintenance needs to take care of this one," Phyllis said.

"You just want Gary to show up and save the day for you," Stacy said.

"Ooh Gary," Chaz said from the other side of the bed.

"Fuck off," Phyllis said. "Gary's not on today." She grinned, showing off her one silver tooth. "And that sucker better not show up today after the way he left me last night."

"Here we go," Stacy said.

"I heard Charley got fired yesterday," Chaz said. Stacy and Phyllis both stopped what they were doing. How did this cat always have the news, Stacy wondered?

"Says who?" Phyllis said.

"I heard it when I dropped off towels at the pool," Chaz said. "Somebody I don't know, a cheese, was talking to Johnno."

"Well, if it was a big cheese," Phyllis began. Stacy laughed. Phyllis took an inordinate amount of pride in knowing who would get canned before it ever showed up in regular gossip, especially if it had to do with housekeeping or maintenance, which Charley had joined at the beginning of the summer. Stacy tried to imagine the bags of cocaine in his greasy automotive fingers, but couldn't. Chaz, though, had to get the drugs from somewhere.

"But it wasn't a cheese. It was Big Daddy," Chaz said.

"You are out your goddamned mind," Stacy said. "That man would never show up in a place like this." The truth was somewhere in between. He'd show up, but it'd never be so openly, getting rid of the ready connection to drugs many of the resort's guests wanted during their honeymoons and vacations. At least a couple housemen and maintenance men made good tip money bringing alcohol and small-time drugs, pot and cocaine, in to the people who needed it.

"Charley got his coke from somewhere," Chaz said.

"Shit. Wait till lunch. I'll find out what's going on," Phyllis said. "Big Daddy my ass."

Stacy nodded to Chaz. "You think you can fish those magnums of champagne out the shower before we go?" Chaz sighed, but leaned over and picked the bottles out of the tiled stall. He also picked up a can of soda heaped over with cigarette ash, dumping some onto the floor accidentally. He turned the water on and rinsed it away without soaping it down.

The crew only split eight dollars per Chalet per crew, plus minimum wage. You could make out pretty well if you got assigned somewhere else, to the Sweetheart Towers or the special timeshare condos the resort set up on the far end of the lake. There were only ten or twelve of these cheap-rate chalets, and they took a long time to clean, so nobody made any real money there. It was a rigged system. The favorite group got the good rooms, and Stacy's crew always ended up on the Lakeside Chalets and Roadside Villas. If they hustled, though, they could clear the whole lake and head over to the Towers, where the real money and the tips were.

Stacy grabbed the tied garbage bag and tossed it over her shoulder as they exited the room. This Charley thing might have created an opening for her, but she fingered the boxcutter in her pocket as she walked to the next Chalet and opened the door from her ring of keys. Careful, was the word.


"So. The deal is, Gary said, that Charley was supposed to do a brake job on the old lady's car, and he didn't do it in time." Phyllis grunted and waved her sandwich. "So that's why he got let go."

"Uh-huh," Chaz said, sneaking a quick look at Stacy. The old lady owned the resort, and often had her car worked on by the maintenance crew, just as she had the housekeeping crew clean her house.

"Don't look at me," Stacy said. "I don't know what the fuck is up with anything around here. Here one day, gone the next." Five minutes later she excused herself to the bathroom and the pay phone. One quarter got her the man she wanted.

"Pablo," a guttural voice said.

"Pablo. This is Stacy. You know which one. I hear you got an opening." Five minutes later she had a meeting set up for 6:30 in the McDonald's parking lot in EastBurg. She whistled between her teeth as she walked back into the laundry room that also served as the breakroom.

"That was the best piss she ever took," Phyllis said. Stacy smiled and flipped her the bird.

"After lunch, you guys take the Towers," Edna said, her hand over the receiver of the phone.

"Yeah, ladies, once in a lifetime" Stacy said. She stood and wadded up her lunch bag and tossed it in the trash. "Let's get this moneymaker rolling."


By 3:00 p.m., they'd cleared out most of the Sweetheart Towers, and wouldn't get any more assignments for the day. They slowed down for a couple cigarette breaks, sitting just outside the truck on the telephone pole pilings that served as rustic-looking fences, the door to Tower 303 gaping open. Chaz and Phyllis smoked Marlboro Reds, and Stacy took one even though she didn't smoke anymore. Chaz looked preoccupied, so Stacy hit him up. "What's up with you, Chaz? You got a girl somewhere in Mt. Pocono, I know. Sharon?"

"I got a couple, if you really want to know," Chaz said. "But the lady you're referring to lives in Reeders."

"Way out in the damned boonies," Stacy said, tapping her cigarette into the gravel road.

"Sharon's a good girl," Chaz said with a lazy smile.

"I'll bet," Phyllis said.

"I only date good girls," Chaz said.

"Is that what they call it now?" Phyllis said. Stacy laughed.

"They still call it dating, yes." Chaz said. Just then the phone in 303 began to ring, and Chaz took long loping strides inside to answer it.

"She tracked us down," Phyllis said.

"Take one damned break," Stacy said, hiking herself to her feet and crushing her cigarette under her sneaker. "They catch you." She heard Chaz's voice risen in a question, and he walked out and waved.

"Edna says there's an early checkout in the condos. We need to turn it around now."

"All right, back on the clock," Stacy said, clapping her hands. The condos paid a lot more than any other units. They'd take the full hour and a half to clean it, too, but her mind was already on her meeting with Big Daddy's man. As she scrubbed the toilets and hustled sheets onto the beds, she thought of every which way the meeting could go down, what she would say, how she would say it, rehearsing in her mind when to act hard and when to act a little aloof. If she could take over Charley's action like she wanted, she could make a lot of money very fast, especially as they were coming into the honeymoon season. The thought of it gave her a strange thrill she hadn't felt in a long time, as well as a little sliver of doubt in the back of her mind. She had a good thing here, made enough money to get by. But she wanted more, like everybody wanted more, and a little something on the side for Sylvia and her would be nice. She was on her way up, and out, she told herself as she clocked out at the end of the day, just a little late, like a good girl. 4:45 exact. Time to get some food and pick up Sylvia from her mother's.


Route 611 at 5:00 p.m. was bumper to bumper with people trying to get back on 80 after stomping up and down the Poconos looking for horseback riding and waterparks and nice restaurants, whatever the fuck these people did with their time after work and after their perfect children came home. Stacy timed her gas pedal to the brake in front of her and fumed. At this rate she wouldn't get there in time to eat anything, or more importantly, get Sylvia something to eat.

Sylvia sat in the backseat playing with a plastic pony and drooling. At three she was slow to use the potty, slow to use words, but her big brown eyes spoke volumes, and Stacy felt just a tick of guilt at what she was taking her daughter into, but it couldn't be helped. If she asked her mother to watch her for even fifteen minutes extra, her mother would get on her something fierce. Who you seeing? What're you doing? Did you work late? Why can't you pick your daughter up on time? On and on it would go, and Stacy, given the free childcare, would take it the same way she took special requests at the resort, teeth clenched behind a closed-mouth smile.

She beat time against the insistent tick of her blinker, making the right into the Mickey D's parking lot. At the end of the lot, behind the drive-through, she saw a powder-blue Mercedes and next to it a small black old-school VW bug. Inside the bug, she saw her man Pablo, next to a huge long-haired white man in a tank shirt who over-slung the entire passenger side. When he shifted, the entire car rocked. Stacy breathed once deeply, and drove through the window first and got Sylvia a Happy Meal. She handed it to her over the back seat, then drove around and backed into the slot the Mercedes had vacated, so the driver's side abutted the person she could only assume was Big Daddy. The things you couldn't guess about a person. She'd always thought he was named after the movie the way these guys named themselves. Never assume: it was a lesson she thought she'd learned already.

She rolled her window down, but the big man's only opened a crack. He had to rare back in his seat to angle the window the rest of the way down, and it took all his fat breath to do it. "You're Stacy?" Stacy nodded, and the big man looked at Pablo and nodded, and then spoke again in a high reedy voice. "You know who I am," the man said. Stacy nodded again, not trusting her voice. The car, the man, had an odor about him like patchouli and pot and something else deep under it, a body smell like nothing she'd ever smelled. And it came all the way out the window and into her car. "You know I take no shit. You know the resort is big business for me during the summer especially. I need an ear to the ground. Pablo knows you and says you're solid. You talk only to Pablo. You talk to someone else about me you get fired. You breathe wrong and my name is on your breath, you get fired."

He glanced at the rear seat. At Sylvia. He breathed out noisily. "No reason for anything to get more ugly. Call Pablo and check in with him periodically." He rared back in the seat again and dug out a wallet attached with a chain and handed her twenty bucks. "I like your daughter," he said. "Cute." Stacy glanced at Pablo, eyes narrowed. Pablo held his hands up in the universal gesture—I don't know—and pulled carefully out of the lot, across traffic and back up 611. Stacy looked in the rearview at Sylvia, and caught a trickle of sweat leaning down her temple.

"Mama," Sylvia said, and threw the pony at the back of Stacy's head and giggled. So, it was on. She ran the drive-through again and got them both sundaes.


Six days later, Stacy happened to be in the resort restaurant dropping off tablecloths and heard Johnno—there he was again, running his mouth. Was he one of Daddy's or just a gossip?—talking about Charley. "Sure was a good mechanic. It was a shame to lose him because of the old lady." Stacy made a mental note. She managed to be around in all the high-traffic areas to catch up on who was sleeping with who, which maintenance man had an alcohol problem, and most of all, who Chaz was supplying. He thought he was quiet about it, he thought he was slick, but poser beard-boy spent a whole lot of time delivering extra towels and pillows to people who requested them, when everyone in housekeeping hated to make those runs. People in the expensive rooms never tipped well, and people in the cheap suites felt entitled. Stacy called Pablo with the information she'd gathered, and at the end of the day Sylvia's Happy Meal had an extra hundred bucks tucked into the nugget basket. Easiest money she'd ever made, and all she had to do was pay attention.

The next day she made a call to Pablo and he told her to come by the McDonald's now.

"I'm in the middle of my shift," she said.

"Daddy wants to see you," Pablo said. "He ain't take kindly to no." Stacy hung up the phone and fingered the box-cutter in her smock pocket.

"Look at her. Still the best shit she ever took," Phyllis cackled. Stacy snorted and went right to Edna, made up a song and dance about how her kid was sick. It wasn't the first time she'd used that excuse, and sometimes it was even true. Edna nodded at her and went back to her phone. Stacy left, stripping off her smock as she went. "Where the fuck does she get off?" she heard Phyllis say as she left. Stacy banged the door shut on her calf in her quick desire to get into the car, and swore. This better be motherfucking important.

Lunchtime at the McDonald's crowded her like nothing since prison. People in line getting their value meals and king-sized sodas. Go large, she heard one young man say. Imma go large on that one and get me a 20-pack of nuggets. Just like last time, Daddy waited in the VW bug, leaning to the side, whether from his size or the weight of his patchouli smell, she didn't know. He rolled down his window and a blast of cold air hit her in the face.

"Don't lean in on me like that," Daddy said, wheezing.

"What do you want?"

"Easy tiger," Daddy said. Pablo kept his eyes straight ahead and expressionless, hands on the wheel. "Chaz is short. By like two large. No product to back up his claims. I need him taken care of."

"Back the truck up right fucking now," Stacy said, banging her palms on the window sill and standing up. "What did you say to me?"

"You heard me. He won't expect it from you. Pablo says you got the heart of a lion."

"How the fuck am I supposed to do this? Why?" Pablo whipped the Mexican blanket off the seat. Sylvia was there, tied up and gagged. She saw her mother and tried to scream.

"Now you know why. The how is up to you. You're a smart bitch. Figure it out. I'll let her go, and give you a nice round figure, say a grand."

"How the hell am I gonna do this?"

"Tie-Dye Dave's in the parking lot. You can catch him there." Stacy looked from side to side, fear sweat trickling down her armpits.

"Don't you hurt her. Motherfucker I will break yo ass."

"That's the spirit. Tonight at 9 he'll be at Dave's. You can nail him there." Daddy leaned out the window. "I want you to tell him it came from me." Stacy nodded. It was all she could do not to scream. "Now go back to work. Play it cool, and she'll be just fine." Daddy laid one meaty hand on top of the blanket, and Stacy blanched.


At 8:30 Stacy was at the head shop, Tie-Dye Dave's, and there was no one there on a weeknight. A Grateful Dead bootleg played on the overhead as she fiddled around, buying a tie-dyed onesie for Sylvia and looking at the hookahs and pipes laid out behind a glass case, dreamcatchers and God's eyes hanging from the rafters with strings of beads and Phish tour T -shirts. Dave himself even made her a paper flower, which she grimaced at as she took it from his hands and paid for her purchases with a limp twenty-dollar bill. Outside she waited for Chaz to show. Fifteen minutes later he pulled up beside her. She had the hood of her car open and looked inside as if searching for something.

"What's up, Stacy? Car trouble?" Chaz slid easily out from his car and looked inside her hood. "Can't get it started?" She swore to a god she didn't believe in and slashed his right hamstring with her box-cutter. He yelped and went down, clutching at his leg and she slammed her knee into the side of his head, bouncing it off the car with a dull thud. Woozy, she picked him up and dragged him into his still-open car door, halfway through, his eyes unfocused and blood dripping out of his ear. Then she laid his neck open to the bone with her boxcutter, barely avoiding the blood that swooped down his throat like a rash. He gagged once. "It comes from Daddy," she whispered, then the light left his eyes. She pushed him the rest of the way into his car and dropped the box-cutter into her pocket and drove off into the empty night sky.


The news at 11 held all the talk of a vicious killer in the midst of it: the honeymoon capital. Pocono Slasher, said the news ticker. Rumored Drug Arrest for Murder Victim. Stacy sat with a hyperventilating Sylvia, soothing her with chicken nuggets she didn't want and a bottle she did, even at three years old. Through it all, Stacy kept her mind off what she'd done with a bump of cocaine. For her baby, anything seemed possible, and right. Tomorrow she might slash that big bitch Phyllis, just for her mouth, but eventually somewhere down the road, her blade and Big Daddy's throat. She knew it. It made her feel warm inside, and eventually Sylvia stopped her labored breathing and went to sleep, and still, Stacy fingered the blade and thought of laying open Big Daddy's throat the way he deserved. She laid Sylvia down gently on the couch and lined up two fat ones and took them down one nostril, then the other. Big Daddy, the no-count sonofabitch, would pay.

# PLEASE DON'T STEAL MY BIKE

## REGAN McGRORY

# 3

"'Cats are okay, but why would you kidnap one?'"

# LOOKING FOR MISHKA
### *A Bart Lasiter Mystery*
### Jim Guigli

*A*pproaching *his sixth-floor office in the Cahuenga Building, Marlowe*—No. That's not it.

*The pulsing red neon sign on Sunset outside his hallway window painted the frosted glass panel in Lew Archer's office door.*

No. That's not it.

The day-dreaming Bart Lasiter was in Sacramento, not Los Angeles. He'd been trying on the personae of his favorite fictional private detectives as he approached his own office door.

Still, there really was a pulsing red light. It was behind the frosted glass panel in the top half of his office door. With each pulse the painted letters on the glass glowed: *Lasiter Investigations*

One hand holding a warm, aluminum-foil-wrapped super burrito, his other turning the key in the lock, Bart entered and moved straight to the answering machine. A new client? Work? Income! Or another offer to refinance a car or house he didn't own. Or buy a hearing aid or some medical device he didn't need. Or maybe vinyl siding.

But Bart did own a car, an '86 Chrysler K-car limo. He'd almost forgotten *The Klimo* because it hadn't recently moved from his landlord's warehouse, out back across Firehouse Alley. Twenty years old, it needed things, things he often couldn't afford. Parts. Gas.

Willing his optimism to vanquish his pessimism, he played the message. Long on garbled dread and short on information, it was delivered in heavily accented, short bursts. No return number. He had to rewind the tape and play it four more times before he was sure of the address, and that it was from a Mrs. Tereshkova.

For a paying job, lunch could wait. He stored his burrito in his mini-fridge and hustled back down to the street.


Her address was only a short walk from Bart's office, and he thought he knew the building. It was one of Old Town Sacramento's historic three-story wood-frame complexes, formerly grand, presently less so, and long ago converted into a warren of odd rooms, offices, businesses, and small apartments.

Pleased that his memory had proven accurate, Bart stepped from the wooden sidewalk into the building's main entrance, a dark, narrow staircase that led up to the second floor. A sputtering neon sign hanging above the stairs provided the only light, *Big River Ink* in red and green.

Bart followed the numbers and arrows on the second-floor hallway walls, past a body piercing shop, a spiritual counselor, then around a corner past a leather goods shop, through more turns to a second-hand curio shop, and then the tattoo parlor, *Big River Ink*. Just beyond *Ink*, he found the room number from her phone message. Under the number, a shaky hand-lettered TERESHKOV-TERESHKOVA filled a small card.

Before he could knock, a man's voice boomed behind the door. Was Bart interrupting something? He knocked politely and waited. He listened until he recognized that the voice came from a radio tuned to a local Russian-language station. He knocked again, harder.

The radio voice stopped, child-like footsteps followed, and the door opened. Six two Bart saw no one until he looked down. An old woman, scarcely five feet tall, looked up, surprised. A patterned dress, black with small white flowers, hung loosely on her thin frame. Her face was crowned with iron-gray-streaked black hair pulled back into a tight bun. Beneath dark thick eyebrows, bursts of wild electricity flew from onyx-black eyes while they searched the hallway beyond Bart.

"You're Mrs. Tereshkova? I'm Bart Lasiter. Got your phone message."

"Oh, oh. You detective? He kihdt-nappdt!" she said, motioning Bart in.

"Who's kidnapped?"

"Mishka."

"Who is Mishka?"

"My boy."

"Your son?"

"Yes, yes . . . my kitty boy."

"A cat? Oh, well, I don't know—"

"Yes—you khelp."

"I'm not sure. How did you hear about me?"

"When police no khelp me, I ask them, who, who? Who, who khelp me, I say to police. They say 'See Bart, Bart Lasiter,' and give me phone number."

Bart detected that someone at Sac PD was having some fun at his expense.

"Then I ask Old Town people. I ask everyone. They say Bart khelp them. They say Bart *everyone* detective. They say Bart find people, you find things. You could find Mishka. Now you khelp me. You find Mishka. You save Mishka."

"I'm still not sure."

She grabbed Bart's arm with two hands and pulled it twice, hard, like she was resetting a dislocated elbow or shoulder. "Yes, yes, you khelp. You save Mishka!"

"Maybe," said Bart, stepping back and rubbing his arm.

Though she looked less than half his weight and was well past seventy, late thirties-Bart didn't want to arm-wrestle with her, unsure of the outcome. From a quick look at her clothes and small apartment, he thought she couldn't have much money. Bart would sometimes barter with a business, especially a restaurant—*will work for food*—but what could *she* do for him?

"What about my fee?"

"Fee? What fee? Don't know fee—you khelp."

"Mrs. Tereshkova, I have bills and rent to pay."

Really, his rent was flexible, given that his tolerant, wealthy landlord was a retired Berkeley cop and friend, but Bart did have a telephone and other bills. And the Klimo.

"Maybe . . . could pay some from Oleg Security check. Every month check come. He work rail yard many year. Oleg is khusband. You khelp, yes?"

"Is your husband here?"

"Yes, but no bother Oleg. Mishka, he *my* kitty. *I* pay."

Bart sighed. No certain money here. This might be another of his Old Town *pro bono publico* jobs. But he didn't have another client right then, and he did want people to call him.

"All right, Mrs. Tereshkova, I'll try to help you. Tell me more."

She smiled. "Yes, yes. Eeez guhdt."

"Good, yes. Now tell me about your cat."

"Mishka, he my love, my Mishka. Sometime he leave for a day—he not like my khusband. But he come back next day, always. Not now. Now he gone two, three day, then come back. Then, five day he gone, but come back. Now, more than week and *no* come back—kihdt-nappdt!"

"Kidnapped? Why?"

"I *know* these thing! Mishka love me. He come back before, always. He not run away. Someone lock him up. This I know!"

"All right. Tell me why. Tell me everything."

Bart regretted his words as soon as they'd passed his lips. Mrs. Tereshkova launched into a 500-page first volume of *Mishka's Life Story*. She told Bart how cute Mishka had been as a kitten, his daily routine, what he liked to eat, what he wouldn't eat, his favorite sleeping places. Non-stop. How did she breathe?

Some Mishka details were familiar to Bart who had his own office cat, Agamemnon, a big fixed-male orange tabby he called Aggie.

Bart listened, but he wasn't a fan of non-stop stream-of-consciousness answers to simple questions. While trying to appear interested, he looked around the apartment. It was more a large room than an apartment, with a bed and nightstand in one corner under a window over Firehouse Alley, and to the right, under an adjacent window, a stove, refrigerator, and kitchen sink. The walls were covered with old mint-green paint and decorated with a few faded travel posters of Russian scenes. The floor, doors, and door frames were dark chocolate-brown stained wood. Opposite the bed and kitchen area two worn overstuffed mohair chairs and a matching sofa commingled with a coffee table and two end tables. No TV, but he saw the radio near the sink.

At the sink end of the room a door stood half-open, revealing a small bathroom. On the bathroom floor near a cat box sat a can of paint, a brush soaking in a jar, and blue masking tape. Next to the bathroom there was a closed door, probably a closet or storage room.

Everything looked clean and well-kept.

Clean, but that smell. The windows were open, and there was a warm September breeze, but a strange mix of odors refused to leave. Maybe she cooked a lot of cabbage, or mysterious Russian dishes, and sometimes left some meat out too long. Cat box, still ammonia-strong after a week with no cat. Paint. Incense. Old people.

While he looked and she talked, he wondered if he could find this cat. He could barely deal with his own cat. Bart, no PhD in Catology, understood cats as much he did women. Aggie had allowed Bart to adopt him, another time that Bart couldn't say no.

Seizing a nanosecond pause in her recitation of Mishka's wonders, Bart jammed in a question. "What does Mishka look like—I mean, do you have a photo?"

"*Konechna*—ach, I mean yes, I get." She went to the nightstand near the bed, opened a drawer, and brought back a cigar box full of photos, all Mishka. After shuffling through several dozen, Bart found one where the cat was adult, right-side-up, and still—not a blur of motion. Mishka was black and white, a handsome Tuxedo, but otherwise ordinary.

She grabbed several photos from Bart. "See, see, look these, when Mishka baby. I find him down by river. I say, 'What this thing—*kartoshka*?'"

"What's a kartoshka?"

"Oh, oh—potato! He like tiny potato, not cat. But then I see it cat, and I take home and feed him. My tiny kartoshka."

Bart rolled his eyes and kept shuffling through the rest of the photos. She watched each photo as Bart looked.

"Look, look." She snatched another photo from Bart's hand and pointed to Mishka's right ear. The ear had a notch where the flesh had been torn away. Not a prison tattoo, thought Bart, but it qualified under *Scars and Distinguishing Marks*.

"Oh, oh, he was attack by big mean, bad, bad orange cat."

Bart decided to avoid mentioning Aggie, who roamed Old Town at will. Aggie's *Agent Orange* persona could be intolerant toward other cats, especially if someone had given him whiskey.

"I want pictures back when you find Mishka."

"What does your husband think about Mishka being kidnapped?"

"Ach! Oleg no care. He sleep. He sleep now." She pointed to the door that Bart had thought led to a storage room.

"What about a reward? Are you offering a reward to anyone who helps us find Mishka?"

Those black eyes stabbed him. "Reward? Ach! I already pay *you*. You find Mishka, yes?"

"All right, Mrs. Tereshkova. I'll get started. Here's my card. Call me right away and leave a message if Mishka comes home, or if you hear anything at all." He looked around again. "You don't have a phone?"

She moved her lips while she read the card. Then she recited his motto from the card: "I ready to khelp." She looked up to Bart and said, "Pay phone third floor."


As soon as he left Mrs. Tereshkova's apartment, Bart started looking for Mishka. A few feet down the hall, he entered the tattoo parlor, *Big River Ink*. The shop was quiet, with no one in sight but the long-haired man behind the counter. He looked half-asleep, leaning back in a chair reading a well-thumbed copy of *Skin & Ink* magazine. Tattoos covered his exposed skin. Advertising begins at home.

"Hi. I'm Bart Lasiter. I'm trying to help your neighbor find her cat." He held up the photo.

The man put the magazine down and stood up. "That cat again. Yeah, sure I know that cat. The old lady's been buggin' us about him for days. If you ask me, the cat just left, because she's nuts. My partner, who won't speak to her anymore, says she's crazier than a outhouse rat. Several times she accused him of kidnapping the cat. When customers are here, trying to relax while they get inked, she comes in yelling about Mishka. Bad for business. Amazing how such a small woman can be such a big pain in the butt. Cats are okay, but why would you kidnap one? They're free all over."

"Sorry, I didn't know . . . what she's been doing."

"Look, I try to be nice to her. But the cat, he could be anywhere. What *I* want to know is, where is her husband, Oleg?"

"Asleep in their apartment. Why?"

"Oleg got a new tat here every third Wednesday, when his SS check came. Steady customer—the best. Same routine for the last year, up until the last few months. No Oleg, no tattoo."

"What kind of tattoos?"

"Nice ones. Not Russian gangster tats. Nothing like that. He'd show me some picture from a magazine, a Russian scene, mountains or rivers, and say, 'This I like. Make it here.' My partner did the rivers. We got good at copying the funny Russian lettering."

"No cat tattoos?"

"No way—never mentioned cats. Only know he had one because of his old lady."

"She was always looking for her cat?"

"Yup. Oleg came here, my partner and me thought, to get away from her and the cat. He was relaxed here. Oleg, he'd sit in the chair or lie on the table and smoke a big stogie—said his wife complained when he smoked at home. I used to keep a few cigars here for him, but now he don't come around. He used'ta just stop in to say hello on his way out, or back from the store. I ask myself why don't he come around—don't he like my art anymore? Is he sick? No, I'll bet anything it's her and that damned cat. She told Oleg to stay away from us."

His face suddenly stiffened. He turned pale. "Oleg's wife and this building are making me feel cramped in. I want to get out. I left San Francisco and came here because I worried about getting caught in the Big One. But even here—" He looked up to the ceiling. "Even here, I can see the roof, the third floor, all that wood and plaster, waiting to fall in on me in a shaker. Man, I want to be outside."

He was silent for a moment, sweat on his brow. Then he smiled. "Hey, how about a tattoo?"

"No, thanks. But I'll tell her husband when I see him that you asked about him." Bart left his sympathy behind and moved down the hall. Visiting businesses in order of proximity to Mrs. Tereshkova's apartment, Bart tried the second-hand curio shop. He entered and saw a woman watching him through hanging displays of old costume jewelry.

"Help you?"

He held Mishka's picture up for her.

"I did *not* take her cat!"

Bart decided this wasn't going to be easy. He detoured to the third floor, where he found that no one had seen Mishka, but they all had heard from Mrs. Tereshkova. He returned to the second floor and stopped at every business and room where he could find someone present. Bart had used up the afternoon and all he had to show for it was an empty stomach and many Mishka sightings, all at least a week old. And everyone knew Mrs. Tereshkova.

Time to take a break. Back in his office Bart quizzed Aggie about Mishka. When it comes to cat affairs and helping humans, cats have a code of silence—*Catomerta*. He fed Aggie, washed down his cold burrito with a bottle of Classic Coke, and resumed searching Old Town.

It was getting dark. Dark, when private detectives and cats prowl the shadows. What would Marlowe do? Maybe Bart would find Mishka in one of Old Town's dark corners. Who knew?


If someone did know, Bart didn't find that person in the bars and businesses that catered to the evening crowd. He returned to his office, checked the answering machine, fed Aggie, and crawled into bed.

He was tired of this case. He didn't quit the Berkeley PD to solve missing pet cases—especially for free. *Bart everyone detective.* He remembered a Lew Archer story, *Find the Woman*. He read a lot of detective fiction in his office to pass the time. He had a lot of time to pass. But as far as Bart knew, no one had written a private eye story called *Find the Cat*.

He was starting to feel depressed.

Then he again reminded himself to be optimistic. If he saw this job as an opportunity to meet potential clients while he looked for Mishka, it could be a positive instead of a negative. He fell asleep with his TV tuned to an old episode of *Rockford Files*.

In the morning, after he made coffee and microwaved a Pop Tart, he set out again looking for Mishka, methodically, one block at a time. Extra, aimless walking was only going to wear out his old Nikes, and they had to last for a while.

By this time Bart had heard variations of the same thing too many times: "That cat —yeah, I've seen'm. He comes and goes a lot. Didn't know he belonged to someone. He seems like a free spirit."

Bart had polished a response: "Here's my card. If you see this cat, call me, leave a message."

"Is there a reward?"

"Yes."

"How much?"

"My client hasn't said exactly yet. But generous, I'm sure."

Bart was tempted to call it a morning and go back to his office, but he wanted to finish this job ASAP. There were two more buildings on this block to check—then he'd stop for lunch.

He entered Randall's Collectibles, a street level second-hand shop, right off the wooden sidewalk. Grateful that he didn't have more stairs to climb, he relaxed and looked. The shop's stock was somewhat better than what you'd find in a charity's thrift shop: miscellaneous tables, upholstered chairs, lamps, and framed pictures. Bart saw a counter at the back with a thin, gray-haired man near the cash register. Weaving a path to the man through the tables and chairs on display, Bart noticed a small table supporting what looked like a black and white cat-shaped lamp base missing its shade. Sure looks like Mishka, Bart thought. Then the lamp moved. "Yikes!" he said. Seeing the torn ear, he smiled. "It *is* Mishka!"

"That's a good boy, Mishka. Hold still for Uncle Bart." Bart carefully picked up Mishka, who leaned into him and purred while Bart carried him to the man at the cash register.

"Hi." Offering one of his cards with his free hand, he said, "I'm Bart Lasiter, and I was hired by the woman who owns this cat to find him and get him back home." The man turned toward a doorway to a back room.

"Martha, we've been saved!"

"What?" came the reply from the back room.

"What?" said Bart.

"Good to see you," said the man. "We've been waiting for someone to come get the cat. I'm Randall. So, his name is Mishka? My wife and I called him 'Cat.' Be my guest, please take him home. We've been trying to get rid of him for weeks, but he won't go. He used to just hang out for a day or two, but now he's moved in and won't leave. We feed him because we don't want him to starve, but we're not really cat people, or we'd already have our own. We've got upholstered furniture here, and sometimes cats scratch. So, if he belongs to this woman, why isn't he home with her?"

"That's a good boy, Mishka," Bart said, stroking his head. "I don't know why, but my client is an old lady, and I'm not sure she is clear about everything. How about if I just take Mishka home?"

"Works for us."

"Thanks. Keep my card and let me know if I can ever help you," Bart said, heading for the door with Mishka purring in his arms. He opened the shop door. When Bart stepped through to the sidewalk, Mishka dug all his claws deep into Bart's shoulder and arm, gaining the grip he needed to launch himself off the paralyzed detective and back into the shop. After Bart had wiped the tears from his eyes and caught his breath, he turned to see Mishka, once again, imitating a lamp on the little table. "Hurts, doesn't it?" said Mr. Randall.


"Mrs. Tereshkova, I found Mishka—"

"Ohhhh!" She looked past Bart to the hallway outside her apartment door. "Where Mishka?"

"But I don't think he's been kidnapped."

"No!"

"He's been staying at Randall's second-hand shop on Front Street, just north of K. They told me he's free to come and go—they've tried to make him go—but he's been sleeping there. They feed him, too. When I tried to bring him home, he wouldn't come."

"Noo!"

"Is there any reason why he wouldn't want to come home?"

"Nooooo!" Her hard, black eyes flashed fury while she stood shaking her head back and forth. She brought a clenched fist up toward Bart's face.

Bart leaned back. "Sorry, it's true."

"Ach! Lies! Not want come home? Eeez not posbill! I give him best food, tickle the ears. Catnip, too—all he want. Give everything! Not believe. Why my Mishka want be somewhere else?"

"That's what I'm asking you, Mrs. Tereshkova."

She pushed Bart down into one of the chairs— "You *SIT*!"—and continued to plead her case to Bart.

While Mrs. Tereshkova droned on, fighting the idea that Mishka would prefer another home, Bart again pretended to listen. His bored eyes scanned the room, seeing all the things he'd seen before: her neatly made bed under an open window, the kitchen area nearby under another open window, a partially open door to the bathroom, the sofa and chairs. She lived in this one room. Poor.

While Mrs. Tereshkova argued for Mishka's return, Bart struggled to escape the mohair and stuffing, slowly, so she wouldn't see. He would have almost asked for permission, but she hadn't noticed, still deep into wailing about Mishka. With a few nods and grunts meant to keep her talking, Bart paced the room, waiting for her to wind down. On his third lap around the room, he noticed something he'd overlooked before. On an end table a box of incense sticks and matches lay next to a hollowed-log-like wooden dish full of burned incense sticks, matches, and ashes. Cabbage, Russian dishes, spoiled meat, cat box, paint, *incense.*

Bart had hoped she would be pleased with his success, his first kidnapping case, solved in less than two days. He was proud that again, *Lasiter Investigations,* using the keystone elements of hard work, optimism, and a little luck, had rendered a service to the community, hopefully not gratis.

Yes, she was poor, but he hoped to see a little of that SS money for his effort. With no sign she would stop talking, he lost patience and interrupted her. "Mrs. Tereshkova, you hired me to find your cat, Mishka. I did. Now, about my fee —"

"No, no, no. Mishka not come back. You fail. I not pay."

Bart sighed. Not unexpected. Close, but no cigar.

Wait . . . no cigar?

No cigar!

In the strange mix of odors in Mrs. Tereshkova's apartment there was no cigar, no cigar odor—none. Bart went back to the table with the incense. Fresh ashes— incense ashes, not cigar ashes. He looked at the door to the closed room—it could be that Oleg only smoked in his room. An ashtray could be in his room.

But then he noticed. The door to her husband's room didn't look right. He finally saw what he had missed before, what he had seen before but hadn't recognized.

"Oleg sleep now," she said, watching Bart study the door.

At the entrance to her husband's room there should have been at least a small gap between the door and frame. He moved closer. He saw no gap. Instead he saw an irregular, wavy surface that had been painted brown to match the wood of the door and frame and floor.

Bart picked at the wavy surface. He saw blue.

"Oh."

The entire perimeter of the door, frame-to-floor, had been sealed in two-inch-wide blue painter's tape. He tried the doorknob, knowing it would be locked. Then he peeled back layers of tape, one from another. Four layers. He pulled enough tape from the frame to expose a few inches of the gap.

He jerked his head back, hit with a familiar, unforgettable odor. In an instant he was again a young cop on patrol in Berkeley.

*"Officer, officer? Can you help me? My tenant doesn't answer the door or telephone, and the mail is piling up."*

She watched Bart. "When Mishka little, he so cute, but Oleg did something, something make Mishka mad. Mad Mishka scratch him— that you must expect, must forgive. But they not like each other no more. Mishka don't want be by Oleg anymore. Oleg just sleep anyway."

Bart turned from the sealed door to face Mrs. Tereshkova, breathing in some fresher air. It would be up to the coroner to say how Oleg had died, but Bart was sure Oleg's death would be news to Social Security.

"Mrs. Tereshkova, because Mishka and Oleg don't like each other, is that why you sealed the door?"

"What mean, sealed?"

"I'm going to call someone I know, to help you. To help you with your husband."

She looked up at Bart. "What?"

"Maybe *after* they help you, *then* Mishka will come home."

"Oh, oh. Thank you. Guhdt!"

BEAK
ALFRED KENNEALLY

"Daniel envied the girl's gentleness with the bird, and to desire something in the land of the living was a revelation for him."

# TENDERNESS
## Estelle Phillips

A pigeon dropped from the sky. It lay on the pavement, broken necked and unmoving, save for a blue ringed eye, which gazed through the window at Grace before its wrinkled lid fell, shuttering in death. Grace took a sharp intake of breath. It hurt her to see the bird die. She worried the pigeon would be trodden on; if quills thrust through the delicate bones of its chest, the bird's soul could not escape.

Grace pulled on her coat, left the coffee house, and went into the street. Was this what happened to birds, she wondered, they'd be flying along, and die? She crouched beside the pigeon, slid her fingers beneath its feathered breast, and walked, cradling the dead bird.

Daniel saw the pigeon fall. He watched the girl begin down the street and followed her to the abbey where a beech hedge grew. When she stopped, he concealed himself in the passage behind the chippie. The smell of boiled oil soured the air, but he did not care; it was nothing to the bite of sulphur in the back of his throat.

The girl placed the pigeon amongst the narrow trunks, covered it with leaves, and marked the grave with a stick. Satisfied, she stepped back, put her hands together, and knelt in solemn prayer. Daniel was amazed.

Chip shop customers passed by him, hugging suppers to their chests. Echoes of homeward conversations reverberated down the street, but the only voice for Daniel's ears came in his sleep; his commander, yelling,

"Johnson! Cover!" through the tut, tut, tut of bullets shot; the thwack of metal through human bone, excavating innards to leave the heart exposed; another life lost. Bodies splayed on buildings, hung decorously from upstairs windows, the plaster behind them splashed with blood; bodies littered streets, and slumped by cars; broken people angled sideways, frontways; heads cracked backwards, elbows screwed forwards, eyes in, eyes out, teeth in, or splattered about; brains blown in chumpy nuggets of person soiling a dusty road; nature shot through with red in every shade, from the brilliant ruby of just torn flesh, to blackening meat in decay. The air was filled with the sound of bodies writhing into death, half breathed agonies, exhalations, and people dying lonely, begging for a moment of love. The white noise of slaughter amplified in Daniel's head, and he'd be at the pit, a dug-out dip with bodies clumsily tumbled in, stained fabric sandwiching mutilated people. The stench of dead human wafted, its pungent odour snaked into his nose, and stayed. Daniel worked on the pit's edge, retching, and shovelling dirt onto men, women and children, burying them in the land they owned. He could not look at the dead boy, maybe four years old, and emptied his spade quickly. Dry earth poured onto the boy's face, covered his skin, and layered his lashes with grey. The child's hand twitched, and the soil around his fingernails crumbled. Instantly, Daniel sank to his knees, and scrabbled at the boy. He tried to kiss some life back in, but had no breath, and snatched wildly, curled out lips straining for oxygen to inflate the boy's lungs. Silent screams came instead: Daniel woke gasping, and rigid with terror. He counted, "One elephant, two elephant, three elephant . . .."


Daniel envied the girl's gentleness with the bird, and to desire something in the land of the living was a revelation for him. That night, as Daniel leant over the boy's tiny chest, searching for breath, the girl appeared at the edge of the pit, the pigeon in her hands. She observed his fight for the boy's small life, and left. Daniel was alone again, surrounded by the dead, and lost for breath.

The next evening, Daniel crept through the streets to the pigeon's grave. Death had dulled the bird's natural wonder; it was beginning to smell, and insects crawled through its feathers. Daniel took a folded note from his pocket. It said, "Thank you for giving me a place to rest." He slid his hands up the textured bark, and found a crook for the note, above the pigeon's resting place. When he slept, he dreamt of the girl standing over the dead.

Two more evenings, Daniel returned to the grave; the odour grew sickly sweet as the pigeon aged. On the fourth evening, only breast feathers remained. Daniel spiralled towards the black. He had been ridiculous, he thought, holding on to a dead bird for life. Bitterness seeped in his gullet, until he spotted a note, jammed in the crook, its paper creased. In the light from the chip shop window, he read, "Thank you for your message. I don't know how the pigeon died. I found it on the pavement."

Daniel made his way home. He spread the note on his kitchen table. Tiny particles of leaves dropped from its folds onto the Formica, bringing the pigeon's grave into his house. He imagined the girl, rummaging in her handbag for biro and paper, and writing, her face and hair in the light. Daniel was in a quandary, should he reply? He slept, questioning, and the girl came to the pit's edge again, waiting. He tried to speak to her but woke, suffocating. Daniel stumbled downstairs, and by morning, screwed up balls of paper were scattered around his chair. He decided upon, "Maybe it was very old. It was nice of you to give it a grave. I think it liked it there." He worried about the last sentence and rewrote the message without it.

After Daniel wedged his note in the branch, he stayed from the pigeon's grave for two days. On the third night, he approached the beeches with hope, and joy grew in him at the sight of a new note. He opened it in the passageway, his heart beating into the wall, "I could not abandon the pigeon. It was beautiful, and suddenly dead. The fox took it. Do you think its soul is free?" Daniel leant back, breathing fast and hard, and rocking against the bricks. He tucked the note in his shirt pocket, and his heartbeat eased.

At home, Daniel pressed the second note to his nose, and ingested her faint aroma, he smoothed it flat, next to the first note. Restless, he paced from the table to the sink, turned on his heels, and paced back to the table, back to the sink, the table, repeat, repeat. Eventually, he went to bed, and his nightmare came: at first, the bodies seemed the same, inert and broken in terrible sadness. Then, a soft gold gleamed from the crevices of the bodies. Open wounds and pulped flesh shimmered, mouths, eyes and ears glistened from golden shadows nestling within the human forms; their souls were departing. One by one, the souls stepped from their bodies, lifted torn skin, and moved jagged bones aside to ease their exit, emerged as lovely human transparencies, which gathered sociably above the pit. At first, they chatted pleasantly, but their exchanges animated, and soon they were shouting. They gestured at the boy, whose soul remained resolutely in his body; Daniel could see its shine behind the boy's still eyes. The girl materialized on the pit's edge, with the pigeon; she was upset, and imploring Daniel to hush the rabbling souls. Daniel listened intently, caught snippets, "He's not ready!" "Make him!" "It's his choice!" Daniel asked, "Make him do what?" but his words got stuck in his breathless throat, and he woke. He staggered down to the kitchen and wrote, "Yes, its soul will be free, because you laid the bird to rest. Do not worry."

The following evening, Daniel attached his note to a lower branch. He fretted about the girl and checked regularly for a reply. The days passed with no word from her, although his nights were full of her asking. Frantic with disappointment, Daniel cleaned his house minutely, except the kitchen table, which he kept untouched, and earthy. On the fourth night, his note was still there. The road swallowed his feet as he dragged himself home. Daniel's nightmares continued, with the souls arguing vociferously, and the girl beseeching him.

Days passed. Daniel attended the pigeon's grave frequently and loitered in vain to see the girl. Hollow emptiness grew in him. He touched the edges of her notes and pushed the earth around the kitchen table with his fingertips, even licking it to check it was real. At night, the souls' agitation increased; the boy's soul refused to leave his body, and the girl's demands on Daniel became more urgent, but he could not utter a word. Once, there was a fistfight, and a soul retreated, its golden glow pocked from strikes. It stood beside its body, contemplating re-entering the slash across its human stomach. Daniel tried to intervene, and woke, thrashing his arms above his head.

Drawn with exhaustion and disappointing pilgrimages, on the tenth day, Daniel kept watch beyond midnight and, as he trailed homewards through the market square, a car screeched to a standstill in the tree-shaded corner. Muffled cries came from it, getting louder when the window opened. Daniel sprinted to the car, he saw the driver twist over his passenger, and slap her across the face,

"You bitch, do as I say!"

"No. No, please, I'm sorry, I'm sorry, Please, no, oh no." The man clenched a knife in his teeth; one hand was wrapped around the passenger's throat, and the other unzipped his flies. The girl pawed desperately at the window and smeared the glass with blood. Daniel yanked the passenger door. It was locked. He slammed his hands on the car roof and the man froze. Daniel forced his hand through the gap in the window, skin from his wrist concertinaed on the metal lip, and his fingers found the inside lever. The door swung open, and the girl tumbled out beneath the man. The knife clattered to the ground. Daniel grabbed the man by his shirt, levered his weight off the girl, and shouted,

"Run!"

She fled into the trees. Daniel punched the man hard on his chin. A tooth shot out. The man lumbered up with a roar, six foot four of muscle on fat. Daniel fought like a tomcat welcoming death. The man smacked Daniel down, sat on his chest, stretched out his arms and ground his knuckles into the tarmac. The butt of the knife dug into Daniel's lower back; he spat in the man's eyes, leant up, plunged his teeth in the drooping jowl, and ripped. The man shrieked and covered the tear with a hand. Daniel head-butted the man, who collapsed on his back, and Daniel thumped his head; it swung from side to side, and the raw cheek became gelatinous, picked up loose gravel into it. Covering the man's ear with his lips, Daniel screamed,

"Have you had enough?" His anger pierced the man's eardrum, and the man was silent, though he lived. Daniel punched his face some more.

"Have you had enough?" The man's head lolled grotesquely.

"Yes." He groaned.

"You piece of shit." Daniel dropped him, kicked him hard in the groin, and shot off, to find the girl.

All night, Daniel searched. He ran bent, from cover to cover, and spied from behind thick tree trunks, boots of cars, and high-rise ramps in the skating park. At dawn, he withdrew to the kitchen table; his dried blood flaked into dusty earth by the notes, and his muscles flicked with sleeplessness. Eventually, Daniel fell asleep on the sofa. The souls were still jabbing at each other, pointing at the soulful boy. The girl stood at the pit's edge, and calm descended; the souls quieted, and turned towards her. Serene, she lifted the pigeon in her hands. Gold glinted on the tips of its flight feathers. This caused a commotion amongst the souls by the boy. They spoke urgently. A soul knelt by the boy's head, shook his shoulder gently, and pointed to the pigeon. The boy's head dropped back, his jaw slacked, and his mouth opened. The girl's arms lifted higher, and the golden fingers of the boy's soul fed through his mouth and clamped onto the boy's teeth. The soul pulled itself up through his throat; first the head, and then his bony chest, his narrow thighs, and finally his skinny legs stepped from his mouth. The soul next to him patted his back, and the souls clapped, and gesticulated excitedly, at the bird. The pigeon's soul was perched on the girl's hands and glittered in the sunlight; it cocked its head, ruffled its feathers, stretched out its neck, flapped its wings, and sprang towards the sun. The souls erupted, cheering and whooping, and leapt into the air, in twos and threes. The soul who had helped the boy took his hand, and the pair floated through the sky; the shapes of them melted as one. The girl stood over the pit of ageing flesh, smiled at Daniel, and left. The sun passed through the sky and started to sink.

When Daniel woke, he cleansed his cuts and ate, and thought about the girl. At dusk, he returned to the pigeon's grave. Her fragrance lingered; he had just missed her. There was a new note, "Thank you for writing. I have to go. Good luck and good bye." Mist enveloped Daniel's head. He raced up the street, but she was not there. He sped past the abbey, through its garden, in and out of the town centre to the edge of the square, where police tape fluttered, and realized late she would not come here; she would travel oppositely, away from the memory. Daniel doubled-back as fast as he could, past the pigeon's grave, and out of town. Sweat wetted his back and dripped down his neck. He fancied he scented her by the canal, but roses in a garden made him doubt himself. Daniel paused under a bridge to catch his breath and smashed his forehead, crying from frustration. Momentarily, he breathed a hint of her. Concentrating, Daniel listened to the air, but no clues hung there. Despair thundered upon him, and a mechanical hum vibrated around, filled his ears and engulfed his body so his organs tremored. Daniel cowered in a cold stone corner, mouthing elephants, and the train passed overhead.

He took off, darted across the road, and ran with the flow of cars. The traffic lights by the station turned red, amber, and green; he held onto their changing pattern while his chest burned and arrived at the station in orange light. The door was locked. Daniel hurtled through the side gate to the platform. The tracks chirped, and a high-pitched whistling skinned his ears; the air squashed, and he was trapped in blasting light. Daniel threw himself to the ground, braced his arms around his head, and his boots convulsed against concrete. Explosion flashed the landscape white; hands and legs fell from the sky, leaked blood through rags of camouflage, and empty helmets bounced beside him, while his nails scoured lines on rock. Metal and metal ground together, the halting grind of wheels on tracks trembled through his ribs and ears, and the whistling stopped. Counting, Daniel opened his eyes and peered under his elbow.

Passengers boarded: a couple carrying a bag between them, a girl with a low-slung rucksack, and a late commuter in full day-glow. In the space at the end, where the tracks entered black, Daniel saw a figure move. He scrambled up, lurched towards it, and stopped. The girl had one foot on the train, and her hand gripped the handle; she looked down the lines ahead. Daniel went closer. The breeze ruffled her hair, and revealed her scar, detail of the night before, written cruelly in her skin. Daniel's throat dried. An alarm summoned, and the girl stepped up. The doors sucked shut behind her. The train revved its engine, and gained momentum, built up speed, and carried the girl away. Daniel stared, shivering. He stared until the tracks stopped humming, and she was gone.

# 5

"Most of the time, I had no idea what he was talking about, but it sure sounded smart, like stuff I sort of remember hearing about in school. Like there might be a big score one day."

# ULTIMATUM GAMES
### James McCrone

"How much did you make last year?" Brian asked me one day.

"I don't know."

"Thirty-five, maybe forty thousand?"

That sounded high, but I didn't want to look bad, so I said, "Yeah, I guess. Between legal, under-the-table work and . . . other stuff. Sure."

I'd just told him about a food truck I'd seen on Washington Avenue that was doing good business—cash only. "Hit 'em on a Friday night," I'd said. "Bet we clear two thousand, maybe two and a half."

"You're gonna have to stick them up," he'd answered in that snotty voice he had when he was telling me something he thought I ought to have known. Like I hadn't thought of needing a gun already. "And once you've used a weapon the whole PRS-OGS sentencing matrix starts getting draconian. So it's not enough."

I figured "draconian" meant bad.

I'd met Brian the Brain like six months earlier. He had a funny way of saying things that I kinda liked. Most of the time. He was the same age as me, 20, but he was tall and kinda sickly skinny. He dressed all in black, except maybe sometimes a scarf or something had some color in it. And he was always reading a book. He'd occasionally get in arguments with some hipster over what he was reading. It almost felt like the way he'd leave the book on a café table was meant to push people's buttons. They'd argue in these hissy whispers about bullshit. It was better than TV, even if sometimes it felt like I was watching PBS.

"Risk and reward," he'd said that day as we sat there sipping coffee, leaving ripe fruit like the food truck just hanging there. The book on the table that day was *The Wealth of Nations*, which sounded like a really big score. "That's how you have to think about it. And if you're going to go away for five or more years for armed robbery—first offense—you'd better be sure the risk was worth the reward. So, $150,000 might be worth it in that sense—five years times $30,000 a year. But then you have to figure that you'll need a partner, and then your take's $75,000 at best . . .."

Sometimes I worried that he talked big but didn't want to actually do anything. He had these big ideas about a crew run by him. I'd glommed onto him more like a partner because he seemed different, smarter than the guys I'd been hanging around. Most of the time, I had no idea what he was talking about, but it sure sounded smart, like stuff I sort of remember hearing about in school. Like there might be a big score one day.

He'd listen to me pining for good old days I'd never known, except through stories my dad and uncles would tell, and he'd say something like: "Yes, it's a sort of market evolution, isn't it? Like from hunter-gathering to agriculture—in the past, you'd take what you need, when you needed it. Now, you have to plant the seed, have to nurture it. Can't be impatient. It takes time and money."

When my dad was working—I guess we can call it that, right?—you'd hijack a truck full of meat or seafood and sell it on. You'd leave the empty truck somewhere and call the truck company from a payphone to tell them where it was. No hard feelings, and an equal share with the guys who did it (which sometimes included the driver, who'd tipped you off). Or you boost a couple dead pigs off the back while the driver was delivering something else. Cheese was good, my dad used to tell me, because you didn't have to sell it right away, didn't have to worry so much about fast spoilage like with meat and seafood. I mean, it's already spoiled, am I right?

I was down to my last $50, and I was figuring I'd leave Brian to his espresso and reading, go see if someone else wanted to help me do a little gathering, when he said: "What if there were something that *was* worth the risk? No guns. Simple B-and-E. We risk nine months to two years."

"Burglary's never simple," I said back to him. That sounded like a smart thing to say.

"Good," said Brian. "Yes." He reached over to another table and grabbed that day's *Inquirer*. He opened the local section to the second page and pointed. The headline read: "Rozovsky Museum and Library to Move Collection." I thought he'd pointed at the wrong thing and took the paper from his hands to scan the whole page.

"Normally," he began, "there'd be no way we could get in there—and get out."

"You're talking about *books*?"

"Yes. Rare. Expensive." I guess he caught my look because he added all snooty: "Some people value books. And they'll pay top dollar for originals and manuscripts."

"It's a fucking museum," I said, reading through the article. "That's some *Mission: Impossible* shit right there. Mostly, I mean impossible."

"Agreed," said Brian. He loved to talk like that, like he was the teacher and he'd been waiting for me to catch up to him. "But they're renovating a whole wing, and a number of items are in a house nearby."

"That's not in here," I said, referring to the news article.

"No, it's not." That same damn tone, like he was talking to a kid. "I saw them moving some things the other day. It looks like it's a two-part move, like maybe the final, secure holding spot isn't ready yet or something. So first, they have to get those collections out of the way, and away from the dust and work."

"And the temporary spot isn't as well guarded?" I asked, catching on.

"Nothing like."

"How'd you know about all this?" I asked. "Were you just waiting for a book heist?"

"They happened to have a rare book I wanted to get a look at, and when I went by, they told me they'd be closing soon for six months. The woman at the front desk even bitched about how crazy and disorganized it all was: 'It was like hurry up and wait, wait some more and then go!' she said. And that got me thinking."


We went up to Center City to check out the "target," as Brian called it. The main museum-library sat mid-block between a bunch of huge, old row houses—a big, modern place carved out of where two or three row houses used to stand. The paper said the museum had bought the row house next to its main building, and they'd started a gut rehab. They were going to break through one of the walls and connect the old with the new. Well, the new*er*. Anyway, the wall demo had started.

The temporary storage building was just an old, empty, expensive looking row house on the corner of the same street. We scoped it out, too. I bought a 40 and we walked down the little street—an alley, really—behind both buildings, like we were just looking for somewhere quiet to drink. Brian would wipe the rim before pretending to take a slug. Well, I thought, that let me know where I stood.

It looked like a slam dunk. The storage house back door was heavy metal, but there were old Bilco doors just to the left of it leading to the basement. We checked out the sightlines at the bottom of the street, too. If we backed up a van, we'd be concealed behind a fence that shielded the house's back driveway. Looking at the back of the building as we pretended to kill off the bottle, there were no cameras there, either. Not even above the heavy metal door.

"No cameras, and no alarms," I noted. "The Bilco doors look really old. That's the way in. Even if we run into more locks coming up out of the basement, we're inside and can just drill them."

"Can you handle alarms?" he asked.

"No," I said.

"Then if we run into any alarms, we abandon it."

"Agreed," I said, hoping he caught *my* tone. "I gotta ask you, if this stuff's worth so much, how come they're not protecting it better?"

He shook his head. "I don't know. I think they're just desperate, and that it's only temporary. I bet they think no one knows they're doing it." He paused and then got real serious. "We need to talk about how this is going to go. I found it, and I'm going to dictate what we take and what we leave behind. I know what's valuable and what isn't. And you don't. Also, I've already got two collectors—"

"Fences, you mean?"

"Pretty much, yeah. I've been talking to two so that I know I'm getting the best deal, like comparison shopping."

I nodded. That was smart. One guy might try to fuck you, but if he knew his competitor might be bidding, too, you were more likely to get a fair offer.

"If we do it my way," he continued, "I see us clearing maybe as much as $100,000. But the split's going to be two-thirds, one-third. Not half and half."

"Sixty-forty?" I offered.

"No. Take it or leave it."

Even by his crazy risk-reward matrix, I was coming out pretty good. A third, $33,000 was as much as I probably made in my best years. And this was all at once. "Ok," I said.

"Very rational," said Brian.

I wasn't sure what he meant by that, but I didn't like it.

We decided that it would be best to go for it that night: "temporary" cut both ways—good for us now, but maybe not if we waited. I got my cousin's van, telling him I needed to do some hauling, and that I'd slip him $50 when I got paid in a week or so. He was cool with that. I spent $12 for some moving blankets from U-Haul and borrowed a laundry dolly from a guy I know. Then I got my dad's old tools out of the shed at the back of my mother's house. The "split" we'd agreed to still rankled, but like I said, it was great money. And there were lots of guys who could do what I did, so he didn't need to use me.

We hit the storage house at just after 1:30 in the morning and worked for an hour or so. My slim jim got us through the Bilco doors and then up through the basement to the main floor where all the stuff was. Turns out we didn't need the laundry cart. I got us in, but Brian took over once we got to the storage area. He'd hand me stuff he thought was valuable, and I'd take the wooden boxes or cases to the van through the back door.

He wore this goofy headlamp flashlight thing on his forehead, so he could "keep his hands free." When we finished, we locked the back door, and then I reset the Bilco doors. They didn't lock completely, but they looked and stayed closed. Unless someone looked carefully it might be days before they realized we'd hit them.

"Like a locked room mystery," Brian said with a smile as we pulled out. I smiled too, except it was because he hadn't taken that stupid light off his head yet.


The Fence we met with next morning ran this crazy shop packed with chandeliers just off South Street. And I mean packed—hanging, like you'd figure, but also on the floor, resting on chairs, some half-in, half-out of boxes. You had to pick your way through it to get to his little desk in the back. I'd noticed the place before. I'd never seen anyone going in or coming out, and I'd wondered how he stayed in business. I figured I knew now. The guy was short and old, kinda used up looking. His hair was a bunch of different shades of gray, and all of it greasy, plastered tight against the top of his head. He looked like he'd slept in his clothes. For like the third time in a row.

If he'd been panhandling outside his own shop, you wouldn't have thought twice about it. He smoked these rank, cheroot cigars, too, all bent and evil smelling. I guess if no one ever comes in the shop you don't have to worry about the smoking police. He and Brian seemed to know each other. I hung around for a bit, listening to them "ooh" and "awe" over the stuff, and trying to out-intellectual each other, but that got dull and I walked up the street to Lorenzo's for one of their massive slices.

By the time I wandered back, they'd opened most of the boxes and were tallying up what was there, and how much it was worth. They were talking in these low whispers, like maybe I wasn't supposed to hear. I walked over to see how it was going, and they stopped talking.

"You know," I said, "we're all in this together, so maybe it's not a bad idea for me to know everything that's going on."

"Of course," said the Fence. "You're absolutely right." He smiled and blinked at me, his eyes absolutely massive behind some seriously thick reading glasses. Brian looked at me like I had embarrassed him. His face got really red.

"I can sell these eight here right away," the Fence said pointing at some books half-in and half-out of their wooden storage boxes. "I have a standing order from various clients. I'm pretty sure I can move these other five quickly, too." He pointed at a different pile. "And I know a collector who'd pay handsomely for these two, though I haven't worked with him before. These," he said, pointing at the rest of the pile, "I might sell on to other dealers, who might be able to get something. I'd have to be careful, of course." He paused, looking at us both. "I can get you the money in four days."

"And how much are we talking about?" I looked at both the Fence and at Brian.

"Seven hundred thousand," said the Fence. "Maybe a little more."

I practically choked. Brian looked upset.

We left behind a couple of select "pieces" as Brian and the Fence called them so he could show his clients, and the Fence took photos of everything else. He told us he'd be in contact when he was set to make the trade. He hoped it would be less than four days.

"I understand," said Brian. "Managing expectations." Whatever the fuck that meant.

He gave us $500 cash to tide us over. I slipped my cousin a $100 so we could keep the van for the rest of the week. I parked it in the yard behind my mother's house, and we both slept in it for the next three nights, guarding our haul, our heads at opposite ends on the floor, pretty much next to each other. I kept a gun in a backpack next to me. There was no way I was going to risk letting this slip out from under me. This haul was the result of neglect, and I didn't like the idea of losing it due to our own carelessness.

"It's kinda like the old days," I said that first night as we both lay there. "You see something, you take it." It wasn't dead pigs, sure, but it felt good.

"It's nothing like that. This took planning and foresight."

"It took someone with the smarts to see that something valuable wasn't being watched the right way. And taking it."

My mother would fix us lunch and dinner in the house. We'd sit in the kitchen, looking out the back window at the van. She never asked what was going on, bless her. But she cooked her famous breaded cutlet two nights in a row, like she knew she could maybe spend a little extra.

For all his smarts and cold, high-class manner, Brian had shitty manners. I mean fine, you're full, but you say "No, thank you, Mrs. Porter, it was great, but I couldn't eat another bite." You don't just say "no." And you don't say, "I'll take another beer," you say "I'd love another beer, if there is any," or something like that. Especially when you've made a sour face about what kind of beer she's serving; and *especially* because now you're gonna make her get up from the table. Not to mention that it's a big fucking thing that she's even got beer in the house. Also, when you're done, you don't just stand up like it's a restaurant and some busboy's going to clean up after you. Obviously, there's no way my mother's gonna let a guest do a lick of work to help, but you're supposed to offer. Sometimes I wondered if he'd evolved at all.

"We have to be careful," said Brian the second night as we lay in the dark, cold van, sleeping bags zipped tight.

"I know," I said.

"You particularly," he said. "You can't be advertising this; can't be buying things everyone knows you can't afford."

"Watch him," my mother said the next morning while she and I ate breakfast and Brian took a shower. (Small consolation: he didn't leave his wet towels on the floor.) "Be careful," she said in a low whisper even though there was no way he could hear with the water running. "I don't know what you two've got going, hon. And I won't ask. But that one . . ." she shook her head and then looked out the back window at the van. "Is it worth it?" she asked.

I nodded.

"All the more reason to watch that creep."


That night in the van, I said, "So far, so good. I haven't seen anything in the papers. If we can settle up before it's even known, we did it . . .."

"Yes," said Brian impatiently. "The only thing that might give us away is some big show."

"Look, I don't know why you think *I'm* the problem. No one in my family's ever had a score like this, but we've had big ones. Things I've heard about much, much later."

"And you're sure it's not just idle bragging, trying to make them seem bigger than they are."

"I'm sure," I said, hating him. "You make sure the stuff that counts is secure, but you don't splash any money around. Maybe take a long weekend at the Shore . . .."

"It all sounds so small," he said.

"It's the big dreams that'll get you busted."

"It was my big dreams, my vision, that got us this score—one bigger than your family ever had before."

I propped myself up to look at him. "My mother doesn't even know what we've done. And she never will. I won't tell my friends because they'd be hitting me up for scratch all the time. And some of those idiots would talk."

I'd thrown in with Brian on this gig, and if the payoff came, I wouldn't regret it. I mean, one-third of $700,000 was $231,000. But it didn't stop me thinking—and worrying—about his big plans. They obviously didn't include me, but frankly, that was fine by me.

I didn't want to tell him my plan—launder some of the money at a casino. Make things nice for my mother inside, but nothing that shows on the outside—a new stove, a new fridge, new HVAC; get an electrician I know to fix some things, a plumber. Maybe get her one of those tall, old people toilets for the first-floor bathroom. I heard those were better for your knees and hips.

"You could get out of Philly," he said.

"Why the hell would I do that? I like it here."

"And that's what I mean by small."


Thank God the Fence came through early, or I'd've probably killed Brian that third night. I thought a lot about the gun in my backpack as I lay there not sleeping, but I couldn't kill him in my mother's back yard. Would've felt weird about getting blood in my cousin's truck. And as far risk-reward goes . . . well, murder's a big step.

Frankly, for all his talk about me doing something stupid, he was the one who needed to worry. I know what I am—a cadger, a criminal. I get it: by the standards of this take, I was seriously penny ante. If we'd pulled that food truck gig, the cops would've been all over me—just the kind of small-time thing I'd pull. But that rep was my strength now. As long as I kept quiet, no one would even think about me as the kind of guy to pull off something like this. And it was Brian's weakness. For me, it was turning out that being lucky was better than being smart. Or so I thought.

We loaded the "pieces" back into the chandelier shop—Brian even helped carry some this time—and the Fence handed us a duffle bag stuffed full of money. "This has been smooth as silk."

"It's been a pleasure doing business," said Brian.

"These will be delivered probably before it's even known that they've been . . . well, that they're gone," said the Fence. "If you guys ever have another idea like this, you let me know right away."

Brian looked at me funny. "We will," he said. But I got the feeling this partnership wasn't going to last much beyond the next hour or so.

We drove down to Pier 70, to a parking lot by some big box stores on Columbus Boulevard near where the cat sanctuary is. The lot was wide open at nine o'clock in the morning—no people, no cameras. We climbed into the back. He opened the bag. "Each band is $10,000," he said.

He started tossing me the bands, counting them as he went. I grabbed my backpack and began stuffing them in around the gun. When he got to 17, he stopped flipping them to me. He rifled through an 18th, which he divided roughly in half, handing me the loose bills. "That's your cut," he said.

"I should be getting 23 of those," I said. "One-third of $700,000 is 231,000. If you wanna get pissy on the last thousand, I'm willing to overlook it. But you owe me six more bands, Brian."

"I've got plans for this," he said. Like that mattered.

"And I'm owed $231,000—one-third of the take, not a quarter of it. We agreed."

"It was my score," he said. "My vision. I saw right away it was going to be worth more than we thought."

"Right. After I got you in."

"Anyone could've done that," he said.

"Not you," I said. "Which is why you needed me. And you agreed to cut me in on a third. Which was already kinda fucked up. Now I'm only getting a quarter?"

"You were content with $33,000. Now you want more—and you're getting it. This is what's wrong with people like you. I've got plans."

"Fuck you and your plans," I said.

"Fuck you," he said. "You're getting *something* when you weren't getting anything before. It's rational to take the money." He actually seemed to think that he was making sense. But to drive his point home, he pulled a gun out of the bag, a short Glock 19, like the cops use. Had the Fence packed it for him? Had he been planning this all along?

"Now, it's just not as much as you thought," he added. "But it's still better than *you* could have ever come up with."

We were kneeling in the back, directly across from each other. I held the backpack in my lap. He held the gun low, aimed at my stomach.

"You're full of shit," I said. "Now you've got the gun, I suppose you're gonna want it all back." I stuffed my hand into the backpack and tossed one of the bands at him. I shoved my hand in again, but this time, deep in the bag, it closed around my gun nestled in with the money. "I'm just supposed to hand this over?"

He took a deep breath, sighed like he was sorry it had come to this. That I was making it difficult.

I shot him in the forehead.

Brian the brain, I thought. Not anymore.

My ears wouldn't stop ringing as I laid him out in the back. Blood was spreading quickly. My cousin was gonna be pissed, but I figured I could just buy him a new van after I torched this one. I zipped him into a sleeping bag, then stood up to peer out the windshield and door windows. Nothing moved. No one had heard or seen a thing.

"A kind of evolution," I remembered Brian had said as the ringing in my ears died down. But some things don't change. A deal's a deal.

# 6

"You get shit on your whole life, it makes you suspicious when something goes right."

# DRYING OUT
## Nils Gilbertson

When the ulcers get bad, I try to dry out for a while. I'm not talking about a little bit of gastric reflux—I mean when it burns like someone's going at my insides with a blowtorch. The damn things are a hell of a way for the Lord to punish my drinking. Sometimes the big man upstairs has a real sick sense of humor. Gives me a habit, the habit gives me a hole in the gut, and—unless I kick the habit—the hole turns to a bloody crater and my puke looks like leftover grounds spoiling at the bottom of some cheap coffee-maker. When it gets real bad, I try to cut the booze for a couple of weeks, let it heal up.

Easier said than done. Especially since Grillionaires, the burger and beer joint where I worked, couldn't stay afloat during the pandemic. Joey, the owner, tried to push the takeout angle, but no one came for the burgers. People came because it's the type of place you take a double-decker with bacon, a basket of cheese fries, and a pitcher of beer to a booth alone, and no one'll look at you sideways. I bitched about the twelve bucks an hour, but compared to the one-time six-hundred-dollar check from Uncle Sam, it didn't look too bad in the rearview. What else was there for a guy to do but drink? Stuck in a studio apartment in a half-dead city without a job to give me some semblance of routine, and barely enough in the bank to pay next month's rent. It's no way to live, but sometimes you don't get much say in the matter. So instead of cutting the booze, looking for a job, and following the recommended dosage on the side of the Advil bottle, I made little compromises with myself. Only drinking beer tonight. That sort of thing. Too bad I wasn't any better at keeping promises to myself than I was at keeping them to others.

I was about a week into a bender that consisted of plastic-bottle gin,

YouTube videos of serial killer interviews, and Wheel of Fortune. As I cursed myself for not solving the puzzle on an episode I'd already seen, my phone rang.

"Yeah?"

"Dev? It's Adam. What's up? How're things?"

I glanced around the small, grimy room. "Could be worse."

"Look, Jill and I are going a little stir crazy with both of us working from home these days, and we're going to stay at this bed and breakfast out in the hills for the week. We were thinking you could stay at our place. Housesit while we're gone."

Stir crazy? They had a closet bigger than my part bedroom—part kitchen—part recycling project. That reminded me, I could make a few bucks off of the bottles huddled in the corner. I didn't give him a hard time, though. Adam had always been a good one. I'd known him since we were kids growing up in apartments across the hall, all the way through high school. After that, he went to college and climbed the professional ladder. Broke guys like me held it in place for him. I chuckled at the self-righteous instinct. I never did a damn thing for him. If anything, I greased the rungs. Still, he kept calling, kept inviting me over. I wondered if, roles reversed, I'd do the same. I took some gin from the bottle.

"You want me to stay at your place?" I asked. "Why?"

"Jill likes someone keeping an eye on it. You know, water the plants, collect the mail. Also," he said, "we're having some issues with the pipes and there's a guy scheduled to come out. We'd like someone to be there. It shouldn't cause you any issues."

"Sure, but me?"

Adam paused. "Times are tough, Dev. I thought you might be having a hard go of it in the city, with the lockdown and everything."

I looked out the window at the empty streets and tried to think of the last face-to-face conversation I had. I couldn't think of a single one, beyond mumbling *thanks* and *have a good one* to the cashier at the local bodega. Their house was about thirty minutes outside of town. Not quite the sticks, but they had room to stretch out. A nice, two-story brick place with the next neighbor half a block away. Not to mention, Jill didn't like having booze around. Her parents had been drinkers. Whenever they had get-togethers it was B.Y.O.B. and take what you don't finish. I winced as a gnawing pain ate its way from my lower back to my sternum.

"I'd be happy to," I said.

It was time I dried out.


Jill greeted me with a hug on the front porch. Her hair smelled like the fruit snacks I liked as a kid and I felt bad for not showering that morning. I hoped I didn't smell as rotten as I felt. Adam gave me a tour of the place while Jill finished packing. I'd been over plenty of times but had never been upstairs before. It was funny the sort of things wealthy folks had in their homes: a shower with two shower heads, a tub so deep you could drown in it, a bed wider than it was long—and it was plenty long. It dawned on me that I'd never lived in a house before. The city'd never loosened its grip on me. I loved how easy it was to disappear in the city—let yourself be swallowed by bustling crowds. No one acknowledged your existence, and I liked that. But these days, the empty, locked-down streets made me feel exposed, naked. Looking out the bedroom at the snow-dusted trees as they obscured the distant roof of the closest home, I sensed you could disappear out here, too. In a different way.

Adam gave me a to-do list. Little things I could finish in under an hour if I put some hustle into it. What in the hell was I going to do the rest of the day? Reading my mind, he showed me how to work the Xbox. It had video games and all the streaming apps. He even had a virtual reality headset, but I didn't want to mess around with that given my alcohol-starved brain. It was great, him letting me crash, but I almost felt bad about it. What did I do to deserve that sort of break? I tried to shake the feeling. You get shit on your whole life, it makes you suspicious when something goes right.

"Oh, and the last thing," he said. "I recommend you stay out of the basement. We had some issues with the pipes and it's a shitstorm down there. Smells like old garbage."

"What's wrong with them?"

He shrugged. "It's beyond my handyman skills. A few pipes are leaking some sort of sludge. But don't worry, the hot water's still running, for now at least. We got a guy coming out in a couple of days. A neighbor recommended him. I hope he can take care of it."

"I'll make sure he has what he needs."

"Great." He gave me the number of the place they were staying.

"Just in case. Doubt there's service out there."

You bet I made the most of the amenities at my disposal. I took a hot bath and even set up Adam's tablet on the fancy wooden bath tray straddling the porcelain tub. Watched some college hoops and ate a couple of vanilla yogurts while I had a good soak. Jill even had some bubble bath gel, but a guy's got to draw the line somewhere. It was good to get some food in me, too, and yogurt was one of the few things that didn't set my stomach on fire.

I stayed in the tub for so damn long that the tablet ran out of juice and the tips of my fingers were like raisins. It was then that I noticed the quiet. Pure, unrelenting silence, which summoned all the times I'd ever felt alone. It scared the hell out of me. I glanced out at the trees. It was getting dark.

I got out pretty quick after that. A chill went through me as I dried off, checking the corners of the room. Nothing. Cutting the booze was never fun. The cravings, the shakes, the sweats, the paranoia. Familiar territory. I felt it coming on, but that wasn't it. No, something else. So damn *quiet*. I couldn't stand it. I also couldn't help wiping myself down with the towel over and over, like I couldn't get dry—like there was some sort of wet mold growing on me. I gave up and threw on some clothes and went downstairs, eager for the T.V.'s company. I flipped on Jeopardy, a thinking man's Wheel of Fortune.

My mind drifted as I watched, reflecting on the terror that came over me in the bathroom. It made sense. Even with the city on lockdown, there was still the constant rumble of construction, the wail of sirens, the sounds of who-knows-what in the alley below my window. You got used to the gritty chorus to the point it was like white noise. Soothing. Alone, in the big house, in the country, it was me and my damn self. Drying out the best I could. I tried not to think about it too much and let my eyelids get heavy.

The quiet woke me. It was three in the morning and the brightness of the T.V. lit the room. I was cold and sweating and my stomach felt like it was trying to digest a rusty nail. Before heading upstairs to the bedroom, I peered out the back window. Pitch black and moving. Like when you close your eyes in the dark and formless clumps of light dance from sight. But, there was something out there, out in the yard. There were specks of light—eyes—in the darkness. Watching.

I don't know how long I stood for, staring into the night. The eyes flickered, but remained. I couldn't feel my hands, so I glanced down to make sure they were still there. Shaking bad. My knuckles were dry and cracked with dabs of dried blood. When I looked back up, the specks of light were gone.

In the morning, I barely got to the toilet in time to puke. There was a little black in it but less than the days before. Last time I'd bothered going to the doc, she told me the black stuff was blood—the stomach acid changes its color. The human body is a fascinating thing. It was a relief to see less of it. I sat by the toilet for a while, spewing strings of warm, grainy spit. It made me feel worse the way I was dirtying their pristine bathroom.

My hands spasmed and I had the chills so bad that I popped a Klonopin. It was good to keep a few on hand when you were drying out. I went downstairs and had a yogurt and water. I couldn't stop fidgeting and wanted a drink like nothing else.

You think back to the good old days when you're out with the boys every Friday and Saturday. Wake up, swear off the poison. The mere thought of another swig makes you shudder. You go about your business for a few days, school or work, until it's Friday again, and the crack of a beer has you salivating. But, before you know it, the time between the hangover and the cravings shrivels and dies. The Friday night craving is there Tuesday morning, after a Monday night six-pack. It's a gradual thing—you give it an inch, it'll take a mile. And put a hole in your gut. Before you know it, it's not a choice. It's an impulse—a compulsion—like a hiccup.

I thought a walk around the neighborhood and the cold air on my face would do me some good. As I started down the street, I saw a man in work overalls and a ball cap loitering in the driveway on the side of the yard. For a second my chest throbbed, but then I remembered what Adam said about the pipes. I walked over to him. He didn't seem to notice and kept on examining the side of the house.

"Hey, you here for the pipes?"

He grinned at me. His teeth were yellow and crooked, a few missing. "That's right. I'm the plumber. You the owner? Mr. . . .." He looked down at a notepad.

"No, I'm a friend of the Vincents, housesitting for them while they're away. I'm Dev."

"That's right, now it's coming back to me." He rubbed the red-brown stubble on his sharp chin.

"I hope they gave you some directions," I said. "Adam didn't tell me much, except that you were coming, and that it's a mess down there in the basement."

He kept grinning at me and I wished he'd stop. "Point me to the pipes," he said. "I'll take it from there."

I showed him the basement and he went back to his van parked out front and brought some tools in. I couldn't remember the van being there before. Why would I? Only a car on a street. Didn't notice it because there was nothing to notice.

I skipped the walk. Call me paranoid, but I felt some sort of responsibility for the place, and who the hell knew who this guy was? Why was he skulking around the side of the house? Why didn't he knock on the door? It didn't sit right with me. Did he even say Adam's name once? Jill's? Frozen with suspicion, I spent the rest of the morning thinking it over, again and again, as though one more time around the anxiety carousel would bring me to lucidity. My body was petrified, but my hands were going like butterfly wings. I tried to hold one with the other.

Summoned by the silence, next came thoughts of all the horrible things I'd done over the years. Appraising my sins, I recognized I was in a better position than I deserved. I thanked Almighty God in heaven that I was a ghost, a nobody. Nobody cared about the sins of a nobody. I thought I'd be sick again. Not wanting to leave the plumber alone, I took laps around the backyard. It was pretty damn big, so it worked out all right. After about fifty times around, I went in for a restless nap, Jeopardy loud in the background.


I woke from a half-sleep to the plumber standing in the doorway, a mangy tan and white cat under his arm.

"This their cat?" he asked. He stared at me like I was a moron while I tried to go back to sleep, assuming it was some sort of waking dream.

"Hey, you dumb or something?" he said. "This their cat? I found him poking around outside the garage door."

"Nuh. Uh—no. What? No, there's no cat here."

He looked down at the animal under his arm. "Looks like a cat to me."

I shook my head. "They don't have a cat here. It's not their cat."

He shrugged. "Seems like it. I tried to shoo him away, but he wouldn't leave." As he spoke, the cat squirmed from his grasp and scampered onto the side of the couch by my outstretched feet. The thing wouldn't take its damn eyes off of me. "It sure looks at home here," he said. "Maybe they forgot to tell you about him. Anyhow, they got a hell of a mess down there, and it's going to get worse before it gets better. I'll need a few days to get it straightened out, so I'll be back tomorrow. That all right?"

"Uh-huh."

He twisted his head and cracked his neck. It sounded like a tree branch breaking. He left and it was silent again. The black ovals in the cat's green eyes bore into me. I thought of the flickering lights in the yard the night before. As it watched me, I started to laugh. It was all so damn surreal—like someone was playing a trick on me. The simplest explanation seemed to be that there was nothing else outside my swollen gray matter. Everyone but me mere characters, nothing more. And why should they be? I laughed and laughed until I felt sick.


The cat wouldn't stop following me. It never made a sound—never a purr, its footsteps muted on the hardwood floor. I couldn't stand it. There I was, trying to sweat the poison out, damn near losing my mind, and now I had this animal following, watching, judging. It had judging eyes. It was a pompous son of a bitch the way it stared at me, like it was my better.

A light snow fell outside. I was so weak and achy that I tried to go to bed. I didn't know what time it was—it was pretty dark out, but the heavy, gray clouds hid the shade of the sky behind it. I got deep under the soft covers. Jesus, they were nice. Too bad Adam and Jill would have to wring the sweat out of them. The cat had perched itself on the long table opposite the bed. In the dim room, its eyes shone hazy yellow.

I ducked my head under the covers and basked in pure blackness. I worried about puking under there, but had no choice. All I could think of was getting to the next moment—one that may be a little less miserable than the last. The bottle of Klonopin in the bathroom wasn't an option—the twenty-step trek was like Everest in my state. No, I'd better stay under. I couldn't even trust my own head. Wind howled and I peeked out and it was much darker than the moment before. The snow came harder. Beckoning from the corner, yellow eyes. Those damn, yellow eyes.

When I came to, I was wet and naked and shivering, the covers on the floor beside me. Brightness flooded through the windows like the sun had swallowed the sky. It was odd because it was nighttime. Light glinted off the sheet of snow that layered the balcony. It must've still been night, though. I knew it was, I don't know why, but I knew it. The cat stood in the doorway, licking its paws until it saw me awake. It stopped and stared.

Ear-splitting clangs and thumps below me. The foreign sounds made my head light. I took a few breaths. More noises. In a way, a relief, stifling the silence. But I hadn't forgotten my duties, watching the house and all. It was the least I could do. I checked the drawer next to the bed and found a hunting knife. I wasn't sure how I knew it'd be there. Had Adam mentioned it? Somehow, I knew.

I started down the stairs, the cat on my heels, the noise like thunder through the hollow halls. I felt it somewhere deep in the house, something wrong. I got to the first floor and kept going down. It smelled like death and rot, but I swallowed the sour heat in the back of my throat and proceeded on my descent. The deeper I went, the more muffled things got. Clangs like hot shards of metal rattling in my skull—something down there—spurting—the acrid smell—a smell like pure evil. I couldn't stand it. My knees buckled and the muscles in my legs surrendered and I let myself plunge into whatever abyss awaited me.

The plumber sat above me on the couch, holding an icepack to my head. The cat watched from the corner.

"You're having a hard time, aren't you, son?" He looked down at my tremoring hands.

"I—I need your body."

He shook his head. "I'm sorry, but I can't do that for you."

"*Please.*"

His mouth churned as though he had to chew on his words before speaking them. "Even if I could, it wouldn't do a damn thing. You'd ruin the next one. No, the body's not the problem, it's a symptom. The problem's your soul." He glanced around the room. "It's sort of like a house. You can patch it up all you want, but if it's poisoned in its roots, its guts, its insides—eventually it's going to seep out. Your friend should've called me a long time ago. It don't look so good down there."

"Can you fix it?"

He looked down at me. His eyebrows were like overgrown weeds. "Might take some time, but sure. Won't be easy, though. I got to figure the source of the mess. Once it's so bad, it's hard to pinpoint the root of the trouble."

"Sometimes things break," I said. "You ignore it for a while. It gets worse."

He chuckled. "I won't argue with that." He checked his watch. "I'll be back tomorrow. There's more work to do."


I couldn't stand it. I writhed and squirmed as though stillness would mean death. The burn in my gut spread like wildfire to the rest of me, all over my skin. My throbbing muscles were alight with torched nerve endings. I felt my bones' sharp edges prodding my insides. The only chance seemed to be to shed my former self like dead skin.

The cat was still there. The night before, in a rage, I'd caught it in the snowy yard, torn it limb from limb, fed on it, its legs like drumsticks. The corpses of men and women and children who'd live there centuries before howled as I scarfed it down.

But it was still there, like some sort of demon.

I tore through the cabinets in the kitchen, looking for a drink. The bedroom, the office, the hallway closet. Adam *had* to keep a bottle somewhere. The cat laughed as I searched. I felt Adam's hands on me, grabbing me, turning me, pointing me in the direction of his stash. Before I could snatch a bottle, Jill's parents—decaying flesh flaking from facial bones—smashing them. I figured I'd put some sort of curse on the house. The poison leaking from me and seeping into its very foundation. I rushed out the front door and puked on the porch. What came out was like wet tar, searing my nostrils, bubbling hot and thick in the back of my throat. When I looked up, there was the plumber, standing in front of his van, watching.

"You gotta help me. You got a bottle? Can you get me to a store for a bottle?"

He nodded. "I'll take care of you, son. I got what you need." He went back into his van and pulled out his tool bag and a mason jar of clear liquid. Moonshine? That'd do it. Without a word, he went towards the house. I followed him.

He helped me onto the couch, went to the kitchen for a glass, and poured a bit of the liquid. "You be careful with this, now."

I threw it back. It tasted like a mixture of vodka and detergent and cotton candy. Vaguely familiar. It numbed my mouth and throat and esophagus on its way down. I gestured for more and he obliged. As he did, there was sadness on his face.

I put five shots of the stuff back. I nestled into the warmness in me and, to my surprise, my stomach felt all right. I lay on the couch, smiling. He started getting a few tools out. The smile glued to my face, all sensation drained from me until I was paralyzed.

The cat watched from the corner as the plumber started going to work on me. He opened me up and removed my liver, kidneys, heart, lungs, you name it. As he did, he'd rinse each organ in the liquid from the mason jar, dry it off with a dirty towel, and fasten it back into me with a few pipe fittings to keep things connected. Last, he took out my soul and gave it a good rinse. I screamed for the duration but my smiling mouth was stitched shut. For a while, I watched the procedure from the corner of the room, through black ovals. Then back inside me, as he closed me up.


The next day the snow had melted. The house was intact, empty but for me. I lay on the couch, reflecting, the past a muddled portrait of regret. The previous day felt as distant as my first memory. I couldn't find the damn cat anywhere—probably found a way out and back home, now that the snow was gone.

There was an invoice on the kitchen counter. $856 for *cleaning and resealing rotten pipes.* I was almost grateful to never own so much as an apartment. But there was a mistake—the charge was to my name, not Adam's. I went to the door of the basement to take a look at the work, but the stench brought splintered memories I couldn't make much of but knew I wanted to forget. As I tried to fend them off, I felt something on my stomach. Something sharp and warm and wet.

I stripped my clothes off in the bathroom and, in the mirror, saw curves of stapled incisions crawling across my chest and gut like centipedes. The sight of it sent me to the sink, but only dry heaves came. As they did, I felt the sharp edges of the staples tear at my skin, loosening, pinging against the marble floor. Without looking, I put a couple of fingers to my stomach. I could feel them sticky, soaked in thick crimson. It was a hell of a thing trying to dry out.

# "Fun w/ Fill-in Stories"
## STORY KEY

*Sure, we'd all like to write noir. The fame, the fortune . . . it can be too much for one person to bear. Unfortunately, not all of us have the proclivity for human darkness that the esteemed writers of RHP possess. But with the help of a fun little game from our youth (just don't call them by their other name, or you'll get us sued), you too can feel like you played a part in creating a noir masterpiece!*

* * *

INSTRUCTIONS: Below is the fill-in key—fill it out, and flip to our fill-in story (pg. 149) to see how your tale shakes out!

1. NAME:_______________________________________

2. ADJECTIVE:___________________________________

3. COLOR:_______________________________________

4. ADVERB:______________________________________

5. ADJECTIVE:___________________________________

6. PAST-TENSE VERB:_____________________________

7. ADJECTIVE:___________________________________

8. ADJECTIVE:___________________________________

9. COLOR:_______________________________________

10. ADVERB:_____________________________________

11. SURNAME:____________________________________

12. SUPERLATIVE:_________________________________________

13. WINTER HOLIDAY:______________________________________

14. RELATION & NAME (i.e. "Aunt Sally"):___________________

15. NOUN:_______________________________________________

16. RELATION & NAME:_____________________________________

17. NOUN:_______________________________________________

18. RELATION:____________________________________________

19. MOOD:_______________________________________________

20. RELATION & NAME:_____________________________________

21. FOOD DISH:___________________________________________

22. RELATION & NAME:_____________________________________

23. DESSERT:_____________________________________________

24. MAIN COURSE DISH:____________________________________

25. ADJECTIVE (-ed):______________________________________

26. EXPLETIVE:___________________________________________

27. VERB (-ing):__________________________________________

28. EXPLETIVE:___________________________________________

29. RELATION & NAME:_____________________________________

30. NUMBER:_____________________________________________

31. VERB (ing):___________________________________________

32. PLURAL NOUN:________________________________________

33. NUMBER:_____________________________________________

34. NOUN (LOCATION):____________________________________

35. ADJECTIVE:___________________________________________

36. RELATION & NAME:_______________________________

37. COLOR:_______________________________________

38. EXPLETIVE:___________________________________

39. NUMBER:_____________________________________

40. ADJECTIVE:___________________________________

41. NUMBER:_____________________________________

42. NAME:_______________________________________

43. ADVERB:_____________________________________

44. EXPLETIVE (ing):______________________________

45. ADJECTIVE:___________________________________

46. VERB:________________________________________

47. ADJECTIVE:___________________________________

48. ADJECTIVE:___________________________________

"He wanted to be reassured that his work there had meant something, that all of the hours he'd sacrificed, the marriage and family he'd thrown over the side, was worth it; that he was—unlike everyone else who had left—irreplaceable. To his dismay, the paper continued to publish without him."

# NEGATIVE TILT
## Bobby Mathews

Corey liked the work, talking people into giving up their friends and family members, finding out where they'd moved. He'd prop one steel-toed Wellington on the bumper of his tow truck, come on with that good-old-boy attitude that it was so hard to say no to, and stay one step ahead of the skip tracers in the corporate office. Those conversations were the best part of his day, a bittersweet reminder of his old life, a life cut off with no apparent way back.

Corey spent less time in the truck than the other drivers. The big tow truck—a Dodge 4500 with a boom folded atop its foreshortened rear end like Jesus carrying a hydraulic steel cross—put people on guard. Being outside the cab made him seem harmless, like someone who could be shined on. It would only be later, after the unit had been scooped up sometime in the middle of the night, that some of them might realize the unassuming, bespectacled driver had put one over on them.

If the conversations were the best part, the constant driving was the worst. He dreaded the long stretches of highway, driving for hours at a time, like a hungry shark churning the water in search of the next meal. That was when his calves swelled painfully in his boots, constricting the blood flow until his feet began to tingle. Diabetes ran in his family, but he'd always tested negative. Now, as the years and the pounds piled up, he worried about his blood sugar as if it were an ancestral curse.

He treated this new career—he'd been doing it for more than a year now, so that counted as a new career as far as he was concerned—like his first newspaper job, working swing-shift hours so that he could talk to debtors during the day and sweep the city at night. He used the conversations like interviews, jotting down notes as soon as he got back into his own vehicle to keep his memory fresh.

That led him to his second-favorite part of the job: slipping through the deserted streets after midnight, using his GPS locator to compare addresses and locate the missing units. Professionally, they never called their prey "cars." In the repo industry, agents always referred to cars or trucks as units—as in, *find the wanted unit*—in everything from official reports to casual telephone conversations. Sometime around 2 a.m. was the magic time of night for Corey, listening to podcasts and letting his mind wander. The company had six trucks working the greater Birmingham area, from Trussville down to Calera, all the way up to Cullman and Jasper.

Mostly, Corey worked southwestern Birmingham, despoiled and rotting neighborhoods like Ensley, Brighton, Midfield, Fairfield, Bessemer, and Roosevelt.

The other agents based out of his office—Corey couldn't quite think of them as co-workers, because they never saw each other— thought he ran the most dangerous territory. But Corey didn't care. He hadn't cared about much at all since the old life had up and left him.


Buyouts, they called them. A month's severance pay for every year a journalist had worked for the paper. For Corey, who had been there twenty-four years, it was a sizable chunk of change. He didn't leap at the money, not at first. He thought about it for a couple of weeks, would have talked it over with Jeanne if she and the kids hadn't already left.

Twenty-four years was a long time in any business. He was only forty-seven, in the news business for nearly half his life. If he wasn't a journalist, what the hell was he?

Upper management increased the pressure. They wanted to hire younger people, get some of the heavier paychecks off the books for whatever merger they could finagle next. The advertising manager was the first one to go. The circulation manager got the ax when he wouldn't take the buyout. A twenty-two-year-old kid took his place.

As the longest-tenured member of the newsroom, Corey carried a heftier salary than most. If he took the buyout, he could take a year off, work on the novel he kept telling himself he should write. He did the math, and then sent an email to the publisher.

"I can't believe it," Nancy Boyette told him while he boxed up the few personal items on his desk. Nancy, his direct supervisor, with her glossy black hair and piercing blue eyes and bottle of Crown Royal in the bottom left-hand drawer of her big cherry desk. She'd been with the paper for eighteen months and always looked a little lost. "I thought you were a lifer."

But that was the problem. Newspaper work was a life sentence. It got in your blood, chasing the story down and wrestling it into print. As the deputy managing editor, he was the one who worked late and put the paper to bed. His phone was the first to ring in the morning if the shit hit the fan. The years made his skin sallow, and his hair had all but disappeared. There were lines on his face and ulcers in his stomach from the long nights and the short deadlines.

"It's time to get out," he told her, patting the check folded carefully in his breast pocket. "I was treading in deep water for a long time, and they finally threw me a lifeline."

"Probably the most money anyone's ever made from this paper," she said. Her voice sounded wistful. "You want to go out back for one last smoke?"

"Sure," Corey said. He left the half-filled cardboard box in his desk chair. There wasn't much left there, anyway. Once he'd decided to take the buyout, he'd started sifting his personal stuff out of the building a little at a time, so as not to cause alarm to the reporters who worked under him.

Corey and Nancy strode back to the loading dock together. This had been an end-of-day ritual for her, and a beginning of shift ritual for him. Each day they'd meet and discuss the budget items for the evening, sketching out the front page, talking through major and minor points like which stories still needed art, or what stories might break overnight and necessitate a flash page on the paper's website.

But that wasn't his problem anymore.

"We're going to miss you around here," Nancy said. She drew hard on her cigarette, which drew the tiny vertical lines along her lips into sharp relief. The first two fingers of her right hand, the ones that held the cigarette, were slightly yellowed, stained with nicotine. When she'd come to work at the paper, her nails had been perfectly lacquered. Now, most of the time the polish was chipped and peeling, and she picked at her fingers absently while the newsroom died its slow silent death around her.

"I've been missing it for a while now already," Corey said. His voice echoed around the open loading dock. When he first started, the dock was where the printers had taken the papers off of the press in freshly wrapped bundles that were warm to the touch. When Corey first started up in the newsroom on the main floor of the building, he could always tell when the press started running because the floor would vibrate softly, bringing even more life into the building. But in some buyout or other down the line, the old web press had been broken down and sold for parts. Now all that was left was the hollowed-out, oil-stained cavern where it had once been. All that is left of the dinosaurs are the bones, petrified relics of a bygone era.

The car was pointed nose-out down a steep driveway, a nearly new Honda Accord, hadn't been off the lot for six months before the debtor fell behind on payments. Corey hopped out, checked the Vehicle Identification Number—a little metal plate visible on the driver's side of the dash—to make sure he had the right vehicle. Back in the truck, the rumble of the engine under his ass, he lowered the boom. He had the newest truck in the fleet, with a hydraulic system that would drop the boom down past zero degrees—they called it negative tilt—so that it could recover units parked down steep driveways like this. Corey used the hydraulic controls to slide the boom under the Honda and lock onto the front wheels.

Corey engaged the boom and lifted the Honda so that only its rear wheels were touching the ground. He shifted the truck into drive and pulled out. No lights in the house behind him came on. No dogs barked. He'd gotten away with it again.

By the time the third day of unemployment rolled around, Corey knew he wasn't going to be able to write anything. It was the noise, or the lack of it. In the newsroom, with a deadline beating down on him and the hum of other journalists doing their own work, he could pound out a thousand words in an hour. No typos. No rewrites. The first draft of history, even if that history was just a recap of a county commission meeting that ended late.

In his sunny little home office, where he'd never done much more than write out checks for the monthly bills, writing anything as vast as a novel seemed impossible. He put the TV on in the living room, just for some noise, but found it impossible to concentrate. He found himself wandering into the living room, plopping down on the couch to check out the second half of *The View* and staying put for the judges, Judy and Mathis. By the time Ellen DeGeneres's show ended each afternoon, he'd be disgusted with himself for another wasted day.

He got a police scanner and placed it on his desk, hoping its familiar noise would help him find that Zen-like place in his mind where the world went away and the words came. It helped for a couple of days, and then it was just background noise. He started lurking on social media, checking out the paper's website. He wanted to be reassured that his work there had meant something, that all of the hours he'd sacrificed, the marriage and family he'd thrown over the side, was worth it; that he was—unlike everyone else who had left—irreplaceable. To his dismay, the paper continued to publish without him.

Nancy would occasionally text, gossiping about who else had gotten the ax. She was safe, of course. She hadn't been with the paper long enough to command a decent salary, and she was young enough that the long hours and the low pay must have seemed sort of romantic to her. But Corey could tell some cracks were appearing at the edges.

"No bonuses this quarter," she messaged one night, out of the blue. "We're still in austerity, whatever that means. FFS, I was counting on that money."

As for Corey, he blew through the buyout money. It wasn't real to him. He applied to other newspapers, but the only one that wanted to hire him was out in the Big Horn mountains of Wyoming. What the hell did he know about Wyoming? He flew out for the interview anyway—on their dime, not his—and found the little shop charming and quaint. The town, about five thousand people total, was mostly one- or two-story buildings, and the mountains surrounding the place painted a blue haze on the horizon. The high plains were scoured by constant wind, and in places bare rock was left scraped raw. The deep folds and creases in the earth looked like something Georgia O'Keefe might have imagined in her earlier and unfinished work.

The first thing he did with the publisher was to settle down on the man's back deck with three months' worth of newspapers and a supply of red Sharpie pens. Corey scanned the papers. He caught typos in headlines and cutlines. He questioned why certain stories got play, and why others didn't. Instead of being embarrassed, the publisher looked eager.

"This is just what we need here," the publisher said. "You

understand local. You understand what I want."

He brought out a bottle of Maker's Mark and they toasted one another. Several times after that, they found reasons to lift a glass until the bottle was empty and they were not. The publisher put him on a plane back to Alabama the next day, with a promise that he'd make an offer soon. But when the offer came, Corey's heart fell. They wanted him to work for half of what he'd been making in Birmingham.

"I can't do it," he finally told the publisher. His voice was calm, but tears flowed freely down his face. "I can't figure out how to make the money work."

Money. That's what it all came down to. Eleven months after he took the buyout, Corey was out of money, so stone-broke that his debit and credit cards were declined at the convenience store where he stopped to buy a soft drink.

He began perusing job websites harder, expanding his search parameters until he found something that caught his eye. DRIVER WANTED IMMEDIATELY, it said, and listed a phone number. That was all. He called the number, and a woman's voice answered.

"I'm calling about the job you listed," he said, and then she cut him off.

"Can you pass a drug test?"

Corey grinned at the phone. He'd never done any kind of illegal drug—not ever—the only one of his friends from high school and college who could say that. He'd often wondered at the lure of a forbidden high. But it had simply never appealed to him, so he never did it. Peer pressure, it seemed, wasn't so inevitable after all.

"Yes," Corey said, and he could feel cool relief flush down his neck. "I can pass it."

"Good," the woman said. "The last three guys who wanted this job couldn't." She gave him an address in Pinson, a small town northeast of Birmingham. He read it back to her.

"All right, so you're not illiterate," she said. "Come in and fill out the application."

"Wait. How much does it pay?"

There was a pause on the woman's end.

"Hundred-and-twenty-five a car." The line went dead. She'd hung up, or gotten cut off. Corey still didn't understand what kind of work it was, but the promise of *hundred-and-twenty-five a car* rang in his ears.

That was the interview. He passed the drug screen and the background check. The woman who'd spoken to him on the phone—Bailey—ran the office for American Repossessors United. She pushed Corey's application through, sent him for a week of training at the company headquarters just outside Memphis, Tennessee, and within two weeks he was behind the wheel of an $80,000 tow truck. He was, in fact, paid $125 for every vehicle—every *unit*—he repossessed, and nothing at all if he didn't find anything. Feast or famine from the get-go.

He seemed to have a natural aptitude for it. Within the first three months on the job, he became the top agent in the Birmingham office, pulling in twenty to thirty units in a week. He ran the new accounts on his list every night, inputting updates on the laptop computer anchored to the dash of the truck while his right foot pressed the gas pedal. He used social media platforms to stalk and find debtors, and he cross-referenced license plate numbers that repeatedly showed up at addresses he was monitoring. He found that he was using the relentless approach he'd taken with journalism, spending hours upon hours behind the wheel. He was in the Dodge or in his own Toyota for sometimes twenty hours a day.

Nancy kept in touch. As the paper's ownership kept chopping staff like loggers felling logs in a dwindling forest, she talked less about what was going on in the newsroom, and more about herself.

"I don't know how much more of this I can take," she texted him one night. It was just after 11 p.m., and he assumed she'd just put the paper to bed. "It's like a ghost town around here. Do you want to meet for a drink?"

Corey had a Tesla on the boom and an angry debtor to sooth when he got her message. He left her on read until the next morning.

"I was already in bed," he told her. "Sorry I missed you. Maybe next time."

The obscene part was that repo work paid better than newspaper work ever had or ever would. The most he'd ever made as a journalist was forty thousand dollars in a year. In six months as a repo agent, he'd passed that benchmark. But as much as he liked the money and genuinely enjoyed the investigative aspect of the job, he still hated parts of the work. He was an anomaly in this new world, college educated and soft, a man with no feel for the lockout kit, a hard plastic wedge used to pry open a unit's window and a long metal rod with a half-hook at the end that the other agents wielded with the deft diplomacy of long use. When they saw one another, which was infrequently, the other agents teased him about his education and his political views.

"Stop being a damned liberal," Nick would say, and laugh. Nick who was not yet thirty and sported a sleeve of tattoos from his left wrist to his shoulder, who chain-smoked Marlboros and listened to artists Corey had never heard of, who would take a shit on a debtor's lawn if he couldn't find the wanted unit at their address.

"Hell, he can't help it," Stevie might chime in, pronouncing can't as *cain't.* Stevie who wore basketball shorts and muscle shirts year-round, no matter how cold it got, who had lost the hearing in his left ear when he was nine when his brother struck him upside the head with a hard pine two-by-four, who would laugh and point at the thick rope of scar tissue that wrapped from behind the ear all the way up to the top of his closely-shorn head. "They done educated him up at that college, and then the newspaper ruined him. He'll be aight if we can keep him in a truck for the next five years. He'll get it outta his system."

Javier, who was also teased by the other agents, rarely said anything either way. He just looked on in silence, sometimes laughing, sometimes watching with dark and brooding eyes that never let on what he was thinking. Javier had come to Alabama as a small child and still spoke with the melodic lilt of the Dominican Republic, even though he'd never been out of the United States. He learned the music of his country's language at home with his mother and three sisters, and it was his dream to visit Paris one day.

"You should go," Corey told him one day. "There's nothing like it anywhere."

Corey had taken his ex-wife to Paris on their honeymoon, a fact that impressed the other agents with its extravagance and romance even if the marriage itself hadn't lasted. But Javier only shook his head sadly.

"I think I'll stay here," he said, casting a sidelong glance at Nick. "I think if I go overseas, they maybe don't let me come back."

Nick laughed.

"I knew you was illegal," he said, his voice full of mirth. "Hey, Stevie—"

"I'm not," Javier said, and the way he said it made the laughter in Nick's words die. Nobody said anything for a minute, so Javier said, "I got a green card and then I got a citizenship test and then I got a Social Security card. I'm as American as you are."

Nick, who was embarrassed that Javier hadn't let his joke go, shook his head and said "Bullshit" in a low voice.

"Hey, fuck you," Javier said. "I earned it. All you had to do was be born here."

Nick threw down a half-smoked cigarette and stepped over to Javier. It might have gotten serious, but Corey and Stevie stepped between them, hustling them out of each other's face and away toward their respective trucks.


Once Nancy called to pick his brain on where to go with a story a young reporter was pursuing. He was good enough to consult for free, but not good enough to pay for his years of experience. Corey was ninety-nine percent sure the consulting call hadn't been her idea. He knew she was getting squeezed, too.

"What are you doing these days?" She asked him when they were done talking about the story.

"Oh, this and that," he said. He didn't know why he didn't talk to her about the new job, the new career. Was he ashamed of it? No. Well, okay, maybe a little. But he also liked it, the silent shark thrashing through the dark waters of the Birmingham night, feasting or starving, depending on how the night went, but always swimming forward.

"I bet you're still living high off the buyout," she said. The jealousy in her voice was thick with pain, like a lonely child. "Jesus, it must have been like hitting the lottery."

If it had, the lottery he'd won had been poisonous, killing off his career, his previous life, as surely as a cyanide capsule would kill the captured spy in a war movie. They hung up, and Corey felt his chest loosen like a clenched fist finally opening.

"We never got that drink," Nancy said. It felt like an invitation.

"You buying?" He asked, hoping that she heard the smile on his face.

She snorted, a wised-up cynical veteran newspaper sound.

"We're in austerity right now," she said, "whatever that means. I gotta take a furlough, a whole week off without pay."

"Well," Corey said. "Maybe I'll run into you soon."


None of the Birmingham agents had ever been shot—not yet—but they'd all had close calls. Stevie had showed up one morning with two neat bullet holes drilled through the glass in the rear windshield of his truck and a pair of slugs buried in the dashboard.

"Probably did it himself," Javier said, checking Stevie's truck. "You know that cracker ain't right in the head."

Corey and Nick watched from a distance. Corey didn't want to get close to the spent rounds. Just looking at the bullet holes made him feel a little weak below his belt line. Javier reached into his back pocket and brought out a heavy folding knife, which he flicked open with one hand. Peering at the dash, he worked the sharp blade carefully around in first one hole and then another until he plucked out two deformed lead mushrooms. He walked over to them and held the shrapnel in his palm for the others to see.

"Twenty-twos," Nick said. "Well, that's not so bad."

"Maybe twenny-fives," Javier said. "Probably just sting a little, you know, from a distance."

They were straight-faced, not looking at Corey. He couldn't tell if they were kidding or not. Probably a little of both. The job required a lot of balls, to go onto someone else's property in the middle of the night, skulk out and pop a VIN on the dashboard with a flashlight, maybe hook up the loud and heavy hydraulic lift, and then scoot away like a thief in the night. They each walked a line somewhere between confident and cocky, but the bullet holes were a reminder of how things could go wrong, and how close Stevie had come to a bad end somewhere in Outer Bumfuck. Corey could picture it in his head, Stevie, half his head blown away, gut sagging in his sleeveless muscle shirt, basketball shorts filling with shit and piss after his bowels let go, sitting in the leather seat behind the steering wheel as the truck leaned cantilevered in a ditch somewhere.

He shook his head to clear the image and walked away. He couldn't think about things like that and continue to do the job.


When her name came up on his hot list, Corey wasn't too surprised. The GPS took him to a large apartment complex off of Highway 150 in Hoover, the largest suburb of Birmingham. The suburbs meant less security than in the city proper, and this particular complex had no gate, no guard. Easy pickings, unless she'd moved and the skip tracers were a step behind.

But he found her building, and then he found her unit, a two-year-old Mazda 3, a sporty hatchback that looked small enough to fit in his palm. But no, better to use the truck. He took the Mazda from behind, raising it up and pulling it deftly from its parking space before leaving it in the middle of the parking lot. He released the hooks and slid away from the unit, circling back around until he could lock onto it from the front, so that he wouldn't have to throw straps over the rear wheels. He drove away with her car trailing behind him like a remora suctioned tight to the back of an apex predator.

His phone was in his lap, his text messages open to Nancy's last missive, the one where she talked about the budget cuts that had come down the pike. The new owners were slashing newsroom salaries by fifteen percent. She was hanging in there, but just barely. In the meantime, she was looking for a new position, she said, but so far there was no good news on the horizon. Corey thought about texting her. He could tell her everything.

He could tell her about the new job, about the top-of-the-line truck with the negative tilt and the hydraulic winch. He could tell her about the money, explain the absurdity of what he did now and how the newspaper business had unexpectedly prepared him for this new life. But it was almost four in the morning, and she would know soon enough that there was no good news anywhere, not anymore.

"I was bone dead tired. So fucking tired. Too tired to deal with her or any of the other overlords who would tell me my attitude wasn't good enough, my energy not high enough, my sales wattage not bright enough, or any of the other corporate double speak that means you suck and you don't even deserve the slave wages we pay you."

# ENTHUSIASM
## Ali Seay

"What do you think?" The woman was tall and bottle-blonde, and her teeth hadn't been real since they'd come in.

I looked at her in the ankle length cashmere "house sweater". It was a stunning charcoal gray and softer than anything I'd ever felt. It also carried the stunning price tag of just over eight hundred dollars.

"It looks very nice," I said, trying to muster some of that good old customer service they pay me twelve whole dollars an hour for.

*Ephemera* charges ridiculous prices for everything from jeans to socks, but they pay their employees just above minimum wage.

Not that I'm complaining.

Oh wait, yes I am.

She turned and twirled, eyeing herself in one of the six-foot mirrors posted at every corner of the store. She smiled at herself as if she were the most stunning creature ever, which I'm sure she considered herself to be.

"I'm not sure if the gray compliments my skin. Thoughts?"

I barely managed to stifle my long exhalation. I sighed so much at work I often sounded as if I'd sprung a sudden leak.

"I think it looks very nice," I said.

She cocked an eyebrow at me. Onto me and my low level of interest, I think.

Her pink painted lips compressed into a thin unamused line and she whipped off the sweater

Uh-oh, I thought. Here we go. Temper tantrum. She won't buy the sweater and then Elaine is going to eat me alive. Again.

Instead, the woman flounced to the very tiny table that held a very tiny register. It was lit from beneath and delicate. The most important thing about taking rich people's money is to make it look as painless and elegant as possible.

After running her card, I folded the sweater carefully and placed it lovingly in a black and white and silver striped paper shopping bag with a complimentary hand lotion in its own separate plastic bag for protection. The bottle condoms, I called them.

"Despite your lack of input, I'll take it," she said, trying to shame me. "It's only eight hundred dollars."

I snorted and then quickly covered with a light cough.

Only?

Only eight *hundred* dollars?

I was worried about whether or not I'd make rent this month, but whatever, lady.

Her card said Abigail Daniels. "Have a lovely night, Ms. Daniels."

We're supposed to call all the women we wait on Ms. instead of Mrs. unless they instruct us otherwise. It's more youthful.

She took the bag and the card and flounced out.

The moment she was out the door, I grabbed the keys. It was the most glorious time of the night—closing time.

But here came Elaine and she had that look on her face. That lecture face.

I rushed toward the door but she was on my heels.

"Kat? Katrina!"

I couldn't act like I didn't hear her. It was only us. It was my sixth night in a row working. I was tired. But I still had ears and she was shrieking at me.

I shoved the key in the door and turned it just as a woman tried to enter. She looked outraged that we'd be closing at closing time, but I shrugged and did my best to act sorry.

"Sorry! So sorry! We're closed."

I turned my back to the window and thusly to her.

"Kat!"

I was worried that Elaine was going to go past me and let the woman in, but instead she blocked my way until I looked at her.

"What?" I asked.

I was bone dead tired. So fucking tired. Too tired to deal with her or any of the other overlords who would tell me my attitude wasn't good enough, my energy not high enough, my sales wattage not bright enough, or any of the other corporate double speak that means you suck and you don't even deserve the slave wages we pay you.

"You need to show more enthusiasm for our customers when they shop."

"You show it," I said, surprising us both. "I'm pretty sure that you, as manager, earn enough to muster up some enthusiasm. Me, not so much."

"You know that's a temporary wage," she said. But her voice had shifted.

The lights flickered and we both looked up.

"I've been here a year, Elaine. I'm on my sixth day in a row so I can get some overtime to hopefully pay my rent."

She put a thin hand on a thin hip and glared at me. "Your personal issues are not my problem. I'm sorry if you're struggling, but if you give this job your all, if you give *Ephemera* your all, your rate can go up and you can get some personal days and—"

"I've heard this shit before, Elaine," I said, stifling a yawn.

If she'd been wearing pearls, she'd have clutched them. Just because I used the word, shit. These are the kind of people I was dealing with.

"Kat—"

"I'm exhausted. I'm on the verge of cracking. I'm going to lose it with these people. I just need to go home, change my clothes, and get a little rest."

The lights flickered again. I looked outside in time to see the lights in the store across the courtyard flicker and blink in tandem.

"I hope this isn't going to be another power outage," she said.

Cold November wind licked the windows. I couldn't see it, of course, but I could hear it howl and I could see the leaves that were left on the trees dancing under the streetlamps.

Then they winked and blinked again.

"Looks like it. But lucky for us, it's time to get going."

"We have to clean up, and I have to do the drawer, and—"

There was a tapping at the door and we looked up to see that woman again.

Elaine started for the door.

"Elaine!" I yelped. "Do not open that. Do not open that door. We are closed."

The lights rallied, sprang to life, then died again.

"Fuck," I said.

"Language," she said, shoving her hand into her pocket for her keys.

"Fuck fuck fuck!" I chanted.

She did it anyway. Opened the door.

"Oh, thank goodness, you're an angel," the woman said to Elaine.

Angel my ass. I had hardly slept more than three hours a night the last week or so. After this, I'd go home, log on, and transcribe legal reports for extra money. All for the privilege of paying rent for a shitty apartment and gas for a crappy car and for the privilege to come back in here every day to deal with people who thought eight hundred dollars was nothing.

Elaine and the woman cooed as the lights flickered yet again.

"I wonder what that's about," the woman said as she made a beeline for a display. "It will only take a moment. I had to have this for a cocktail party tomorrow and I have a meeting for a new charity extravaganza in the morning so I won't be able to shop."

By all means, keep us here later than we should be. Prevent us—by us I mean me—from doing my *other* job just to make ends meet.

"We understand," Elaine said. "Please take your time."

We do not.

Please do not.

She brought up a cocktail dress not much bigger than a dinner napkin and brandished a black credit card just as the power failed.

I sighed.

"It's fine. We keep those runner things for times like this," Elaine said. She looked beneath the register to no avail.

"And if I can't find one, Ms. Flynn is one of our regulars. Let me just . . .."

Elaine straightened, looking a little panicked. Even Elaine answered to someone and that someone might not be too gung-ho with Ms. Flynn walking out of the shop with a—I glanced at the tag and smiled—$1,200 dress.

"What's funny?" Ms. Flynn asked. Now that Elaine had fled to the back, she looked a little less friendly or thankful.

"Nothing," I said, trying to just get through the time with this princess.

"Is it possibly that you thought it was okay to lock me out when I needed a dress?"

I looked at her steadily and smiled. "We were closed. We do have business hours. And you came after them. Ms. Flynn."

"I'll be complaining about you," she said.

"That's fine. I'll probably be complaining about you for a while, too."

She pointedly glanced at my name tag.

I stuck my tits out. "Kat," I said, enunciating slowly. Which made me giggle.

I was cracking.

Elaine came rushing out looking a little frantic herself. She was waving an ancient credit card machine. Those rarely made an appearance. And a place like this would never trust us to run a credit card on our personal phone.

"Sorry, sorry! I got it. It's fine."

I started to wrap the dress for her highness as Elaine held her hand out for the credit card. But Ms. Flynn wasn't satisfied with that. Oh, no. She had a lesson to teach me.

"Let her do it," she said.

Elaine looked confused.

"Her. *Kat.* Let her do her job."

Elaine looked at me. The look on her face was part determination, part pleading. She was just trying to get through the day, too. The only difference was, she was paid handsomely to put up with this shit. I was paid shit to deal with shit.

"Sure," I said. I took the card and placed it in the machine. I tried to get it to fit right but it didn't want to. Finally, I got it to snap in and then tried to shove the runner over the top. It got jammed.

"I can help—" Elaine said.

"So common she can't even take a credit card impression," Ms. Flynn said.

I looked up and smiled at her. Then I took a wide swing with the machine. The impact with her over made-up face was satisfying. The crunch of her nose breaking and then collapsing was satisfying as well.

The screaming had to stop, though.

I rounded the counter and took swing after swing as blood and hair flew.

Elaine was shrieking my name and fumbling her phone. Our store line would be out along with the power. I had to do something, but the credit card machine turned club was stuck in the dented, barely breathing mass of Ms. Flynn's head.

I had to think fast.

I let go of the chunk of metal and rounded the counter. The closest thing I could find was a suede four-inch heel. The display shoe. Perfect.

The heel was steel with a painted black tip. Manufacturer's trademark.

It pierced Elaine's eye socket like a surgical instrument. She dropped to her knees, then her ass, then fell on her back.

"Well, those are worth the money, aren't they?" I said aloud as I yanked it free. I had to brace my foot on her chest and yank. The heel came free with a wet, victorious sound.

Her fingers were still scrabbling at her phone. Working. Trying to push buttons that weren't there. Touch screens can be a bitch when you can't see.

"I'm very tired," I told Elaine as she struggled to breathe. I jammed the heel into her eye once more, pushing down with my weight until the sound and the amount of blood I encountered assured me that the deed was done. There was a crunching wet squelch, a spasm, then silence.

"How's that for enthusiasm?" I asked Elaine.

I saw that Ms. Flynn was still trying to rally. It could only be dumb animal instinct at this point but it was still an inconvenience. Like everything she did. Like her and every other member of the elite who thought they were more valuable, more deserving, more more more.

I used the heel on her quickly. One eye, two eyes, red eye, goo eye.

I laughed.

"Lucky for me," I explained. "The power is out. And as rich as this fucking place is, they don't spring for backup generators. Which means, no footage. No proof. If I take this," I said, shoving the shoe in my back pocket where it hung comically. "And this," I said, waving the antique credit card machine. "I should be fine."

I looked at Elaine. "And if they even come looking for me, and they might not if you doctored the schedule again to look like I didn't work overtime so you could pay me my regular hourly rate, I say I left as you were letting queen bitch inside."

I kicked Ms. Flynn just to get some relief.

Everything else would have my fingerprints, but I worked there so . . ..

"We'll see what happens," I said to the women on the floor.

Then I made sure my shoes were clean, walked out the front door, and locked the door behind me.

I went home and slept for twelve hours straight. I deserved it.


She stood beneath the *Walk a mile in someone else's shoes. Save the world. Shop used.* sign. Thin with long fluffy blond hair. She shrugged into the oversized herringbone coat. It was long with enormous shoulder pads. Circa 1980-something. Great condition.

"What do you think, Kat?"

She was one of our newest customers at the thrift shop. Everything she wore had once belonged to someone else. It worked on her.

"I like it," I said. "It's very *Working Girl.*"

I'd taken a dollar an hour pay cut to go from chic to thrifty. It had been worth it. I made that dollar back in peace of mind and appreciation. No one had ever come looking for me, but I was prepared to face the music if they did.

For now, I was happy to work with people who saw me. Valued me.

She twirled, fingered the tag, glanced into the faded scratched mirror. "I mean, it does look good."

I nodded. "It looks great, actually."

"You wouldn't lie to me, would you?" she asked, pinning me with her waifish gaze. "I mean it is . . .." She looked at the tag again. "*Twenty* dollars."

I had to stifle a laugh. "And worth every penny."

MAFIA

RENÉ BÖHMER

"He'll live.

"It's nothing compared to what he should have got, fucking
up the way he did."

# THE TWO OF US ARE GOING
## TO HAVE A PROBLEM
Daniel Vlasaty

Sometimes jobs go bad and you got to lay low a while. Keep your head down. Stay out of the way until shit cools down. It's all a part of the game.

Something I been knowing a long time. All these years, all these jobs.

That's how it is.

Sometimes jobs just go bad.

But it's the kid that don't know it. The kid thinking he's some hard G and he's got the whole fucking thing figured out.

This kid. His name's Colin something but he tried to get me to call him Cash Money. Cash for short. Said that's what everyone on the street calls him.

Long time since I had a good laugh like that.

That was nice of him.

Less nice of Peele to put me here. Like I'm some fucking babysitter.

He found the kid somewhere and had him shadowing me and I could tell right off the bat he was going to be a flop.

Didn't think it could go this bad. But the kid's first real job and here we are.

And now he's not talking to me. Sitting in the passenger seat, got his head buried in his hoody. Sulking or crying or whatever because I had to smack him around a bit to get him to shut the fuck up so we could get on the road.

So we could get out of town before the whole thing blew up even more in our faces.

But Peele's got us all set up.

A little motel room, somewhere out of the city. Some quiet for a day or two so he's got the time to see how this whole thing's going to shake out.

This fuck-up.

Would have been a smooth one, too. The cash was right there. Fucking in and out.

But then the kid had to go and fuck it all up, shoot the lady.

And after I fucking told him to be cool, don't do anything stupid, just take it easy, breathe, and the shit will be over soon enough.


"We're here," I say and pull up to the motel.

The kid pulls his hood down and looks around. His face is a little beat up, some dried blood, a few cuts, a little bruising.

He's good, though. He'll live.

It's nothing compared to what he should have got, fucking up the way he did.

Peele had some of his other guys beat on the kid a little bit too, before he sent us away. Because that's what you got to do when some shit like this happens.

Lessons to teach when one of your people fucks up so bad.

Peele told me to keep my head down, and to make sure the kid does the same. Just sit back and wait for a call. That's all we got to do.

Wait for Peele to make his decision on how he wants to handle this.

Whatever that means.

And with Peele, I mean—

Sometimes you don't know what he's going to do or how he's going to react.

Maybe he shrugs it off or maybe he has the whole fuck-up crew done to cover his own ass.

I step out of the car and stretch away all those hours spent behind the wheel.

I light a cig and the kid gets out of the car, looks up at the motel. "This can't be . . ." he says, spits out a wad of his bullshit that smacks against the pavement. "Peele's just fucking with us, yeah? This place is—"

"What?"

"It's kind of—"

"It's fine," I say.

"It's a fucking shithole."

"It's quiet and—"

"It's a fucking—"

"It's *quiet*," I say again. "And that's all that fucking matters. That it's quiet and it's out of the way. Kid, you got to understand how bad this shit is. You know that, right? Tell me you know how fucked this is."

"But I mean . . . I know Peele's fucking loaded. You'd think the man could put us up somewhere a little nice—"

"He don't owe us shit."

The kid shrugs. He pulls out his own pack of cigs, says, "He did send us out on the job, though. It's not like we were there on our own. I mean, he's got to take some responsibility—"

"He might have sent us there but he's not the one fucked up."

He turns toward me quick. "How many times I got to tell you it wasn't my . . . that fucking lady, man. It was her . . . if she didn't reach for the fucking alarm I wouldn't have—"

I hold my hand up to get him to shut the fuck up.

I'm sick of his voice, sick of hearing his fucking bullshit. Wish he'd go back to hiding in his hoody for the next day or two. Would be fine with me to ride this thing out in silence.

Until Peele comes calling.

"I'll get us checked in," I say. "Get the bags out of the back and maybe try not to fucking shoot anyone else while I'm gone."

I turn to leave him to it and he mumbles, "Fucking shoot you," under his breath.

But I let him have this one and keep walking over to the office.

"Where's my key?" he asks when I come back out of the office.

And I laugh at him again, shake my head.

This fucking kid. He don't know shit about shit.

"Where the fuck do you think we are?" I say.

"What do you . . . I don't kn—"

"What I mean is: look around you, kid. Look where we are. You were right about one thing. This place is a shithole. Peele sent us to this dump to lay low and that's it. If he was going to spring for separate rooms, let us live it up, he never would have sent us all the fucking way out here to begin with."

I start to walk down to our room, last one on the right side.

The kid follows. "I don't . . ." he starts to say. But his slow fucking brain must finally catch up with the rest of the world and he gets this look on his face like maybe he's starting to understand that you don't shoot a citizen and fuck up a job so spectacularly and get to just walk away.

I don't know. Maybe he knows it, maybe he don't. He'll figure it out eventually.

Fucking has to.

I open the door to our room, step inside. The kid takes a deep breath before following me in.

"Been told I snore," I say with a laugh.

And he shakes his head, sighs.

The room's bad. But it's not much different than any other motel room I ever stayed in.

Maybe just a little dirtier and sadder and bed-buggier.

The kid steps in behind me. "You got to be kidding . . ." he starts to say. But he just drops his bag and shuts his mouth again.

He walks over to the table and sits in one of the chairs, sulks, lights another cig.

I set my own bag on one of the beds and look around.

"Motherfuck—" the kid says and tosses something across the room and drops himself heavy into one of the chairs at the small table.

I sit up in bed, must have passed out, and I see that it's a crushed and empty pack of cigs he threw across the room.

I also see that the ashtray on the table is mostly full and the kid's got an antsy look about him.

I cross the room and sit at the table with him.

"You good?" I say.

Because now I'm also a fucking guidance counselor or some shit, I guess.

Because looking at him now, I can tell he's starting to crack.

But he don't answer. Just puffs on his cig, sighs, and taps his fingers against the tabletop in a frantic pattern. His feet are going too. Tapping against the table's legs, shaking the whole thing.

He holds the cig he's smoking out for me to see, says, "Last smoke."

And I nod my head, feel my own almost-empty pack in my pocket.

He's going stir crazy already. I know the feeling. Can't sit still but there ain't shit to do either. Got him thinking all the smoking will even him out, calm him down.

Don't work like that in my experience.

The curtains are pulled but I can still see the sun glowing yellow but fading behind them.

I stand up, say, "No worries, should be dark soon enough and I'll go make a food run for us. I'll grab us both some cigs, too. So just chill out for a bit."

I grab some shit out of my bag, tell the kid I'm going to shower real quick. Wash the day's bullshit off me.

Tell myself *you're getting too old for this shit.*

But what does that mean?

"Try to get a little rest," I say before I close the bathroom door. "It'll be dark soon and I'll make that run."


The shower's hot and that's the only thing I care about. I stand under the spray as long as I can, until it starts to go cold.

The first thing I notice when I step back into the room are the cases of beer on the table. Two 30-packs, one of them torn open like in a frenzy, cardboard scattered, cans spilling out.

And then I see all the packs of cigs, five of them, and the chair missing from the table.

"What the . . ."

I look over and see the door sitting open.

The fucking kid's nowhere to be seen.

But I hear him talking.

"—yeah, babe, I'm saying," he's saying. "I'm telling you, it's a fucking joke. He's a fucking dick. I don't know what the fuck he think's going to happen but I mean—"

And I cross the small room in a few steps, stick my head out through the open door.

The kid's sitting outside right next to the door. He's got a beer in one hand, his cell up to his ear in the other, a fresh cig dangling from his lips.

I step out so that I'm standing over him. Slap the phone out of his hand and it goes clattering across the pavement. Grab him by the front of his shirt and lift him out of the chair, slam him back against the wall.

"What the fuck?" I say, and look around us to see if anyone's watching or listening.

But there's no one.

Fucking ghost town.

He squirms out of my hands. "You motherfucker," he says and goes crawling after his dropped phone. Picks it up and looks back at me. "Babe," he says into the phone, "you still there? Yeah, I got to call you back, this motherfucker right here's on some bullsh—"

But I'm on him again quick. Grab the phone out of his hand and throw it down as hard as I can. It shatters into dozens of pieces, spraying our legs like blowback.

"What are you—" he starts to say but I grab his face like a basketball, my hand covering his mouth.

Pull him close so that his eyes are inches from mine.

"Shut your fucking mouth and get in the room," I say.

And he makes like he's going to do something, protest in some way, a little gesture, a movement. But he sees me standing here, ready for whatever, and he stops. Looks around too. But there still ain't shit.

"Motherfucker," he mumbles under his breath, kicking at his dropped beer can on his way into the room.

He stops to look back at the shattered remains of his phone and says, "Owe me a fucking phone, too."


He's already cracking open a fresh beer when I get back into the room.

"That shit's not cool, man," he says, before I can get anything out.

"What the fuck did I tell—"

"Look, man, whatever," he says. "Okay, you're pissed at me. I went to the liquor store. Big fucking deal—"

"It is a big fucking deal. I told you. I fucking said it. Don't go anywhere. Don't do anything. That's what Peele said and that's what I fucking said, too. We're supposed to be laying low. We're not supposed to be doing shit else."

"It's like a block away. I didn't even see anybody else. Just the sad fucking guy worked there."

"And then you're sitting out there, kicked back, chatting away on the phone like a bitch. Don't know how many times I got to tell you, kid, we ain't on some fucking vacation here."

He waves me off. "Oh, fuck you. I was talking to my girl, just letting her know—"

"You fucking idiot. You're not supposed to be letting anyone know shit about anything. No one's supposed to know where we are. That's the whole fucking point of this."

"It was . . . I mean, like I said, it was just my girl. I wasn't telling her shit. I was ju—"

"I know I keep saying this," I say. "But I wish you'd fucking listen to me. This is some serious fucking shit we're in here."

And he opens his mouth to start spitting more of his bullshit but I hold my hand up to stop him.

"You fucking shot a citizen during a robbery. That's not some shit that just gets brushed—"

"If she didn't press the fucking alarm—"

"But she did. She did press the alarm and then you fucking shot her."

The kid doesn't say anything. He sparks another cig, stares off at nothing over my shoulder, sucks on his beer.

"So, yeah," I say because he still doesn't seem to be catching on. "We don't know if some cops or whoever got to your girl, are listening in, whatever. And if they are, well then you just fucking wrapped it all up in a nice and neat little bow for them."

He closes his eyes. "How would they even—"

"And, see, that right there's what I been fucking saying. We don't know what anyone knows or what anyone's saying or doing. We don't know shit. And that's why Peele's got us here. So, he could figure it out."

The kid rolls his eyes, drinks more beer.

"Which is why when I say don't fucking go anywhere you don't fucking go anywhere."

"But you were going to go out for a run, so what's the big fucking deal? I don't—"

"Yeah. I was going to go. *Me.* Because I'm not the stupid fucking asshole that won't listen to what the fuck I'm saying. I'm not the one going to get us busted because you can't wait twenty fucking minutes for a cig and a beer."

He slams his beer down on the table, starts to come at me. "Look, man, you need to stop talking to me like I'm some pu—"

And I hit him once in the face and his whole body crumbles to the ground and he's out like a light.


"Shit, man, you all barely been there a whole damn day and you already calling for relief," Peele says.

"Listen," I say. "It's just the—"

"You going soft in your old age, Gerry, my man?"

Peele's laugh echoes through the phone and I let him have his fun.

Once he stops, I say, "I'm just calling to see what you been hearing."

"Things, man, lots of fucking things."

"Yeah, and?"

"And not any of them sounding really good to me."

We're both quiet a second, let those words hang between us like the ominous shit they are.

"Okay, but what are you thinking? Because the kid, he's . . . he's—"

"Don't you worry about him. That's already being taken care of."

Which means either a bullet in the back of the head or an envelope with his name on it.

"I just need another day or two to put it into action."

"Kid ain't going to make it another day or two, he's cracking. Shit I probably won't make it much longer, not with his fucking—"

"I knew it. You are going fucking soft on me."

Peele's laughing again and I'm tired and it's been a long day.

"I'm not getting fucking soft," I snap.

And Peele pulls back. "Shit, man," he says. "Okay, okay. We all friends here. No reason to bite my fucking head o—"

"I'm saying I don't think we got another day or two, is all."

"Seems like you got him pretty settled now, from what you saying. You should be good until then."

"I'm supposed to, what, keep him knocked out for another—"

And Peele's laughing in my ear again.

"I know. I know," he says. "I'm thinking about back in the day how you—"

"Not really feeling a stroll down memory lane here."

"Okay, alright, you're right. Thinking about how you'da handled someone like him back in the day, but now like I was saying—"

"You want me to handle the kid, I'll handle him. Don't even got to ask twice. Just give me the word and I'm ready."

"Look, just give me 'til the morning. I'll move some things around, could have some people there first thing."

"Okay, yeah," I say.

That's sounding a bit better.

"That is if you think you can handle—and I don't mean *handle*-handle—but if you think you can sit on him that long. It'll all be over in the morning."

"Yeah, okay. First thing then. Because, I'm telling you, if it's much longer than that the two of us are going to have a problem."

"Ho, whoa," he says. "The two of who?"

"You fucking know who. Me and the . . ." I sigh. The kid's not going to be my problem much longer so fuck him. "You fucking know who I mean."

Peele takes a breath, says: "I know, I know. You need to chillax a bit. Okay. Just fucking take a breath and . . ." He exhales slowly, making a show of it. "I'm saying."

And we're quiet for a second. But I guess he can hear something in my breathing. I've been working for Peele a lot of years now and maybe he knows me better than I think he does. "What's on your mind here, Gerry, man?"

"Noth—" I start to say but stop myself. "Okay, look, I'm just wondering where all this leaves us? You know, like where it leaves me. I was with the kid at the fucking thing and I tried—"

"You don't got to worry about that right now. Just be ready first thing, yeah?"

*Don't got to worry about that right now.*

Which means, like with the kid, first thing tomorrow morning's about to greet me with either a bullet in the head or an envelope with my name on it.

And again, with Peele you never fucking know.


The kid's sitting up and staring at me as I hang the phone up.

"What the fuck?" he says.

And I don't know if it's because I knocked him the fuck out or because he saw me using a phone.

He tries to stand up but it's like he can't get his legs all the way under him. He reaches over and uses the edge of the dresser to pull himself up.

He says, "All that shit you talking and here you are on the fucking phone. Can't fucking believe—"

"It was Peele," I say. "And this is a fucking burner."

And I pull the phone's battery, remove the SIM, and snap it in two. Bend the phone back until it cracks, too.

"I'm not fucking stupid about this shit," I say.

He makes his way over to the table, falls back into the chair, and looks at me.

"And?" he says.

"And what?"

"What did Peele say, you fucking—"

"Said he's gonna send some people out tomorrow."

He nods, cracks open another beer. "And what does that mean?"

"What do you think it means?" I say.

He drinks more of his beer, stares at me. "What's your problem—"

"I don't have a problem. We just got to make it through the rest of the night and . . ."

I stop myself. Not worth it to waste the energy trying to talk to him.

A few more hours and Peele's guys will get here and that will be that.

"Let's just ride out these last few hours," I say.

And again, he doesn't say anything, just drinks his beer at me.

It takes him a few hours to drink and smoke himself to sleep. Puts a pretty good dent into the opened 30-pack.

It's close to four in the morning when he finally drags himself into bed.

And I sit and watch him the whole night.

Because I don't trust him. And I don't know what he might do if he ever sobers up enough to figure out how the morning's probably going to go for him.


I hear the car pull up into one of the spaces near our door at about seven a.m. The crunch of the gravel under the tires, the idling chug of the engine, a car door opening and closing.

I'm dead tired and the kid's barely moved since he passed out.

There's a knock at the door and I peel myself out of the chair and open it.

Find myself face to face with a guy I've never seen before. But he's got a face like any other guy Peele's got working for him.

"You Gerry?" he says. His voice gravel in a tin can.

"Yeah."

And he reaches into his jacket pocket. I hold my breath a second, expecting a bullet in the face. But his hand comes out holding an envelope.

"Peele asked me to give this to you. Said for you to have yourself a nice vacation. He'll be in touch when he needs you."

I nod my head and take the envelope. It's thick and heavy and I slide it into my pocket.

"Where's the other one?" he says.

I gesture back into the room. "The kid's still passed out."

And he looks back over his shoulder, nods back at the car. The driver side door opens and another guy with the same look climbs out of the car and approaches the room.

"What are you going to—" I start to say.

But he gives me a look that tells me everything I need to know.

# EMPTY HOUSE, HIGHWAY 1

**IAN USHER**

# 10

"Barely a badge flash before sixty rounds got pumped into a sixteen-year-old with a sandwich. Time enough for four clips yet not enough to tell the difference between a sub and a submachine gun."

# DAMNED IF YOU DO
## J. Rohr

The ashes of empires sent up choking clouds. Days turned blue to gray. Out on the streets Chicago typewriters spit the writing on the wall. Red ink spread the names of rising royalty. Some went to knife parties doing the blade ballet, while others favored the unsubtle language of explosives. Yet it all amounted to the same mess. Bone-clogged boulevards and no one on the throne. Then, when the power vacuum sucked enough innocents into the blender, shit really hit the fan.

Cops got left off what little leash the city strapped on. They went from rowdy pigs to bloodthirsty boars overnight. Some might say just another gang vying for control.

Barely a badge flash before sixty rounds got pumped into a sixteen-year-old with a sandwich. Time enough for four clips yet not enough to tell the difference between a sub and a submachine gun. Though, off the record, that tin foil can be confusing after four days of coke-fueled head cracking. All, supposedly, in the name of justice.

That gave a devil a chance to make a deal. The mayor wanted the scandal gone but reelection on the horizon, no way to renew rule without the police union backing him. Odds against charging the cop, he turned to a marvelous Mephistopheles.

Pitching, "I can make your problematic police office go away in such a way that'll please the public, but in exchange, perhaps Your Honor might send the boys in blue like a flood washing out the competition."

"Agreed."

No need for blood on the dotted line, but both knew the high stakes of failure. Prison? No worries. Neither would ever make it there.

Mayors aren't bulletproof, and revenge minded pigs just needed a name to go hog wild. Even Beelzebub can't survive a baton beat down.

"Into the darkness," the devil said raising a glass of wine.

"It's not my first rodeo," the mayor sighed—clink and swallow. "There's no one wearing white in city hall, if you catch my drift."

*Extra, extra!* Crooked cop whacked in the West Loop. Stabbed sixteen times, one for every year he stole. Coked to the gills, initial reports said the corpse twitched all the way to the morgue. Headlines sang like Munchkins crooning over dead witches as the scandal died down. The last mention of it: fifteen seconds on the evening news reporting the teen's burial. Brief shot of a weeping mother then let's see who the Cubs are playing this weekend.

Not long after, the flood came. Cops cleansed parts of the city in a way that made citizens wonder why the hell it never happened before. Their success almost seemed to imply law enforcement allowed certain things until now.

Eventually, bullet swarms stopped flying down streets. The bombs went quiet. Knife dancers gave it a rest. The war ended, but peace never has one price.

Before swearing fealty, the remaining crime lords demanded sacrifices.

Feeling magnanimous, "Who do you want?"

A list of reprobates no one'd miss. Rats, skimmers, and incompetent triggers, the whole crooked lot destined to make more trouble eventually. Asking for their executions almost seemed like a gift. Cunning appetizers, though, revving up the devourer to blind gluttonous slaughter.

"We'd also like you to do something about El Sepulturero."

"Done."

Agreed to as if it would be that easy. Leaving the question, who'd be dumb enough to do the deed?


Palms sweaty, Diego paced around his apartment. He felt everything except ready. For the sixth time in an hour, he checked the setup.

Eighty gallons of booze. Some liquid gems but mostly rot gut. No sense wasting cents since it all tasted the same after a certain point. Not that he knew. Never really touched the stuff for fear of ending up like his dad; didn't want to be one of those folks people don't mind seeing dead.

Focusing—he turned away from the past. Eyes on the future, Diego examined the fridge. Top to bottom full of beers. On the lowest shelf behind a row of brown bottles lurked a sawed-off shotgun. He got that trick from an old Italian, a retired assassin's ingenieur.

"Guy asks for a beer; you get him one," he said. "Calm, no worries. Then, when you go back for another, come back with the *lupara—pow!*"

It sounded so simple. Yet, to be on the safe side he stashed a few pistols around the apartment. In the arm of the couch, the tank of the toilet, taped under the table—a veritable arsenal to kill one man.

"It's just one person," he said checking the action on a .45.

Person—the word implied someone human. El Sepulturero amounted to a monster. During the recent war, The Gravedigger saw a familiar face headed into a Roger's Park dive. He double parked, got a machine gun out of the trunk, and went in spraying. He killed twelve people then went home. Only one was a soldier from another faction.

Now, the powers that be wanted the monster put down.

"Lucky me," Diego thought. "I get to help."

He sighed. He never pictured a life of crime as one of subsistence living. He amounted to a criminal day laborer, often called last minute to fill in for some goon.

"Yeah, Freddy 'Gills' got iced last night, so we need eyes. You interested?"

Rent and bills due, saying no never seemed like an option. Diego sometimes wondered if that's how the bosses liked it. The low tier hoods too desperate to turn down a job. So hungry for more—just an inch enough to sleep comfortable on the cliff's edge—they sprang at any opportunity. Like him volunteering to host an assassination.

The buzzer squawked.

"Here we go," Diego said.

Swallowing hard, he went to the door.

"Hello?" he said hitting the intercom.

"It's Irish. Open up."

Diego buzzed the visitor in. He heard the thud of the door five floors below. Soon the thumps of someone hurrying upstairs. He opened the door catching Irish about to knock.

The hitman entered without hesitation. Diego stepped aside to avoid getting shouldered through. Irish looked like a goat in a flat cap. Carrying a battered briefcase, he stopped in the middle of the room.

"Nice place," he said.

"Thanks," Diego said. "I just moved in actually."

"Oh yeah?"

"Yeah, like two days ago. Boss set it up. He didn't think a Buck Town studio would be the right spot."

"Makes sense," Irish said. "Plus, you're moving up in the world, eh?"

He grinned. Nodding, Diego thrust his hands deep in his pockets. It certainly seemed that way.

He showed Irish around the apartment. Mainly he revealed the hidden weapons.

"I do applaud your initiative," Irish said, fishing the shotgun out of the fridge. "But just follow my lead."

"I know you got your own plan," Diego said. "I'm just trying to be helpful."

Irish patted him on the back. He went over to the side table covered in booze. He laid the lupara behind it. Then he set the briefcase beside the bar. Irish took off his leather jacket, tossed it to Diego, and started fixing a drink. While Diego hung the coat on a hook, Irish reminisced.

Back in the day he got started at the ripe age of fifteen. Picking up takeout, he walked in on a hit at Jimmy's Pizza Café on Lincoln and Foster.

"They got good pizza," Diego said.

"Oh, the best," Irish said. "Anyway, I just thought it was a robbery, so I stabbed the guy with a switchblade like fuck you, not in my neighborhood, ya know? He ran away, but he didn't last. I got him good in the kidney. Then a week later, some Ukrainian shows up offering me a job. Now, here I am, a celebrated professional."

He raised a glass of whiskey. Diego quirked. He got his first job around the same age. His dad went into debt with a loan shark. Unable to squeeze a penny out of the booze bag, they gladly took his kid to work off what he owed. Diego sometimes wondered if that's why he never rose up the ranks. No one respected an indentured servant.

But he never complained. Whenever arrested, he never gave the cops anything. Even when detectives let him rot in Chicago's black hole, Homan Square, vanished off the face of the earth for three weeks, Diego said nothing. One day, he kept telling himself, they'll reward me. Now, the final hoop seemed here at last. Once he jumped through, dreams could come true.

He just needed to kill one of the most dangerous people in the city. If nothing else, it inspired him to be sure of success. Otherwise, he risked El Sepulturero's wrath.

"So," Diego said. "What's the plan?"

According to Irish, El Sepulturero couldn't pass up a party. Like others who thought themselves clever, he disguised his alcoholism as social drinking.

"All we gotta do is get him to the bottom of a bottle then—*pop, pop.*"

Irish slapped the back of his head for emphasis. He asked about the bathroom. Diego directed him.

Alone in the room, Diego heard a faint beeping. Curious, he followed the sound to the briefcase. Peaking inside, he saw a bomb.

The toilet flushed. He snapped the case shut. Putting it back, he stepped away as Irish returned.

"Let's get this party started," the hitman said.


Two hours later, the celebration hit high gear. Guests arrived from all over the city. Glasses raised high celebrating the recent victory. Diego heard legendary names getting introduced to gutter trash nobodies. Dead-end career criminals hobnobbing with a mix of rising stars and certified myths. Wise guys in twenty-five-thousand-dollar suits swapping jokes with fellas in thrift store ensembles. It reminded Diego of benchwarmers whooping it up in the locker room after a championship game. Chugging the same champagne as MVPs and the real winners.

Perhaps that's why, carting drinks around, his ear kept catching snippets of conversation.

"What the fuck is that loser doing here?"

"He's part of the party plan."

"Oh, this is that blast?"

Delivering sections of a sub, he overheard more jigsaws.

"A grave for the gravedigger."

"Yeah, but he ain't gonna be alone."

"Do you know why? I mean, why now?"

Irish shrugged.

"People only want a devil they can deal with."

Nagging notions kept tugging Diego's thoughts. Like the way Irish lurked by the *lupara*. Always keeping himself between anyone and the briefcase.

"I said you got any good beer?"

Diego snapped to attention. Ronnie Hurenko stood swaying by a window. In a track suit and sneakers, he looked like someone who wandered in off the street. He took a swig from a bottle then spit it out the window.

"This is piss!" he shouted.

"I'll see what I can do," Diego said.

Hurrying into the kitchen, Diego found Mr. Dobbs sipping brandy. It felt like walking in on the pope at a kegger. A person like him didn't belong here. He partied in mansions, on yachts, in clubs that charged a thousand dollars just to walk in the door. On the one hand, it seemed like an honor, but those meat hook doubts kept snagging Diego's brain. He made attendance mandatory.

"When is he getting here?" Mr. Dobbs said.

"Soon," Benny the Bear said. "I invited him myself."

"Good," Mr. Dobbs said, his voice dropping to a whisper. "If this doesn't happen, the peace is at risk."

The men around him nodded solemnly. No one wanted another round of war. Diego cleared his throat. All eyes went to him. It felt like being judged at the gates of heaven. Shuffling closer, Diego addressed Mr. Dobbs.

"Don't worry, sir," he said. "I'm taking care of it."

"Who are you?" Mr. Dobbs asked.

Benny leaned over to whisper in his ear.

"Ah," Mr. Dobbs nodded. "You're doing a good thing Domingo. We won't forget it."

Diego put on a smile. So extensively practiced the expression came across as genuine.

"Good boy," Mr. Dobbs said.

Leaving the kitchen, he patted Diego's cheek on the way out. The others followed him, leaving Diego alone. He couldn't help thinking about three years ago. He got a call saying some boss's kid got into trouble. They needed someone to take the rap. Promises of rewards a plenty got Diego thinking this must be his shot. So, he went to prison. Two years later he got out on good behavior, and no one seemed to remember him on the outside.

Nowhere to live, not a dime to his name, and the whole damn syndicate acted like he should be grateful. He got to serve. There is no higher honor.

This felt the same as then.

"Where's my fuckin' beer?" Ronnie hollered.

Throwing open the fridge, Diego grabbed a bottle. He stormed out. Passing Ronnie, he practically threw it at him.

"This is the same piss," Ronnie said chucking it out the window.

"Then check the fridge," Diego snapped. "I don't know what you want."

Throwing up his hands, Ronnie staggered towards the kitchen. Diego frowned. He stormed over to Irish beside the bar. Diego grabbed a shot, fired it down, and winced.

"I'm gonna step out for a minute," he said.

"You can't go," Irish said. "The guest of honor is coming, and you got the most important job."

"Isn't that what you're here for?"

Irish cocked an eyebrow. The buzzer screeched. Some guest hit the button shouting, "Come on up!"

"It's a two-man job," Irish said.

"Then what the hell am I even supposed to do?" Diego said.

A cold chill filled the room. The general clamor of conversation died down a degree. Diego turned. The crowd parted as the new arrival entered. He resembled a retired math teacher. Combover, bowling ball paunch, and thick glasses, he approached the bar in a pigeon toe shuffle.

"Glad you could make it El Sepulturero," Irish said. "This is Diego. He's gonna be your personal bartender."

"Pleased to meet you," El Sepulturero said. "I'd like a Rob Roy."

For the next few hours, Diego attended to The Gravedigger. He made sure the killer's cup never went empty. A booze brook ran through him, yet he barely seemed affected. Only after killing a bottle of scotch did any hints of drunkenness surface.

Most of the other guests avoided him. The killer drifted into conversations and his presence caused folks to disperse. However, Diego always kept him company. Eventually they stood alone in a corner. El Sepulturero talking and drinking. Diego pouring and listening.

"Normally I don't stay this long," El Sepulturero said. "If there's no one to talk to, what's the point of a party?"

"It is supposed to bring people together, I suppose."

As they chit-chatted about baseball, Diego began noticing some of the more celebrity gangsters slipping away. One or two, like Mr. Dobbs, said their goodbyes, but most made their exits discrete. Gradually, only the dregs remained. An apartment full of losers, a monster, and one bomb. Diego grimaced. It didn't take genius to guess the plan.

When El Sepulturero went to the bathroom, Irish approached Diego.

"I'm gonna get some ice," he said.

"Need a hand?" Diego asked.

"Nah," Irish said. "You just make sure no leaves. Party ain't over yet."

He slapped Diego on the shoulder then vanished out the door. Diego felt a sinking session like someone lowering him into a grave. He looked around the room. If he warned anyone, they'd live, but he'd get wrapped in plastic, weighted, and tossed in the Chicago River.

Plus, if the peace failed, that meant blood in the streets again. Dying to stop that sounded honorable. Although that stunk of the same bullshit that got him a thankless prison stint. Now, they expected him to die happily for the empire. No longer wasting his life, they wanted it all.

El Sepulturero returned from the bathroom.

"Where was I?" he said. "Ah yes. The league average for on-base percentage was around .300 during the dead-ball era. By the by, my drink is empty."

Diego handed him the bottle.

"Excuse me," he said.

Making his way through the crowd, Diego went to his bedroom. Shutting the door, he rushed to the window. He went out onto the fire escape and started down quick as a wink.

He tried not to think what this meant. Rushing off with no money, no prospects, no real options, just the chance to stay alive. He certainly couldn't stay in the city anymore.

An explosion rocked the building—derailed his thoughts. Diego looked up. He saw a chance to shine, so flew up the fire escape. In through the blasted window, he crept into the apartment.

A smokey haze filled the place. Small fires burnt in various spots, but mostly charred ruins, the interior smoldered. Pieces of burnt bodies littered the living room. Some still alive, blackened beyond recognition, rolled and rocked, moaning in agony. He found El Sepulturero dead in the corner. Somehow, he seemed scarier in death. His expression one of disappointment and anger.

Diego heard the thumps of someone headed upstairs. Probably Irish coming to clip whatever threads survivors clung to. Diego bolted into the bathroom. Getting the pistol from the toilet tank, he returned to the front door. He caught Irish about to step inside. Savoring the hitman's shock and confusion, Diego shot him.

Feeling dangerous yet merciful he went around the room silencing the dying. Hushing agony with a bullet; it didn't feel like murder. Then he went down to the street. He saw a black sedan parked across the road. A rear window rolled down revealing Mr. Dobbs in the back. Diego approached the car.

"It's done," he said. "I took care of it like I said I would."

"Good boy," Mr. Dobbs nodded. "We won't forget this, Domingo."

"My name is Diego."

VASILY LEDOVSKY

# 11

"She knew she had to leave just as bad as Tara but she didn't believe her chance would come so soon. Life doesn't happen on your schedule though. You have to take advantage of the opportunity when it presented itself."

# AS LONG AS YOU LOOK FARAWAY
Rob D. Smith

Rachel watched the Moonlite Motel parking lot from the second-floor railing through her gas station mirrored sunglasses. No one was paying her or Tara any attention. She said, "Clear."

Tara stuck the pass key she had swiped from her Aunt Jenny who used to work as a cleaning woman at the motel almost two years ago. The lock clicked open and Rachel followed her friend into room 201. Tara walked right to the bathroom door. Rachel locked the door then drew the curtains across the wide window facing the parking lot. Tara said, "Oh my god Rach. You got to see this."

Rachel didn't like the sound of this. She baby-stepped towards the bathroom. Eyes wide expecting anything. When she rounded the corner, she saw Tara staring into the toilet bowl. Tara said, "This turd is bigger than a hornet's nest."

"Gross." Rachel couldn't help herself. She moved into the brightly lit bathroom to get a peek. It was horrendous.

"Okay, enough wasting time. Must be a big dude to crap something like that out and proud enough not to flush it down." Tara lifted the porcelain lid off the toilet's reservoir. She saw in a movie once that people hid their valuables in a Ziploc bag inside. In the two years and hundreds of rooms they've pilfered, she'd never struck gold.

Rachel left the bathroom and checked the bedside table drawers. Nothing but brochures and the Cave City phone book. The room was ice cold from the air conditioning being left on high. Tara had made it out of the bathroom and was pulling out all the drawers on the dresser. Bottom drawer first. She pushed some clothing around, searching for cash or other valuables. Rachel peered out through the curtain. No one coming.

Tara said, "Help me with the bed."

Rachel gave her a hand lifting the mattress off the bed frame. This was usually paydirt for them. A Crackerjack box that always held a prize. You may not like what you got but you always got something. Nothing under the left side. Tara said, "Rotate it towards you."

A little lifting and sliding and Tara's side opened up. She had found something but nothing of value. She reached down and pulled up a couple of porn magazines. "For your split, do want Cherry magazine or Tight Teen Butts?"

"Put them back."

"No. I'm swiping his porn. For wasting our time. He can jack off to Spanktro-Vision." She slid the magazines into the hidden sleeve in her beach towel. They had sewn in pouches to two beach towels. It was less conspicuous than carrying their stolen goods in backpacks or tote bags. No one paid any attention to two girls going to the pool at the motel with their swimsuits and towels. Rachel wore shorts and a t-shirt over her suit. Tara was comfortable in just her two-piece bikini and pristine white Nike shoes.

"Such a bitch. Let's put the room back together." They got to it and had everything tucked away as if they had never been there. They never drew unwanted attention by leaving a messy room they rousted. Boys get caught. Girls run free. It didn't take long to cover their tracks and Rachel was soon shutting the door to room 201.

She pointed in the direction of the motel's pool. "Let's go take a dip before the next room."

"Just one more room." Tara stood on her toes.

"You want to get caught, don't you?"

"We won't get caught."

Rachel knew good luck wasn't forever. Someone would eventually catch them. It wouldn't be the Steinrocks who owned the place. They were so cheap they fired their cleaning service and did it themselves after their guests checked out. Rachel and Tara might be able to pull the scared little girl's routine and get off with a warning. What then? Go work at Dizzy Whizz or the Headhunter Hair Salon. Ride in a carpool two hours to Blue Label Publishing where her Mom and Grandma worked. Cave City was a parking lot for the afterlife. It was purgatory personified.

"One more room then, we can be cautious grandma's again." Tara pulled on her friend's arm.

"No one suspects grandma." Rachel took in the parking lot with a glance. A couple of people milling about.

"One more Rach. One more. I got a feeling."

Rachel pulled her arm free. It had been a fruitless day. All week had been slim pickings. If they were going to save enough money to leave town and get a place in Bowling Green, they would need some bigger scores. She held up her middle finger to Tara. "Okay, one more."

Her partner in crime grabbed her finger and laughed. "You're the best. Let's hit room 101 on the first floor."

Rachel sucked in air through her teeth. "Too close. We're going to the last room by the stairs."

"210? We've never gotten anything good out of that one. Loose change and that purple hairbrush. Might as well go to the pool." She pouted.

Rachel put an arm around her shoulder and began to walk her towards the last room on the second floor. "210 is the safest bet if we want to try another room so fast."

"I just think if we took some risks that we might make more money. More money and we can get the hell out of this town sooner."

"Joe messing with you again?"

"Stood in my doorway Sunday night with his hands inside his jeans. I took the butcher knife from under my pillow. Told him the next time I see his pecker is the last time anyone sees it."

Tara's stepbrother was two years older than her. He worked seasonally on local farms. Her mom had married Stan in their freshman year. He was an overnight truck driver. Tara's mom was a lush. Rachel let her spend the night whenever she could.

Rachel's family life wasn't so bad. Just her, Mom, and Grandma. They scratched by but there was no future here. And Rachel wasn't a great student or athlete. No scholarships coming to her rescue. She would be just another citizen of purgatory and that she could not abide.

"I want out too but if we get greedy, we won't make it."

As they passed a garbage can near the railing, Tara pulled out the porn mags and tossed them in the bin. "I get first dibs on the best thing in room 210."

"Sure sis. You can have the purple hairbrush this time."

Tara slung her towel over her shoulder and whipped her long brown hair to one side. "About time I get some respect around here."

They reached the end of the second floor. There wasn't a Do Not Disturb sign on the door handle. Shades were drawn. Tara slipped to the railing as the lookout. Rachel took out the key and tapped on the door. "Housekeeping."

No one stirred but sometimes you had to try louder. Some people liked to take a siesta on their vacation of hiking through Mammoth Cave or swimming at the pool. She tapped three times louder than the last on the door. She called again, "Housekeeping."

She put her ear to the door and halted her breathing. She had gotten pretty good at sensing if a room was clear. She had only gotten that one wrong when that couple left their toddler in the room unattended and he cried as soon as he saw them. A mess but the parents were afraid they would get in trouble so she and Tara escaped any trouble. Rachel asked, "Clear?"

"Good to go," said her lookout.

Rachel slid the card in and the lock clicked open. She stepped into an empty room with just a bedside lamp turned on. She flipped the switches turning the overhead light on. First one in checks the bathroom so after not seeing anyone in the main room she moved towards there. She heard Tara enter the room behind her and began to rifle the place.

The door was shut to the bathroom. She reached out to grasp the handle and when her fingers touched it static electricity gave her a jolt that caught her off guard. She tapped it to make sure the charge was gone when she noticed an odor. She hoped there wasn't another mess left in the bowl or worse, diarrhea.

She swung the door open and the foul smell overwhelmed her stinging her eyes. Made her blink. She covered her nose with one hand and rubbed her eyes clear with the other. Hanging limply from the bent shower rod was a dead man. The noose was made out of clothesline. Brown eyes wide open looking faraway. He was shirtless with a distended belly. He did have cargo shorts on. His legs were bent back into the bathtub. He could have stood up anytime. This was no accident.

She should have called for Tara but her brain just recorded all the details it could. On the toilet seat was a red Hawaiian shirt folded up. On top of the shirt was a nickel-plated revolver. Shiny as the chrome bumper on Tara's stepdad's rig. The man gave himself options. Gun or noose. She wondered why he chose to hang.

Tara yelled in delight from the main room. Rachel too stricken by the suicide aftermath to respond. Her friend rushed into the bathroom jabbering about something then she was shaking Rachel and pulling her from the bathroom. The change in scenery stopped her mind from cataloging the death scene. She began to tremble.

"Are you okay?" Tara held her cheeks with both hands and searched her eyes.

"I . . . I can't stop shaking."

Tara led her into the main room and pulled a comforter off the bed wrapping it around her. "You don't look so good."

Rachel plopped down on the bed. Her muscles and brain weren't connecting right at this moment. "He could have just stood up."

"Stay here and get warm. I'm going to check it out." She headed for the bathroom.

"Wait. Don't look at his eyes." Tara didn't hear her or didn't care. Rachel huddled in the blanket trying to calm down. She noticed a white envelope on the dresser. It was stuffed full of something. The shaking receded so she went to inspect the envelope. It wasn't sealed shut and she pulled the contents out onto the dresser top. She fanned the one hundred dollar bills out.

Tara came back into the room carrying a wallet and the revolver. "Dude's name was Harry Palmer."

Rachel said, "Why do you have that gun?"

Tara ignored her question. "Did you see how much money is in there?"

"I'm still shook up. How much is it?" She scooped the bills back into the envelope.

"Three thousand dollars. Enough for us to finally leave."

"Leave? We have senior year left."

"Fuck senior year. If I stay here any longer, something bad is going to happen at home." She tossed the dead man's wallet on the dresser top but she held fast to the pistol.

"We need to finish senior year. Maybe I could talk my Mom into letting you stay with us."

"I need to leave today. Not tomorrow. Not a year from now. Now." Tara noticed something on the dress and scooped it in a jangle with her free hand. She wagged car keys in Rachel's face. "And with his wheels, we can leave right now."

"You can't steal his car. The cops will find you."

"We just take it to Bowling Green or hell even Nashville and ditch it when we get there. No one will be looking for us."

Rachel remembered that familiar look in the dead man's eyes. That faraway look. She knew she had to leave just as bad as Tara but she didn't believe her chance would come so soon. Life doesn't happen on your schedule though. You have to take advantage of the opportunity when it presented itself.

Rachel said, "We need to swing by our homes and get our stash. I have almost two thousand saved up."

Her friend dropped her gaze to the thick beige carpet. "I only got 700."

"Jesus, where did the rest go?"

"My Momma found my hiding place. Took it for rent she said but I don't think you can rent a liquor store."

"With this three-grand combined with our money we should be able to get an apartment then look for jobs. Should be enough to start over."

Tara smiled. "Thanks."

"For what?"

"For keeping your promise. I never thought it would happen."

"I always knew it would." Rachel kept inside that she knew she would leave but might have to leave alone. "What are we going to do about him?"

"Harry Palmer?" Tara waved her hand like she shooed a fly. "We clean up the room like we always do and leave him for the Steinrocks to find in a couple of days."

Rachel helped her friend tidy up the room after turning the A/C up to arctic levels. She thought that might preserve the dead guy and keep anyone from noticing his smell. They got everything straightened up. Rachel avoided the bathroom. Her senses overloaded once already from the sight of hanging Harry Palmer. She wished she never knew his name.

They were ready to go. Rachel put the envelope full of money into her hidden towel pocket. She noticed Tara had the dead guy's red Hawaiian shirt tied around her waist. "Why the hell are you wearing that shirt?"

"Because when I stuck the gun in my bikini the weight pulled them down. The shirt keeps it from slipping." Tara showed the handle of the pistol sticking out of the tied shirt.

"Can't you just leave the gun?"

"We could use protection where we're going. Two hot country chicks in the big city? The wolves will be all over us." She threw her towel over her shoulder and it hung down far enough to cover the pistol's handle.

"It makes me uncomfortable."

"No shit. That's what guns do. Let's go see what our new ride is." Tara left the room without checking outside. Breaking their rules already.

Luckily no one was on the second-floor walkway. They went down the steps to the parking lot below. Tara pushed a button on the key fob and a dark blue Nissan Sentra's headlights flickered in the second-row parked nose out. With no hesitation, she ran to the driver's side, opened the door. Started the car right up. Rachel came over as Tara rolled down the window.

"I'll meet you at your place after I grab my clothes and stuff. Want to flip a coin on Bowling Green or Nashville." Her smile was so wide.

Rachel said, "Let's stick with Bowling Green for right now."

"Cool. Be at your place in a minute." Tara accelerated pretty quickly out of the parking spot for not having a driver's license. And a gun jammed down her bikini. She had always been lucky with other people, just awful unlucky with her family.

Rachel tried to walk as naturally as she could back across the parking lot to her Grandma's 1982 rusted-out Ranger. It wasn't easy when she wanted to dash as fast as she could. Her dream of leaving town could slip away just as the hanging man's hopes did. She made it to the truck like a regular human and not the alien she felt like under her skin.


Rachel tugged on jeans to go with her black tee and red plaid long sleeve western shirt. Under her bed, she kept her sayonara bag packed and ready to go. She bought the large Wilson duffel bag at the Barren County Flea Market two years ago. She didn't believe anyone used it to carry tennis rackets or shoes in it. The interior smelled like weed but she had cleaned it out with some watered-down Murphy's Oil soap. For two years she's had it packed and now it was time.

She had written the note to her mom and grandma in her head on the drive home. Now she got out her spiral notebook and committed it to paper. It wasn't flowery. She did say she loved them but it wasn't enough to keep her in Cave City. She said she would call when she could. She didn't tell them where she was going.

Letter written and her sayonara bag slung over her shoulder she left out the side door of the little house on Pearl Street. She made sure the door was locked tight with the screen door propped open on her hip. The aluminum metal door whacked shut like a mousetrap. The last time she would hear that familiar sound. She walked down the sidewalk where her home sat at the corner of Pearl and Washington. She sat on the short leaning concrete wall that ran down their narrow front lawn.

Rachel heard the car coming before she saw it. The compact car came to a stop with the passenger's door facing her. Tara waved for her to get in. When Rachel reached the door, it was locked. They played that game of unlocking and locking for a few seconds until her friend just reaches across and pulled the handle. Rachel got in and put her bag on the floor.

"Are you messing with me on purpose?" Tara's eyes were wild.

"What's wrong?" Rachel didn't like how her friend sweated while the air conditioning blowers were turned up.

"Nothing." She took off before Rachel could even shut the door.

Rachel watched Tara as she attached her seatbelt. She looked in the backseat and on the floorboards. Nothing of concern. All the bad juju was coming from her buddy driving the dead man's car. She was riding in a stolen car with her best friend out of town. Her dream and a nightmare all at once. She looked at Tara's sacred white Nike Airs. Tara cleaned them nightly with an old toothbrush. She was so proud of them but now there were little spatters of dark crimson on her pristine shoes.

"Are you okay?"

"Okay? We're finally shaking the dust off of us from this shitty place. I'm fine."

Rachel wondered where the gun was. She wondered what would happen to them now. Her wish finally granted by the small gods of Cave City. She was leaving and she could never come home again. She gazed out the passenger window and looked as far away as she could into the cloudy sky.

# 12

"Frank Kennedy was royalty around here at one time—, a walking, talking, living legend. The past moves on. Instead of the man he could have been, he stood in the little office at the back of the car lot pointing a gun at me and Mags."

# ONE LAST ROUND
### James Lilley

*"Ever since I came into this world, I've been fighting to stay alive and live a reasonably normal life. I've never been able to do it."*
-Sonny Liston

I knew his hand wasn't trembling out of fear. Frank didn't fear much; his hand shook all the same. Was it the weight of the Magnum he held or was it from the drink? Frank was a big bastard and the stink of stale whiskey clung to him like a blanket.

I felt sweat run down my back in rivers, pooling under the armpits of my work shirt. All I knew, it wasn't from the summer's heat—I was sweating out of fear.

I hated guns and I sure as fuck didn't like them pointed at me by a pissed off, ex-heavyweight champion.

Frank was a hero of mine from way back when. First guy from our little burb to win a professional boxing title. Only the NABF title but still a title. Frank Kennedy was royalty around here at one time—a walking, talking, living legend. The past moves on. Instead of the man he could have been, he stood in the little office at the back of the car lot pointing a gun at me and Mags.

July heat cooked the streets, and rose in waves from the asphalt. Frank spun away from me, his arm out stiff, and pointed the gun at Mags, who bucked and thrashed in the chair he was tied to. His eyes popped out of his head in fear.

"Mags, I know you screwed me. Fess up."

Mags shook his head so furiously I could see the sweat spray in the sunlight beaming through a split in the blinds. He screamed his protests through the gag. My heart beat a little faster when I realized this wasn't the first time Frank had people tied up. Of course, I'd heard the stories of his extreme acts of violence inside and outside the ring.

"I'm going to pull the gag out, Mags. Give you a chance to defend yourself." Frank lowered the gun and took a few steps towards Mags. He reached out for the gag but stopped slightly short.

"I don't need to tell you what will happen if you scream, Mags." He nodded in the direction of the door where Billy's body lay, blood pooled around him. "Get me, fuck-face?"

With two fingers he pulled the cloth down so Mags could speak and without taking a breath he started talking.

"It weren't me, Frankie baby. We go way back. We knew they wanted us to make the kid look good. Fuck, I wanted us to win—it was our ticket back to the big time."

Without warning Frank back-handed Mags hard. The smack was audible and if I hadn't been so scared, I probably would have shit my pants.

"I can't stand liars, kid," he said turning to me. "Let me tell you what I know."


In the eighties after the Ali era and before Iron Mike rolled into town, the heavyweight division had grown stale. They were crying out for the next big name. The next star.

Frank Kennedy was our hope. Son of an Irish father and Italian mother, he was the epitome of the American dream. Working class, good looking and he could punch like a mule. His star rose rapidly. Everyone knew him. A couple fights and he'd be looking at a title shot. A world title.

But best laid plans in boxing often have a way of not working out, and in his next fight he was iced in two rounds by an over-the-hill fighter. Frank was derailed and his career fell off. The loss should have been a bump in the road, but he rebounded into the bottom of a bottle and his career nosedived.


We were nearly forty miles from Boston. Far enough to be a sleepy little town, not far enough so the Irish mob's reach didn't touch us. My life in boxing and crime intersected and began through one man. Mickey "Mags" McDonald. He was nothing more than a seedy second-hand car dealer, but he had connections, and had done a few jobs for some known guys up in Boston. Nothing major, nothing to put him in the category of gangster, but enough so people feared him, and he fucking thrived off it.

I'd grown up loving boxing. Mainly through my father. He let me stay up late as a kid watching the big fights when my Ma was working nights. The old man screamed at the box while I shadow-boxed along with the fighters.

I'd gone to the local gym but getting punched in the face wasn't for me. Few bloodied noses and I'd had enough. My Ma didn't want me to fight anyhow. I still trained there but never for a fight—I was just happy to be around the sport.

The old sawdust and spit gym was where I met Paddy, a little man who'd been here since he was about twelve years old but never fully lost his thick Dublin accent. Paddy knew my father, even trained him for a while until he hit the bottle. Then he was a bearer after my father's car hit a truck.

When I finished high school, Paddy got me a job with Mags, the local businessman with his fingers in more than a few pies, not all of them legit. Mags like every other kid in the neighborhood had tried boxing or baseball. He saw the money to be made from the sport. I saw this as an opportunity to get closer to the fighters who visited his office. I started out washing cars in the lot, but the more I hung out there, the more I learned about boxing promotion. You see Mags didn't care how he made money as long as he made it. He had no love for the sport. He had a love for money. Through his connections up in Boston he managed to get a few over-the-hill boxers signed up.


Late winter in a freezing rain which hadn't quit for a day, I sat in the little cabin we used as an office at the back of the used car lot, waiting for Mags to call it a day when the door swung open and the hulking figure of Frank Kennedy walked in, dripping wet. His shadow blocked out most of the light. I looked up from the magazine I was reading, and my jaw dropped. I shot a glance over at Mags. The skinny arrogant prick didn't even look up from his paper.

"We're closing up, pal. Come back tomorrow."

Frank chuckled.

"Now, little Mags. You ain't got time for a broken-down old fighter like me? Shit, I hear all the bums are coming to you."

Mags looked up and nearly leapt out his chair.

"Frankie fucking Kennedy. Mary mother of Christ."

After the shock defeat, he took five or six losses in a row and had his license revoked. He went on to work as a bouncer in some fancy club up in Boston. Rumors circulated down that he was up to quite a bit more. He got himself into debt down the track. He got points off guys he couldn't pay back. So, when they couldn't collect, they let him work it off, and they started putting his tools to good use as an enforcer, shaking down anyone else who owed. I even seen him once up at a big new fancy mall with my friends. I asked for an autograph but all I got was: "Not today, kid."

Now, here he was. In Mags's office. Asking Mags to get him his license back. Get him a few fights to finish his career on a high note. Sure, he was the wrong side of forty and hadn't boxed for ten years, but if big George Foreman was doing it why couldn't he? I stood next to Mags, nervously drinking in the features of the ex-champion. Crooked nose, dark-black slicked-back hair, murky grey eyes. You could tell he was a ladies' man the way he carried himself, and the clothes were pristine. Mags was babbling on about opportunities and big fights down the line, but I wasn't paying much attention. I still couldn't believe the man dripping all over the floor was Frank Kennedy.

He signed with us and it took our little promotion in the next direction. The comeback was the talk of the town. There was a buzz. You see the Rocky movie when he's running through the streets, and everyone is cheering him on and clapping? The movie mirrored Frank's life when he was fighting.

A couple fights in, and things started to go sideways. He was down the track again. Losing more than he had. I asked Mags what to do one night as we closed up. He smiled in his weasel-like way.

"Mind your business, kid. I'll sort Frank."

A few fights fell through, and business went quiet. We hadn't seen or heard of Frank in a month. I was taking a slow stroll home one evening. The days were getting longer, and the weather was turning; summer was finally on its way.

I always walked to the little one-bed apartment I called home. It took longer and I didn't like to be in my place on my own for too long. I went past the Irish bar near the car lot, through the dirty window, someone caught my eye. In the gloom inside, I saw a shape I had become accustomed to. I snuck in through the swinging door. The bar was empty except for Frank slumped over the bar. Something muffled was playing over the sound system.

The place smelled like Frank; stale booze and hopelessness clung to the place like a disease. As I took a few paces into the darkness I caught the singer—it was Nina Simone, singing a sad love song. The buzz from the faulty green neon sign hanging behind the bar drilled into my brain and overpowered the music.

"Hey Frank." I called, walking across the barroom floor unsteadily, trying to act like this was my regular haunt. The bar was empty but I felt like I was being watched, tested. He turned to me and even in the dim light I could see his bloodshot eyes. He looked at me and then turned back to his empty glass.

"How you been keeping, champ? Haven't seen you around for a while." I pulled a bar stool out next to him and perched myself on it, resting my arms on the sticky bar. The bartender appeared from nowhere, a huge man with a pure white beard and flowing long hair. He wore a cut off tee and his arms were covered in tattoos, a big red "8" on one forearm and a big red "1" on the other.

"You twenty-one?" he barked in a graveled voice ruined by tobacco.

"Umm, yes."

"When's your birthday?" he countered.

I tried doing the math in my head quickly, but my brain froze. The two huge men watched in silence.

"Ah . . .."

Both men burst out laughing at some private joke.

"Kid, you're alright in here with Frank. Don't let anyone in blue see you come in or leave, you feel me? Another whiskey, champ?"

Frank nodded and the man behind the bar retrieved a bottle and poured into the empty glass. He disappeared into the back again.

"He's Hal. This is his joint. He's not Irish, but don't hold it against him." Frank chuckled to himself "You see his tattoos? Guy used to be patched."

"Patched?" I asked

"Never mind. What you doing here, kid?"

I felt my throat go dry. No matter how many hours I spent around a former hero I still couldn't help getting nervous.

"Why don't you come to the gym in the morning with me Frank? Get back on track? I know there is nothing lined up, but we can stay ready."

"Kid, listen. I been in the game a long time. I been screwed, used, chewed up, and spat out. I know how it works. You tell Mags to get me a fight and I'll put down this glass and put on the gloves. Until then, I'll see ya round." He lifted the glass as if to toast me.

"Frank . . .."

"Fuck outta here, kid. You're starting to piss me off. I wanna get drunk and fall off the stool. Stop bothering me." He slid off the stool and stumbled to the back of the bar and started thumbing some coins into the jukebox and smashed the buttons until Motley Crue came on over the speakers. He stood. leaning against the jukebox as I left the bar. The sky had gone pink as the sun sank.


Boxing is a lonely sport. Being a promoter, or whatever the fuck I was trying to be, was just as bad. I got into my little one bed apartment, about to call it a night, when my phone rang. I picked it up and knew it was Mags by the fast words he spat at me.

"Where the fuck have you been, kid? I gotta speak to you? Do you know where Frank is? Shut your trap. Listen. We got a fight! A big one. Go find the big guy and get back to the car lot. Hurry up, kid!"

The line clicked off.


Four weeks is all they gave us. Four weeks to get Frank off the booze and fighting fit. Frank didn't care. As soon as I pulled him out of Hal's bar, he hit the gym hard. Even with the hangover the next day, he done ten rounds on the mitts. Paddy and I watched the life seep back into him.

Darnell Abraham was who they gave us. An ex-football star who'd lost his love of the game and retired at twenty six. He'd been in a

couple of TV movies and moved into boxing to raise his profile. He'd
been put in with a string of bums who he'd dispatch in no time. "He
has explosive power!" One of the commentators said once during a
fight and Darnell was blessed with Dynamite as his moniker. Frank was
the next target. Everyone knew about Frank. He needed money. He
was an ex-champ. He was in the bar more than the gym. Easy target
and would be the big step up to validate Dynamite. Of course, we had
other plans.


Walking into the arena I could feel the buzz, even with half empty
seats. We were co-main event in the biggest arena we'd been in so far.
Five thousand were expected. I looked up at the bright lights shining
down on the ring. I'd be up there soon with Frank; he'd asked me to
help corner. I was no Paddy but Frank said I saved him.

We waited in the changing rooms for the call. Frank was his usual
self: shooting the shit with everyone, shadow-boxing, every now and
then bursting into a song. The atmosphere was relaxed. He'd done this
a hundred times and it wasn't anything new. The only one who didn't
seem to be himself was Mags. I'd never seen him look so nervous. We
got the knock, and Frank pulled on a green robe with a shamrock
etched around his surname. It glistened like jewelry in the lights.

Mötley Crüe came blasting over the sound system and we made
the walk. I couldn't make out much with the lights on us and the music
blasting. I held my breath until the bell rang to start proceedings.


An overhand right—more of a hopeful last-ditch attempt—caught
Frank high on his left temple, freezing him in place. I glanced over at
Paddy on the other side of the turnbuckle and saw the panicked look
on his fat, red face. Something wasn't right with Frank.

The first round he'd looked like the Frank of fifteen years ago,
bobbing, weaving, and floating like he was a lightweight instead of an
over-the-hill overweight heavyweight. He'd come back to the corner
full of smiles and jokes. I don't think he'd even been hit. Going out
into the second as the bell sounded, he had a spring in his step. If this
was to be his swan song, he was going to go out looking good. I even
felt sorry for the young opponent opposite him.

But something happened about thirty seconds into the round.
Frank dropped his hands slightly as if they were too heavy. He glanced

around, as if he'd forgotten where he was, as if he was walking through quicksand. Abraham took the opportunity to fire off a quick combo, but Frank had enough about him to ride the shots and slide out of the way, firing his right hand off to keep the younger man at bay.

I was hopeful it was a momentary lapse but when Frank reached the ropes, he lay back on them, a bewildered *what the fuck am I doing in here?* look on his face. Abraham, like a predator sensing weakness, charged forward, throwing big heavy shots, but in his eagerness, he got too close and Frank managed to grab a hold of him, smothering him. The referee who didn't look like he weighed more than a hundred and fifty pounds, struggled to pull the giants apart. The bell sounded to our relief and Frank wobbled over to the corner like he'd been back on the drink.

Paddy dived through the ropes as Frank slumped onto the stool I held under him. The little Irishman was barking at Frank and waving his arms in the air. I gently put a cold sponge on the back of the boxer's neck, squeezing out freezing cold water, trying to revive him a little. Completely oblivious to Paddy, he turned his head to me and was mouthing something. Over the noise of the crowd and Paddy barking I couldn't quite catch what he was saying so I leant in so he could whisper in my ear like a lover.

"They are going to try and screw us, kid." He said gently.

"Don't worry, Frank. Get your head right. This kid ain't got shit on you."

"One last round."

I passed him up the water bottle and he sprayed a mouthful into him. He pulled away from us, clambering up to his feet. He leant down and kissed Paddy on the forehead.

"Seconds Out!" a call came from ringside, the bell sounded, and the dance began again.

Climbing down from the apron, I glanced over my shoulder. Ringside near the rich seats, I saw Mags staring at me. Waiting for me to make a mistake. He wanted to be in the corner and he fucking hated that Frank asked me. He nodded at me and melted back into the crowd.

Only a few seconds into the final round, Abraham threw the overhand right. It hit home and stopped Frank in his tracks. Then, Abraham unloaded on him. The referee was slow to act as the round had only begun and Frank took a bunch of unanswered blows before the ref got between them to wave it off. Abraham threw his hands in the air screaming with joy, as our man toppled, the referee desperately trying to catch him. They went down together in a heap. Frank face-first twitching on the blue canvas floor. The crowd fell silent as Paddy screamed.


The three of us stood around the hospital room, not speaking, but the room was loud from all the machines: the beeping, the hiss of the ventilator. Frank was lying in the middle of us, oblivious to it all.

"What'd the doc say, Paddy? They have any idea what happened?" Mags asked in a hushed voice, as if not wanting to wake our friend.

Paddy lowered his head fighting back the tears.

"Nothing. They've done tests. Scans. All shit. They say big words and stuff I don't understand, I told them he was fine then came over all funny-like. They said it might have been a concussion. Can you fucking believe it? Concussion? Bum didn't land a punch on him." The old man looked tiny as he clutched his flat cap in his hand. One hand released the cap and clamped over his mouth, choking back tears. He stormed out the room, leaving me and Mags standing over the man.

"Come on, kid. He won't be going any place soon. Let's get back to the car lot."

I took a long look at Frank: a man who would rather be carried out on his shield than quit. Lying there, frail and weak, having machines breathe for him.


"The doctor found Flunitrazepam in my system. Any idea what they use Flunitrazepam for kid?"

I shook my head.

"It's a date rape drug. Weasels like Mags here call them roofies. They find a broad and whisper sweet serenades in her ear and slip a little in their drink. About right, Mags?"

"Frankie, I didn't do nothing. How could I of got some roofies into you?"

Frank smiled and raised the hand cannon once more. Mags bucked in his chair again, trying to get up, and a dark patch began spreading around the groin of his hideous burgundy track pants.

"It was the kid, Frank. He slipped you the mixed water. I didn't do nothing."

I couldn't believe it. The accusation stung like a slap, but it also hurt knowing I was so stupid not to question why Mags had appeared the night of the fight and why he handed me the water bottle, I thought he was concerned. How could I have been so gullible? So fucking stupid. I opened my mouth to protest my innocence, but the words caught in my throat again.

Frank looked back over my shoulder, a sullen look on his usually cheerful face.

"Don't worry about it, kid."

He pulled the trigger, and an almighty roar filled the room like we were in the middle of a thunderclap. The gun smoke stung my eyes instantly, when my vision cleared I saw Mags slumped in a broken heap on the floor, office chair tumbled over, gaping red raw wound in his chest. Frank, calm as the ocean on a summer's day, walked over and raised the gun again and pulled once more. This time I closed my eyes, but I still managed to see Mags's face disintegrate in a gruesome cloud of gun smoke and grey mater.

I heard Frank's sneakers treading over toward me, and then the sound stopped. I could sense his presence looming over me, filling the space.

"Open your eyes, kid."

I clamped my eye lids down tighter and shock my head viciously.

"One last round, kid."

I heard him pulling back on the hammer. I waited for the end.

I didn't expect to hear the gun shot. I thought I'd be dead and heading toward whatever came next. What I heard was a deafening roar so loud it spilt my head in two. Then, nothing. Silence. I cautiously opened my eyes and saw Frank lying at my feet, down for good.

## "Fun w/ Fill-in Stories"
# STORY

*Time to see how you did with your noir masterpiece, a heart-warming holiday tale filled with family, festivities, and some light B&E. Fill in the spaces with your responses from the Story Key and enjoy!*

* * *

______________, looking rather ______________ and wearing a
      1                      2

______________ hood over their face, slid the window open and pulled
   3

themself inside ______________. The bright, ______________ presents
              4                      5

were ______________ under the tree. Throughout the house there was
       6

only ______________ silence.
       7

Carting a ______________ ______________ sack, the intruder slid
          8             9

first one tightly-laced combat boot over the window sill, then the other.

______________ couldn't help but rub their hands together
   1

______________.
   10

This looked like it was the _____________'s
                                 11

___________ ___________ yet. It appeared ___________ got
      12              13                              14

the ___________ they'd been asking for. ___________ had a
        15                                      16

large box with their name on it, and he guessed it was that

___________ their ___________ had hinted about.
      17                18

Feeling ___________, ___________ shook open their sack
             19              1

and made ready to shovel the presents in. This wasn't their fault. They

wouldn't have to do this if they'd been invited like the rest of the

family. In fact, just thinking about ___________'s
                                         20

___________ made their mouth water, not to mention
      21

___________'s ___________. And of course,
      22            23

___________ that would be cooked. But no, ___________hadn't
      24                                           1

been invited, and this is what the family had driven them to.

Only three presents were in the sack when a sudden click made

___________ freeze, then squint as the sudden light
      1

___________ their eyes.
      25

"SURPRISE!" the gathered family yelled.

"_____________" _____________ yelled back. "I was just
      26              1

_____________ these presents!"
   27

"_____________!" laughed _____________. "You can't rob us
   28                 29

_____________ holidays in a row and expect us to sit here and take it
   30

like _____________ _____________."
      31          32

_____________ dropped their head. So much for the
   1

_____________s of dollars they were going to make. There would be
   33

nothing like detoxing in a _____________ during the holiday. They
                         34

just hoped they didn't get the _____________ vomit again.
                         35

"Cheer up, _____________!" said _____________. "We didn't
              1               36

set all this up to stop you. It was just the only way we knew how to find

you to give you your gift."

They held out a thick, _____________ envelope and as
                     37

_____________ looked inside, they saw a stack of cash.
   1

______________, but there must have been at least
    38

______________ dollars inside. They could score not just the
    39

______________ shit, but enough for all their friends, too. Or, you
    40

know, just keep themselves supplied for a whole

______________ weeks.
    41

"I don't know what to say. Thank you so much. I'll pay you back

when—"

"No, you won't," said ______________, ______________. "Now get
                              42                43

out of here so we can quit this ______________ shit and go to bed."
                                      44

______________ went back out the window they'd come in
    1

through, wiping away a tear before sliding it shut behind them. They

couldn't believe the family had done that just for them—stayed up late,

collected money, and surprised them with it. It was going to be a(n)

______________ holiday indeed.
    45

Especially, they thought as they _______________ in the
46

_______________ bushes, when everyone went to bed for real and they
47

could get their hands on that _______________ stack of presents for
48

keeps this time.

# 13

"The cinderblock cell in County wasn't so different from a coffin vault, just upright and missing that last slab of concrete. Ern was sobering up. He wished he wouldn't."

# DEAD MAN'S COCKTAIL
### Chris Harding Thornton

The night Celia landed Ern in a Garfield County holding cell, he'd been in Enid six months. He'd moved to Oklahoma when an unbonded contractor in Omaha tried to pin a four-alarm fire on Ern and some other cut-rate welders. Ern had priors, so he didn't wait to see how it played out. Mom said she had an extra room, and he took it.

He'd got a job at Memorial Gardens, a cemetery north of town. It was the only job that ever suited him. He worked alone, on days there weren't services or after funerals, once the family had cleared out. When he wasn't mowing, gouging out new eternal resting places with the backhoe, or shifting slabs of concrete over coffins so the sod didn't sink, all he heard out there was wind. That and birds. Ern hated birds, but out there even the birds were all right.

The cinderblock cell in County wasn't so different from a coffin vault, just upright and missing that last slab of concrete. Ern was sobering up. He wished he wouldn't. He also wished he'd never met Celia. But he supposed if he hadn't, he wouldn't have the boys.

Celia had brought them, Ern Junior and Ashton, from wherever she'd moved them, some town in Arkansas he'd never heard of. Ern had braced himself for her arrival by getting half lit, and not long after she got there, they were both glaze-eyed. She waited till then, till they were both good and drunk, to show him the band on her finger. She waited till then to say the boys had a new last name.

Ern Junior was playing outside. Ashton was in the living room, climbing the entertainment center, the end tables, the couch arms. She yelled at him to stop climbing. Ern said to let him be, and that set her off. The hell did he know about raising kids, she said. She railed on about what a piece of shit Ern was, right in front of the boy, and soon enough, Ern felt the blood pressure pounding in his head. It got to pounding so hard he saw stars, and that was when he shot his mom's .38 at the ceiling. He did it to shut Celia up and keep from having a stroke. Little bits of crumbled drywall had landed in his hair and moustache.

She'd called him in on anything she could think of: possession (they didn't find anything), domestic (he hadn't laid a hand on her), unregistered gun (not against the law in Oklahoma), and pipe bombs. It was true he'd made them on occasion. Some people liked ham radio, Ern liked building pipe bombs. It was a hobby. But he hadn't made one since he'd been in Oklahoma, and when the cops didn't find any, they nailed him for a defused hand grenade in his underwear drawer. In hindsight, he shouldn't have let them search, but Ern didn't think he had anything to hide.


Ern waived the preliminary hearing, and a paperweight and ceiling hole landed him in Big Mac. One count "possession and/or manufacture of incendiary device (85 percent)," two counts assault and battery with a dangerous weapon. The one shot, at nobody, was two counts because Celia and Ashton were inside the house. There'd been a dozen other charges, all of the same ilk, suspended or deferred. He got five years.

He lay on the cot that was bolted to the cell wall. Everything in there was bolted down. Ern lay there and knew he couldn't do five years. Plenty of men did, but the most time Ern ever served was eleven months in Nebraska. DUI and paraphernalia were the charges, but what did him in was a litany of catch-22s beforehand—tickets for no insurance, outdated plates, driving under suspension because he had to get to work, legally or not. Then there'd been the juvenile record. He'd thought it'd been sealed, or expunged, or whatever the hell they did with those, but it hadn't. Either Mom was supposed to have taken care of it or somebody made a clerical error. Didn't matter. Eleven months was enough to teach him he couldn't do five years.

Ern's back ached against the flat slab of a cot, and when a guard came to get him for dinner, Ern wasn't up for it. He said his back was out. He couldn't move. They called his bluff, brought him a wheelchair, and sent him to the infirmary. The guard, like Ern, must've thought he'd be laid out in his cell again in twenty. Ern figured they'd give him a Norco or two and he'd kill a few hours.

What he hadn't counted on was the pen contracted with a hospital. And Ern had pretty well shattered himself thirty-some years before in a motorcycle wreck. He'd healed all right, got around, worked, but that hospital read Ern's X-rays and saw dollar signs. He needed surgery, they said; it was some kind of miracle he was even walking around. He did the math. Back surgery would eat up a week or two, pain meds a few weeks more.

Then one surgery turned to four, each followed by a push-button morphine drip. He'd max it out, and if he didn't fall asleep he'd picture the boys. Both were towheaded. Ern's hair was near black and going gray. They took after their mother in looks, but Ern knew he was in there somewhere. He'd find it when he taught them to drive or rebuild a carburetor. In the midst of imagining parts spread across newsprint, he'd drift. He'd drift and always end up back at Memorial, taking a smoke break next to the backhoe, sun beating down but not too hot, breeze filling his head with a rush that shut out any other sound.

The surgeries were followed by a daily diet of three different flavors of pharmacy-heroin. Two brands for pain, one for sleep. "Dead man's cocktail," the prison GP called it. But Ern didn't feel dead. What he felt was a constant buzzing between his ears and under his skin, like the wind at Memorial rushing through his head. Whenever he felt it fading, the edges of everything in the cell or the yard or the cafeteria getting sharper, another dose was at the ready. He'd pop it and wait for the static in his ears and the prickles washing down through his chest and limbs. The pills made everything too loud, especially his own voice, but he rarely used it.

Since the first surgery, that'd been another bonus: nobody fucked with him. Nobody talked to him. He was jaundiced from hepatitis he hadn't known he had, bloated up by meds, and moving like half his body had rigor mortis. He looked like death.


The day Ern walked out of Big Mac, his mom, freshly blue-rinsed, met him in a used Geo Prizm. With effort, he squatted low enough to prop himself in the passenger side. He could bend at the hip, but the rest, all the way up through the neck, was fused. They said he'd need another surgery, but once Medicaid was footing the bill, he could delay it indefinitely. Ride however many years he had left on that cocktail.

Mom said he looked a fright. Hepatitis, he said. She hadn't been down since the first month, before he knew he had it. He couldn't turn his head, but he felt her shrink away, molding herself against the driver's side door. Ern wasn't offended. Ern appreciated quiet and distance.

But Mom could never be quiet long, so for the next three hours and change, she rattled. She'd found a townhome and hated it. She said he needed to stay out of trouble with that woman, for the kids' sake, if not his own. She said he needed to get right with God.

Ern let her rattle, gave an occasional grunt to be polite. Two things he didn't need told about were Celia and God. Celia was proof-positive there was no God. Inside, he'd heard about some boys in Wyoming who could make it look like she'd been eaten by a bear. But he wouldn't do it. She was a witch, but she was the mother of his kids.

When Mom finally pulled up to the "townhome," it turned out to be an apartment in a four-plex. The building looked like it'd been a clinic or something—part of a strip mall. Half of Enid was a strip mall.

Inside, Mom had dedicated a shelf in the hall closet to Ern's clothes. He'd sleep on a foldaway in her QVC room. Not like the whole apartment wasn't one middling-sized QVC room. She'd run up her credit while he was inside until they'd cut her off. Ern didn't know if creditors garnished SSI, but if they did, he'd be paying off blankets that doubled as capes and cubic zirconium earrings till whenever he finally died.

They sat in the living room, Ern on the couch that was too soft and low, Mom in her rocker-recliner. She flipped on the TV. There'd be roast and potatoes for dinner, she told him. "And Celia's bringing the boys."

He tried and failed to scoot forward, to push against the couch arm and stand. "Thought I'd head up to Memorial," he said. His reactions were slowed, but that one was knee-jerk. "See if they could use some part-time help." He knew he couldn't do half the job he'd done before, but he imagined he could still drive a backhoe. With enough mirrors, he bet he could.

"You can't be using my car," she said. "And the boys want to see you."

He doubted it. They'd be six and eight by now. "I doubt they remember."

"You're their father," she said, flipping channels. A station came on too loud with an ad for car insurance, plans tailored to people who'd let their coverage lapse or run somebody over. Ern could've used insurance like that back in the day.

Mom tried to find the volume-down button but turned the set up till he winced. "*They don't know me from Adam*," he yelled over the TV. Mom found the volume-down and stared at Ern like he'd yelled for no reason.

"Keep your voice down." She looked startled. Ern remembered what he looked like. Sallow, bloated, stiff as a corpse. She seemed to force her eyes back to the TV. "Boys need a father."

He wanted to think that was true, though he supposed Celia had got them one.

If Ern walked to Memorial, he'd have to pass the cop shop, and this part of Enid had no sidewalks. He'd be hoofing it through strip mall parking lots. There was about an eight percent chance, looking and moving like some B-film rip-off of Frankenstein, that the nosy manager of a Family Dollar wouldn't call him in as a suspicious-looking character. He could wind up spending the night in County, which was only about three miles down the road.

The roast was cooking. Ern could smell it, though it didn't make him hungry. Nothing did anymore. Mom got up to check on it and stayed over in the kitchen. When she was done boiling the potatoes and started mashing, there was a knock on the door. It was only a warning, apparently, because Celia let herself in.

Ashton jetted past her and into the hallway. Celia closed the door behind them.

"Ern Junior outside?" Mom asked.

Celia said he had little league. Ern wondered if the boy was good at it. He pictured himself in the stands, eating popcorn, watching the boy slide into second.

She flipped her shoes off and stood in front of the TV. She was getting jowls. Looking more and more like her mother. Celia's mother always hated Ern. She was a hateful woman in the general sense, though Ern supposed she had decent reasons for hating him specifically.

Celia stared at the TV like she'd been watching it for hours. She wore a cowl-necked sweater, iridescent orange. Strands poked from it so it looked fuzzy, like the yarn was charged by static electricity. Maybe the effect was supposed to be like airbrushing. She sure as hell couldn't airbrush away the paunch beneath it, and her ass had gone wide and flat in a pair of Lee's. Ashton would've had plenty of room if he'd wanted to hide behind her, but he was off slamming a rubber ball, the kind from one of those quarter machines at the grocery store, against the walls of the hallway. He stomped as it ricocheted.

"Ashton Lee, goddammit," Celia yelled.

"He's all right," Ern said.

Over in the kitchen, Mom's mouth was a tight line. Celia must've sensed it. "Boys and their balls," she said, loud as ever.

A court show was on. It went to commercial, and she finally looked Ern up and down. "You look like shit."

"Had back surgery," he said.

"You're yellow as a canary."

He thought to tell her about the hepatitis. Depending on how long he'd had it, she might have it, too. And if she did, she could somehow accidentally give it to the boys. But if Ern told her and she lunged at him, he couldn't very well defend himself, all fused up. For once, Mom didn't say a word.

"The meds," he said. He wanted to tell her she looked like a goddamn muppet the size of the sun. Her hair matched the sweater. Frizzy strands poked from the perm she'd gotten, which was like a poodle dog's. She had a puff up top and a haze of curls jutting down and out like a triangle.

"How's the old man?" he asked her.

She scowled at him. "Dad's been dead eight, nine years. What kind of meds you on?"

"I meant your husband."

"Clint," she said and went back to the court show. "Clint Havelock. He stays out of jail and holds down a job. A good one."

"Hope everybody's hungry," Mom cut in.

Mom had a cloth-covered card table in the space next to the kitchen. Each of them took a side. Mom sat across from Celia, and Ern sat facing Ashton, who stared, a little gap-mouthed and squinting. While Mom said grace, Ern and the boy didn't bow their heads. Ern tried to see some sign of himself. He thought he could. There was an old photo where Ern couldn't have been three and looked half-asleep. Ashton looked a little bit like that. Ern wondered if Ashton was studying him the same way. For the same kind of recognition.

Back in the hospital bed, Ern had pictured the boys to try and miss them, but the morphine drip kept him too numb. He was still numb. But as he stared into his son's eyes, he felt something. He wasn't sure what to call it. It was like the boy was an organ Ern hadn't known he was missing. A hole in his lower chest, near his stomach. There'd been a time, years back, when Ern thought he'd take this boy and Ern Junior fishing. Hunting. They'd catch and clean turtles. As Ern stared, the hole seemed to widen, deepen.

Then Ashton turned to Celia. "Is he dead?"

"*Ashton,*" Celia hissed, but she had an elbow on the table and hid her mouth with a fist. Mom said nothing. She looked down at her lap.

Ern used his legs to scoot back from the table, braced his hands on the folding chair's seat, and managed to heave himself up.

He went to the door and opened it, stepped out, and closed it behind him. Outside, the sky was still light, but dusk was setting in. Memorial was a good six, seven miles away. Before he took a step, he thought to stretch. He reached upward, but nothing gave anymore. Everything in him was bolted down.

# 14

"'I'm afraid I'm going to have to ask you to give me everything in your pockets,' she said."

# THE BORDER
## Gregory Wolos

The tall, pregnant woman with the dark curls spilling around her pie dish face sat alone in the back row of the chairs arranged for Leonard's Barnes & Noble reading. In front of her an audience of a dozen tired mothers and wriggling children watched and listened as the author read from *Mend My Tail, Doc*, the latest in his series of *Emergency Vet* picture books. He'd retired from his veterinary practice and now lived a nomadic life on the road promoting his stories. Leonard displayed the illustrations: here was the cat being fitted for a prosthetic leg; here the pig with its snout stuck in a peanut butter jar; here the monkey with its hand super-glued to its tail.

The expecting young woman remained for the question-answer period.

"How long did it take you to make the pictures?" a chubby boy asked around the finger in his mouth.

"I don't do the illustrations. We have an artist for those," Leonard explained.

"But how long? And what's the matter with your eye?"

"Shh, Jake, be polite," his mother hushed.

"It's okay, ma'am." Leonard was walleyed. He'd been born with the imperfection his mother had reassured him a thousand times was "slight." Frown lines framed her smile whenever she patted his cheek and called him "my handsome boy." Leonard's gaze flitted to and from the pregnant woman. She wore a yellow raincoat. "I keep an eye pointed to the side so I can see if anyone's sneaking up on me," he told the boy. "Did you know that a chameleon's eyes work independently? Can you imagine looking at two different things at once?"

The boy blinked, spun his eyes around the room, shook his head and groaned.

"Do you have a pet?" a little girl called from her mother's lap.

"Nope," Leonard said. "Traveling around to talk about my books, I can't really keep an animal. Sometimes I think a companion for the road would be nice, though."

"What about children?" It was the pregnant woman. Leonard flinched when she batted her eyes at him: on one of her lids, the left, an extra eye had been tattooed.

"No children, no pets," he said. "I'm not married."

The pregnant woman stood nearby as Leonard signed his books for mothers whose children were tugging them toward the exit. Her belly swelled out of her yellow raincoat, stretching her orange maternity shirt as smooth as a pumpkin. She held a large paisley bag by its strap. When he finished, she approached. She was tall—taller than Leonard.

"Your book title's a pun." Her hands slid over her stomach as if she were polishing it. "Doesn't docking a tail mean to cut it off? Like for cocker spaniels? So, 'doc' is a pun, right? You can't mend something and cut it off at the same time."

Leonard wagged his head, a nervous habit. He was trying not to stare at her eye tattoo. "The publisher titled it. But good catch. You're the first to notice."

"I saw you on *Denver Today* this morning. You told the monkey story. *Loved* it! Would you want to get some coffee? If that doesn't cross some kind of author-fan boundary. Not here, though— somewhere more private. You drive us, and I'll treat. It's hard for me to squeeze behind a steering wheel these days. I'm Mindy." She held out her hand, and Leonard shook it. It was dry and cold and strong.

When they'd settled into Leonard's Escalade in the mall parking lot, the sun was setting. Mindy rummaged in her bag and pulled out a pistol. She held it by her belly so it couldn't be seen through the SUV's windows and angled it at Leonard's face. "I'm afraid I'm going to have to ask you to give me everything in your pockets," she said. "Keep your keys for now. But I want your phone, wallet, everything else." The gun didn't look like a toy. "I'm not joking, Doctor Friedman."

"You're robbing me?"

"No. You won't lose a thing. This isn't a robbery. It's a kidnapping. Or no, a *doc*-napping." She paused, licking her lips as her attention dipped to her swollen stomach. "Though I guess it *is* a kidnapping, too. That depends on who you think this baby belongs to." Her eyes flashed at Leonard, and she grinned. "I'm a surrogate mama," she said. "Somebody else's zygote has grown to full term inside me. But I'm calling it mine. I've got a promise of fifty thousand for it in Mexico City. That's double what my contract here calls for." She extended a palm toward Leonard. "So the wallet and the phone—and whatever else you've got that identifies you. Keep the keys in the ignition. Start up and get us out of here—take the Interstate south." Without lowering the pistol, she took in the SUV's interior. "Nice car. How's it on fuel? It's about ten hours to the border and twenty more to Mexico City."

Leonard couldn't think of the questions he knew he should ask. He tugged his wallet out of his back pocket and his phone out of his front and placed both in Mindy's hand. He started the Escalade.

"So—you want me to be your chauffeur?"

"Oh, you'll be that and maybe much more, Doctor. I'm going to call you 'Doc,' okay? Listen, I could have picked anybody to drive. But I chose you after I saw you on TV and heard you were going to be reading right here in town. What you are is my insurance policy." She glanced around the parking lot, clutching the gun like it was a small animal needing restraint. "Just get us out of here. We'll get food and gas on the road. There's a long way to go. I pee often, by the way."


An hour later, Mindy pinned her gun between her knees while she peeled the plastic wrap from the sandwiches she'd bought with Leonard's cash. It had gotten dark. The only light in the SUV was the luminescence of the dashboard and the occasional swimming beams of northbound cars and trucks.

"Do you ever use your four-wheel drive?" she asked with a full mouth.

"No," Leonard said. "I don't even know how it works."

Mindy swallowed, then rested her sandwich on her belly. "You got what I meant by 'insurance policy,' right? You understand your purpose?"

Leonard wished he was taller—long-legged Mindy had pushed her seat back to its limit, and, because his right eye was weak, he had to screw his head like an owl to see her face. He hadn't much of an appetite for his sandwich and chewed mechanically. He'd been thinking about a coincidence: Mindy was a surrogate, and he had once attempted to donate his sperm.

"Is it because being in the car with a celebrity will help if there are border issues?" he asked.

Mindy laughed. "You're not *that* well-known, Doc. You think customs guys read? I guess they might watch talk shows, though. And they are trained to recognize faces. But, no, don't you get it? You're a *doc*, Doc! I'm due any second—what if my time comes before Mexico City?"

"I'm a veterinarian, not an obstetrician."

"A baby animal is a baby animal—a delivery's a delivery. I've got towels and alcohol and scissors and a threaded needle in my bag here. I hope we don't need them. There's a clinic waiting for me in Mexico City—if I hold out that long."

"You could just take some of my money for a plane ticket," Leonard said.

Mindy patted his shoulder—he felt the thrum of each long finger. "That's a nice offer, Doc. Really. But why would I pass up an opportunity to travel with the Emergency Vet? I love your stories! The truth is, I've got passport issues. As in, maybe I've misplaced mine. Or I never got one, I guess. Besides, air travel's unsafe this late in a pregnancy."

"You'll need a passport to drive into Mexico, or a passport card. I have one in my wallet."

"We'll cross that bridge when we come to it—so to speak. It's funny—we're sneaking somebody into Mexico when everybody else is sneaking out. But keep both eyes on the road, Doc!"

Leonard had edged onto the shoulder and eased the SUV back into the center of the lane. "I've got a problem with my eye," he murmured.

"Yeah." She purred a laugh. "I saw. For a minute there I thought you were getting a little crush on me, sneaking peeks—getting a little Stockholm-ish. You know—Stockholm Syndrome? Everybody falls in love with their captor, right? I've got an eye thing, too—this extra one on my eyelid—I got it when I was fifteen. It's supposed to be spiritual.

Hey—" She touched Leonard's shoulder again. "—we could get matching eye-patches. Like a couple of pirates. Ouch!" She wrenched herself back in the seat, and her huge stomach rose beside him. The gun was still between her knees. "Christ, it's hard to get comfortable." Her pale hands floated like lily pads on her belly as she settled herself.

They drove in silence through the tunnel the Escalade's headlights cut through the darkness. The tattooed lid made it impossible for him to tell if Mindy slept. An excess of stars swam through the sky—like crystallized sperm, Leonard imagined. Would he share the story of his failure on the long drive to Mexico City? He'd been warned by the clinician: "Only five percent of potential donors are approved. Frankly, most are college students, much younger than you." Leonard had continued doggedly through the process—physicals, paperwork, interviews. One night he dreamed that he'd been chosen: he'd been ushered into a gleaming white bathroom where, with the aid of *Penthouse Magazine's* Miss October—a petite redhead wielding a glass dildo—he'd ejaculated into a plastic cup. Upon exiting, product in hand, he'd been greeted by a crowd of a thousand children, boys and girls who resembled his third-grade photo—the one his mother had framed because his eyes were shut. He'd awakened full of hope, only to receive his blunt rejection in the morning mail.

Mindy's voice startled him. "This little monkey inside me is a blondie."

"Excuse me?" Leonard shivered himself alert. He'd need to rest soon.

"This baby I'm carrying—there are rumors about him," Mindy said. "I'm not supposed to know who the parents are—sometimes that's part of the agreement. But I heard nurses talking at the fertility clinic. Sperm from a dead actor, they were saying. I didn't recognize his name, so I Googled him. He was old—he died two years ago. But he was blond and very handsome when he was young. I never saw any of his movies. Wikipedia said he was married to a model I never heard of either, much younger than him—also a blonde—natural, I think. I read that she had cancer, but recovered. I know chemo makes you sterile, so I figure she had her eggs harvested first—then they cooked up a zygote for the widow with her husband's sperm, and voila!" She patted her stomach. "But this one's mine now. She's got more frozen zygotes, I'm sure. I wish I could advertise this baby as Hollywood royalty. Can you imagine what he'd be worth?"

Leonard shrugged.

"I saw the way those young mommies were looking at you in the bookstore," Mindy teased. "Is that what you're thinking about? Can you tell which moms are single? Or don't you care."

Leonard's face warmed. His head wagged. "Never—"

Mindy sighed. "Doc, here's what's going to happen next—" She hoisted herself up as if she were pinned under a boulder, and when he glanced over, he saw that she again aimed the pistol at his head. She cupped it in both hands as if it were a kitten. "The next cheap motel we come to, we're going to get a room. Both of us need to sleep. I'm going to handcuff you to the bathroom sink. Underneath. Don't worry, I'll give you a pillow and some blankets. It'll probably be a little uncomfortable—sorry in advance. I'll be stepping around you to pee in the middle of the night. Or maybe I'll need you to deliver the Hollywood royalty. That'd be a riot. Think I can keep the gun on you while that's going on? This is my third pregnancy, you know. First one I gave up for adoption. The second was a surrogacy like this one. But that baby had something wrong with it—they never told me what. I did my part—and was paid in full even for a defective—" The sudden illumination of a carcass on the side of the road stopped her short. "Ugh—what do you think that used to be?"

Leonard blinked at the body as they flashed by—only a long torso, really, its head long gone, its legs crushed to a ruby froth. "I don't know," he said. His joints ached—he'd be sleeping on a bathroom floor? But escape was out of the question—he was too weary. "A coyote, maybe. An antelope?"

"Save *that* one, Emergency Vet." Mindy yawned. "Yuch."


The Blue Daisy Motel had one room left with a private bathroom. In it, Mindy offered suggestions for Leonard's comfort: "You'll have to lie on your back, and we'll cuff your right wrist to the pipe. Wedge your pillow in the corner there. See—you can stretch your legs around the toilet." The cuff she pulled from her bag and snapped around his wrist pinched slightly. She grunted as she kneeled to fasten the other end to the drainpipe. "My stomach's in the way," she puffed. "You do it." After Leonard locked himself up securely, Mindy lurched to her feet. A meaty odor wafted from under her skirt and mingled with the cool air beneath the sink. Leonard stared up at the filthy underside and closed his eyes—how many more bathrooms before Mexico City?

"I'm leaving the light on and the door open. I'll try to tiptoe around you," Mindy announced. Leonard could only see her legs. Her blue running shoes looked new, and her ankles were swollen and chafed. A quarter-sized bruise yellowed on her shin. The bed springs squeaked under her weight. "Oh—" she called, "if you need to go, just give a shout. I'm a pretty heavy sleeper, though. Maybe you'd better hold it."

Leonard woke, stiff, unsure of where he was. His wrist touched something cold and metal, and he jerked it, thinking *gun*—and he remembered that he was chained up and why. He strained for sounds of Mindy's breathing, but heard only the faucet dripping above him. Mindy liked his stories, she'd said. He imagined that she couldn't sleep and called to him: "Tell me a story about a time you wanted to save something but couldn't—or you *didn't* want to save something, but had to." Leonard thought hard. Absent from *Mend My Tail, Doc* were the more lurid stories he'd been saving for an adult version: a frantic, semi-carved steer savaging a slaughterhouse; a manatee with an anchor through its head; a shih tzu and an eagle locked in a thousand-foot death plunge. Then he remembered a rural emergency from his internship—a distressed cow with Madonna eyes suffering through a breech delivery. The cow stood trembling, and the twig-legs protruding from the leaking opening beneath her tail shook with her.

"Pull!" Leonard's supervisor had shouted, and Leonard had grasped a warm, slick leg and yanked. The calf slid free, and as he and the newborn slipped to the floor, he'd hugged it to his chest. The smell of blood and raw flesh washed over him. Then his supervisor and the dairy farmer swore at the same time: there was a second calf, a twin, left in the womb. "Stillborn," his supervisor had determined with a plumbing arm. The cow and the senior veterinarian struggled to deliver the dead calf while its sibling shivered next to Leonard on the barn's dirt floor, waiting for its mother to lick it to its feet.

Mindy's legs! Her greeting dropped from above: "Morning, Doc. You sleep okay? You were dead out when I came through to pee. Both times. I'm going to wash up, then I'll give you the key so you can free yourself." She straddled his hips. Water hummed through the pipes and splashed in the sink over Leonard's head. A hand descended with a wet washcloth, and she washed her legs. Her skirt rose and fell with each stroke. He caught a glimpse of her pale underbelly and closed his eyes, opening them when he heard the jingle of the handcuff key.

By the time Leonard released himself, Mindy sat on the edge of the bed, watching him. He craved a long, groaning stretch, but resisted, unwilling to admit his discomfort.

"Hurry up and do what you've got to do," Mindy said. She clasped her paisley bag under one arm. "Leave the door open, please. Any funny business and you'll be sorry for it. I'll shut my eyes—that's the best I can do for privacy. What're you staring at?"

The tattoo of the eyeball was missing. There was only a dark smudge on Mindy's lid. "Your third eye—it's gone."

She snorted. "Oh—yeah—that was washable marker. You don't think I'd really tattoo something on my eyelid, do you? Who'd do that to themselves?" She picked up her gun and looked at its muzzle. "This is all the 'third eye' I need, right, Doc?"

Leonard didn't answer. He washed his face and rinsed his mouth, then used the toilet, peeking now and then at Mindy, who, to her word, didn't open her eyes. A smudge instead of a tattoo on her lid was a disappointment—no twin patches; no pirate gang.


Back in the Escalade, Leonard behind the wheel, they breakfasted on Twinkies, corn chips and Mountain Dew from the machines in the tiny lobby of the Blue Daisy Motel. The morning sunlight sharpened the borders of the black highway that sliced through parched land. The broken white line leapt at them like machine gun flak as they made their way south, and the blue sky spread over them as if they were in an enormous tent. Mindy's thumbs fluttered over Leonard's phone.

"I'm going to crack your access code," she said. She bent over her beachball belly, her unwashed curls hiding her face. "What's your date of birth?"

"Why don't I just tell you the code?"

"No—I want to figure it out. I'm good at it."

"My birthday's June 28, 1970."

"6-28-70—no—no—" she grunted as she tested permutations.

Leonard peeked at the gun in the folds of her skirt. "Hey—that's tomorrow! Happy birthday, Doc."

"Thank you," he said, surprised. He searched for a birthday memory, but found nothing. Instead, the moment when he realized he'd never marry arose: he'd just finished neutering a ferret and was transferring it to a recovery pen. Its limp body hung from his gloved hands like a necktie. He'd looked at its tiny, shut eyes and thought, "I will never have a wife." The words struck him like a chest punch, and he'd had to sit down, the ferret still dripping from his hands. His failed sperm donation had come soon after.

"I'm in!" Mindy laughed. "Wow—'628vet.' I'll check your messages. Then I'll send some. I'll tell all your contacts that you're on your way to Alaska. Okay, good, the GPS works—I see where we are and—there's Mexico! I love the GPS! It's like a big eye in heaven that's picked us out of nowhere. Mmm—looks like no text or voicemail messages for you, Doc."


"Thank God for air conditioning," Mindy sighed. Even with open vents blasting at full power, she was flushed and sweating. They weren't far from the Mexican border, according to the last highway signs they'd seen, a fact corroborated by the GPS. The blue had drained from the morning sky, leaving a pale midday haze. Leonard suspected Mindy was planning their assault on the border, and his heart beat faster. She'd been texting busily for an hour—his phone hummed like a jar of bees in her hand. Now and then she mumbled or laughed at something she read without telling him why, and he wished she trusted him enough to share. It had been years since he'd been in the company of another person for so long.

"I have an idea," Mindy said. "Let's pretend we're refugees. We're on the run—"

*Weren't they?* Leonard wondered.

"—There's a joke my father used to make—I think it's from my father—I heard it when I was little. Whoever it was said that Mexico and Canada were planning to attack the United States together. There'd be Eskimos attacking from the north, pulled by sled dogs and waving harpoons. Riding up on horseback from the south would be Mexicans with big floppy hats and rifles and those bullet belts crossed on their chests."

"Bandoliers."

"Right, okay. They were going to squeeze in on us from the top and bottom. They'd call themselves the 'Meximo Army'—Mexicans and Eskimos, get it? You and I are running away from them. We're refugees of the Meximo invasion!"

"We don't use 'Eskimos' anymore," Leonard said. "It's 'Inuit.'"

Mindy hesitated. "That spoils the joke. It's so easy to ruin a joke. What if—" she began matter-of-factly, "what if my mother died giving birth to me?" Leonard pictured his own dead mother and the *handsome boy* lines that marred her smile. He prepared a "sorry," for Mindy's loss, but hesitated to offer it for a "what if." Mindy patted her belly and huffed: "Woof. Sometimes I forget what I've got going on here. But never for long. If I had no mom, that would explain why I lack a nurturing impulse—no maternal role model. Incubation would be my limit. Would you please pull off here at this exit? Take me off the Interstate. I've got to pee before our next move."


Off the highway, they headed due west along a narrow tar road. Weeds grew in its cracks. The dry land, the sparse brush, the gullies and arroyos, the distant hills and cattle fences looked the same as they had from the Interstate, but Leonard felt different, as if the scene had swallowed them, and they were seeing things from the inside. He wondered how difficult it would be to engage the four-wheel drive. The Escalade's owner's manual was in the glove compartment. Would they have to ford a river? Would there be a border patrol that shot first and asked questions later? He sneaked a look at Mindy. She had picked him, something no woman had ever done before. Though they weren't pirates, they shared something. They were pioneers of modern survival. Leonard had been rejected as a sperm donor, but Mindy had given him a new purpose: she was an incubator in need—an *entrepreneurial* incubator—and he was a deliverer.

"Here is good," Mindy said when the road cut through a sandy stretch along a dry creek bed. Leonard slid the SUV to a stop, the tires crackling and shushing. Mindy still toted the gun, but Leonard doubted she'd force him to follow her while she went off to squat behind a bush or outcrop. She probably wouldn't even ask for the keys. After she did her business, they'd plan the crossing—from north to south, right through the southern outpost of the Meximo Army.

But Mindy didn't budge. "I think I just saw an animal in distress," she said, staring straight at Leonard, her face as cold and flat as a china plate. "I did. Definitely. Down that empty creek bed. It was limping." Leonard peered past her, to the right and left. There wasn't a sign of movement, and he could see for miles. "It was a burro, I think," she added. "Probably escaped from a ranch. Poor thing. A burro or a mule. What's the difference?"

Leonard focused on the gun, which seemed to have woken up and taken an interest in his chest. Mindy braced it on her belly next to the phone. He choked the wheel. "A mule is the offspring of a horse and a donkey," he said. "Mules are sterile."

Mindy shook her head. "I meant what's the difference *what* it is? You've got to investigate, right? You're the Emergency Vet." She started a deep breath, then cut it short. "Doc, there's no Mexico City. I couldn't drive that far in my condition. But we're less than an hour from the border now, and my associates are going to meet me when I cross. I'll flash your passport card. Believe me, nobody'll give it a second look. We kind of resemble each other, in a way."

Leonard's thoughts unspooled—he felt light-headed.

"No contractions yet," Mindy said. "I don't need insurance anymore. But it's been nice talking to you. What I would like now is for you to get out and walk down the creek bed—off the road a ways, please. Leave the keys. Just right there in the ignition, thank you. This is a beautiful vehicle. Real value." Mindy gazed up and down the road. Leonard noticed for the first time that her eyes were the color of lilacs. "Let's go, Doc. Think of that suffering creature out there. Who's going to investigate if you don't?" She gestured with the gun. The phone hummed, but she ignored it. "Go on—open the door and step out."

Leonard lost his balance as he swung the door open, staggering as he set his shaking legs on the baked ground. Fresh tar oozed from the cracks in the road. The air above it shimmered with heat in both directions. His cheek muscles tightened, and he held his hands out to his sides as if he'd dropped something. His gaze swept across the terrain to the horizon. There was no injured animal.

"Which way did you see it go?" In spite of the dry air, his voice came back to him as if he was underwater.

"It doesn't matter," Mindy said. "Just start walking. And don't look back. That way, I guess, off the road. Hurry up." As he shuffled around the Escalade, Leonard heard the passenger window whine open. He kicked up dust on his way to the creek bed and glared at his feet: his brown moccasins looked new—when had he bought them? Where? He passed rocks and pebbles striped with glitter. When he was a kid, he would have collected stones like them, pretending they'd make him rich. Maybe it had been a hundred years since anyone had looked at these. Maybe they'd never been noticed by a soul.

"Keep going!" Mindy's voice sounded as if she were just a few feet behind him, but he'd walked at least thirty paces. He shivered a breath. His shadow leaned away from him, and he watched it pass over larger rocks and the shriveled bushes that would become tumbleweeds when they broke off in the wind. A half-hope rose in his throat—maybe Mindy didn't mean to shoot him. She wouldn't have to—she was going to Mexico. His elbows brushed his hips; he regretted never having learned to walk proudly, and he tried to stand straight. But he didn't want to march. He waited for an instinct to tell him to run. The Escalade started, and the drone of its engine rolled out to him. This would end up no worse than a desertion, he reasoned. He'd need water.

*What if Mindy's water broke?* What if, as she lowered her smudged lid and tightened her finger on the trigger, she suddenly exploded? The water would gush between her legs and flood the upholstery. Her dress would be soaked. Contractions would begin. Driving would be impossible, and she'd need her insurance policy once again. She'd call Leonard back to the Escalade, but he would plant his feet in the dust, fold his arms over his chest, and wait. Until she begged. Time would crawl by. He'd outlast her. Where are your associates now, he might chide. Leonard would have to deliver the baby.

*There might be complications.* The newborn, a fine boy, would slip into Leonard's steady hands, but Mindy, lying back on the reclined passenger seat of the Escalade, might hemorrhage uncontrollably. He'd drag her bloody and unresponsive body from the car while the infant squalled. Leonard would cover the young woman—she'd either be dead or the next worst thing—with brush and rocks and sand. Then he'd drive south overland while the phone buzzed with orphan messages and all of nature drew toward Mindy's body. Scavengers, sun, and wind would pick her clean until her bones merged with the country.

*The boy belonged as much to Leonard as to anyone.* Years in the future, Leonard would share with the handsome child the true story of how they came to live in their villa. The Meximo invasion would have dissolved all borders, but Leonard would faithfully describe the world as it had been: he saw himself flipping through a picture book, lingering over each illustration, pointing out details.

But each turn of a page was a scuffed step into the plain, and, as Leonard edged further from the SUV, a question rose like a monument—would he hear the shot before he felt it?

# 15

"Before he disappeared into the dark, Tim looked back at me. I didn't say anything more than a promise I'd check on him tomorrow. I felt as though I were leaving a stray with its fate undetermined, and the most I could do was make its life easier by feeding it until it died."

# THE BLUE LIGHT NIRVANA
## Christopher Witty

**W** *ednesday*

Tim dropped the Dice situation on me at 8:36am over coffee at Three-J's Diner.

"Jesus H., T," I said. I placed my palms on the table and leaned back against the faux leather headrest. We'd taken a booth at the far end of the diner to keep out of earshot, even though we were the only customers. From my place, I could see the owner, Jo-Jo Junior, wiping down the counter.

Tim picked at something on the table. "Sorry, Bac," he said, "I think I might have screwed up big this time."

"No shit," I said a little too loudly. "Of all the people to rip off, you chose Dice?"

"Rip off's a little strong, man. We were gonna make good with him."

"Yeah? When?"

Tim held out his hands and made a face like I was the stupid one. "When it paid off. Obviously."

Just like that. I could have smacked him in his teeth, him sitting there in that red leather jacket he wore almost every day.

"Alright," I said. "How long do we have?"

"Well, I told Dice I'd shift it by Saturday."

"And he wants paying right away?"

"That's what he said. 'No layaways, Tim. If they can't afford it today . . .'"

"'Then they're not gonna be able to afford it tomorrow.' Right."

Tim brushed his hair away from his eyes, leaving a brittle, sandy strand clinging to his finger. He stared at a spot somewhere just above my head while he searched for something lost in the fog. "What's today?" he said.

"Wednesday."

"It is? Shit. That gives me four days. I told Dice I'd shift it by Saturday."

"You said that already."

I held his eyes for as long as I could stand it. When he dropped his, I let mine drift up to the EcoZap placed high on the wall above our booth. A fly popped on its bars, the promise of a life no longer eating shit burnt up in a fire of electric blue.

I eased out of the booth.

"I need to get to work," I said. "Maybe I could ask Leo for an advance." I dropped four dollars on the table. "I'll get this."

I could tell Tim thought I was going to make everything right, the way he looked up at me, all hopeful and needy. Like I had six thousand dollars lying around. Who had that?

"Thanks," he said. "I owe you one."

"Only one?" I said.


My name's Bacuda. Nobody calls me by my real name anymore. Tim's an addict, a burden, and my closest friend. I love him like a brother and hate him almost as much. When we were ten years old, he saved my life. That was how we met, with him pulling me out of the river, forcing his own breath down my throat and into my lungs. I remember his mouth tasted like the strawberry soda he'd been drinking when he saw me flailing around in the water. Said he'd do it all over again if he had to. That was twelve years ago and counting. He's been making me pay for it ever since.

He'll die before his time, that I'm sure of. I sometimes think it'd be better for me if he did. But then I think maybe it should be me who dies, and that when my death comes, he'll be to blame. That way the slate would be cleared. That could be my gift to him. My final show of gratitude.

My drive to work took me past Kim-So's, a boarded-up convenience store that had been robbed so many times the owner finally packed up and moved back to North Korea. Or maybe it was South. Wherever the hell he'd run to, he'd had the good sense to move his ass far away from here. Kim-So's stood in front of a vacated lot where Tim's dad, Rick, used to run a scrap metal business. Rick sold the land to a supermarket chain two years ago, but they didn't finish building. All that remained of the deal was a rusted frame. For three months after, broken down dishwashers, refrigerators and microwaves lined the sidewalks waiting for Rick to show. Finally, the neighbours moved the scrap into their yards and Rick moved to Phoenix. Said he needed a break from the rain and from Tim using his mom abandoning him when he was seven as an excuse for his bad habits. Rick paid off the mortgage on the house Tim stayed behind in, which I guess went some way to easing his conscience. I couldn't blame him for leaving. If I had that kind of money, I'd have left too.


Tim and I had always been into drugs, but I didn't share his taste for the harder stuff. He still dropped acid and smoked hash, but that was more to keep me company. He preferred to shoot speed and freebase. You hear about friends drifting apart when their drugs of choice don't match up, but that never happened with us. I wouldn't have let it. I knew that sooner or later the path I sometimes let him walk alone would lead somewhere bad, like the Dice situation, and I promised myself I'd always be at the other end to meet him. So, when Tim had asked me to go meet him at Triple-J's, I went. This is what he told me:

Dice had ordered Tim to work for him, telling him it was the only way he could pay for what he used. But when Tim took hold of the package and felt the weight of it, the junkie in him saw an opportunity there. He showed the package to his friend Morris, and together they formulated a plan. They'd keep a quantity of the coke for themselves, then step on the rest to make up the weight. The quality wouldn't be as good, but then nobody complained to Dice about his product anyway. Free coke and a cut of the profits for moving it. Simple. Until Morris, bubble head that he is, fell asleep in the car while Tim was in the store buying baking soda and detergent. When Tim got back, he found the back window down and the coke gone. Seemed they weren't the only two in town who knew an opportunity when they saw it.

Now, let me put this as clearly as I can. Dice was not a man to be fucked with. To make sure maximum effort was made to get his money, he'd take a piece of you as collateral. To show you he still had a semblance of good in him, he'd take a piece that could be easily sewn back on again. He had a surgeon friend who did the work for him. For that you were supposed to be grateful. He kept the pieces in a box freezer in his garage. If the money didn't turn up, he'd feed the pieces to his dog, a mongrel whose breeding could only be guessed at.


I worked at Barnaby's Burgers and Shakes. It was a shitty job, but it paid my rent and left enough over to get high. The steady green almost made me forget I was working for some prick I went to school with. Leonard Barnaby, the regional manager, handled three of the sixty-seven restaurants his Pops owned across the Pacific North-West. The Barnaby's in our town was just about breaking even, and it was no secret that Leo was given the manager's role because he didn't have much else to do.

I arrived five minutes late. Before I could finish tying my apron Leonard was at my shoulder like a parrot with bad breath.

"You're late, Bac," he said.

"Five minutes, Leo. I'll take it out of my break."

"I need to put it down on your report card anyway. Pops needs to know who's pulling weight. He's looking to make some changes."

I told Leo that was fine, and that I just wanted to get my shift over with. When he asked me what was so important, I pushed passed him and headed to my work station. With hardly any customers, Leo hovered around like a fly, griping about how much he'd been screwed by his Pops for not giving him a PR job. Lucky for me he took a call in his office within an hour of me arriving. Whatever was said must have pissed him off because he drew the blinds and didn't come out again for the rest of my shift. I clocked out at 2pm without saying goodbye.

Back home I called Tim. He told me he was one his way to Top Dollar, a pawn shop and one of the few businesses left open in town. I brought up my bank account on my laptop. Six hundred and change in savings. After that, I didn't know what. I was tired of Tim's shit, and at the same time tired of welcoming it just to break up the monotony. I took my car keys off the hook by the phone and drove into town. I made the withdrawal at the bank and set off to find my friend.

I found him outside Top Dollar. He was standing with a guy named Flue, an amateur boxer and small-time dealer. When they saw me pull to the kerb, they bumped fists and Flue took off. Tim leaned his head through the window.

"You've gotta be fucking kidding me," I said. "You're copping? You've just walked out of the pawn shop, for Christ's sake."

He opened the door and climbed in, a bag of weed between two fingers.

"Here," he said. "A little thank you for helping me out."

"Who's to say I'm going to? And I don't want that, it's stolen."

"Stolen from who? I paid for it out of my own money. Jesus, Bac, I hocked my fucking toaster for this."

"Tim, listen to me. As long as you owe Dice, you don't have any money. You stole from him, remember? So, from here on, anything you buy is bought with his money. Technically, this is stolen weed. So, no, I don't want it."

"I thought maybe we could drive up to the hills. I can leave my car here, pick it up later. I'm right over there."

He nodded to where his dad's old station wagon sat parked across the street.

"I don't know," I said.

Tim left the weed dangling between us.

"So you don't want it then?"

"What did I just say?"

"Suit yourself. But you're the one always telling me it helps you think."

That much was true. Weed, not too strong, and hills, not too high. That's what helped me think.

"Just give me the weed," I said. I stuffed the bag into my breast pocket and put the car in drive.

We parked in our usual spot away from the walking paths and picnic areas. I rolled a tight joint, fired it and passed it to Tim.

"So how much did you get?" I asked.

"A hundred and twenty-five. That was for the TV, DVD player, stereo and toaster."

"That it?"

Tim took a hit and passed it back. "He said everything was too old."

I held out a hand. Tim reached inside his jacket and placed the money in my palm. "A hundred and five," he said. "Less the twenty for your present."

"You're all heart." I put the money in the glove compartment. "I'll add it to what I got from the bank. You need to speak to Morris, see what he can come up with."

"Morris doesn't have a thing, Bac. You know that."

"Shit," I said, "We'll be lucky to get a grand between us. We need to think of something else. How about your dad?"

"My dad won't give me anything, I can tell you that for certain. Maybe I should split."

"And go where?" I said.

"I don't know," he said. "Someplace." He nodded to himself, scratched hard at the bridge of his nose. "I need to go piss," he said.

I climbed up onto the roof of the car, put a little of the weed into a pipe and fired it up. I looked up at the trees, smelt the air and the scent of the pines, imagined myself as a trapper, living out in the wilderness alone, measuring time by the stars and my worth by my instincts. Kicking back against the daydream, the weed had given me the clarity I needed to see, irrefutably, that there was no way of raising six thousand dollars in three days.

I looked over to where Tim was standing with his back to me. A smell like kerosene but perfumed drifted back toward me. I looked back at the trees, tried to enjoy my high while Tim enjoyed his.


By the time we got back to town the sun was dipping. A light rain had started to fall. I flicked on the wipers and listened to the swish and click ticking away the minutes as the day drew to a close. I pulled in across the street from Tim's car. He was working on a hangnail with his teeth. The dash lights caught the mist on his brow.

"I'm a dead man walking," he said.

This time I didn't nod or try to tell him he was wrong or anything. Tim got out of the car and walked into the rain. I watched him blur through the window. Then he came back to the car at a run, swung the door open and jumped in beside me.

"Drive!" he said. "Go, now."

"What is it?" I said.

"Just fucking drive, man! Go!"

I put the car in gear and drove up the street. Tim directed me to the lot behind Kim-So's. I parked and asked what had happened, but he was already tapping out a number on his phone.

"I've got to call Morris," he said.

"What the hell happened, Tim?"

"Morris," he said into the phone, "are you okay?"

"Put it on loudspeaker," I said.

Tim switched the phone to loudspeaker. Morris's voice then: "Tim? You scared me, man. I thought it was Dice again."

Tim looked at me. Said, "What are you talking about, Morris? Why would Dice be calling you?"

Morris said, "Now listen. I know I fucked up, but listen, okay?" He took in a sharp intake of breath, like something was paining him. "It's alright. I told Dice what happened, thought maybe I could take the heat off you."

Sickness washed over me. I said, "Why would you do that, Morris?"

"Who's that, Bacuda? Tim, is Bacuda with you?"

"Yeah, Morris," I said, "it's me."

"Hey, Bac. Jesus, this is fucked right?"

"Just tell me what happened," Tim said.

"Okay, well I went to see Dice today. I tried to tell him it was my fault, but . . . he wants you to go see him tonight."

"Why didn't you call me, Morris?" Tim said.

"I tried but your phone was dead."

"I've been in the hills with Bac."

"Right," Morris said, "that's why I couldn't get a hold of you."

Said it like he was some kind of sage, all wise and knowing. Then he started to make these noises, like he was struggling to breathe.

"Morris, are you okay?" I said.

He started sobbing. "He took my fucking thumb, man! Said he

wants his money by Saturday or he's gonna feed it to his dog."

Tim buried his face in his hands.

"Where are you, Morris?" I said.

"Well, I ain't home," he said.

He told us where he was hiding out and we went to collect him. On the drive over Tim told me how his car had been wrecked. A rock buried in the windscreen and the driver's side window smashed through, the battery taken out. He didn't have to say who had done it.

Tim and Morris hid out in Kim-So's store. Tim helped me pry free a loose board from a back window while Morris looked on, one hand wrapped in a frayed bandage. It led to a small room at the back where Kim-So used to sit and watch TV. Before he disappeared into the dark, Tim looked back at me. I didn't say anything more than a promise I'd check on him tomorrow. I felt as though I were leaving a stray with its fate undetermined, and the most I could do was make its life easier by feeding it until it died.

When I arrived home, I microwaved a pizza and watched TV on low volume through the night. At some point, I thought I heard someone knocking. I stayed frozen to the chair, even after I was sure they'd gone.


*Thursday*

The next morning, I stopped at the store on the way to Kim-So's. Picked up two Cokes, a bag of chips, and some sandwiches. When I passed them through the gap to Tim the smell of crack burning hit me. Without me inviting a lie, he told me Morris was already holding.

When I pulled into Barnaby's, the shutters were down. The cleaning lady, a short lady in both height and temper, was standing outside smoking a cigarette. She told me how Leonard had locked her out and wouldn't speak to anyone. I went around to the rear of the building and banged on the door marked "'STAFF ONLY.'"

"Leonard!" I called. "Open up, man. It's Bac."

The sound of keys and the slide of a chain and the door swung open. I walked into the dimness of the storeroom. Leonard took a seat on an upturned crate.

"What's going on, Leo?"

He looked up at me. I could tell he'd been crying.

"I spoke to Pops yesterday," he said.

"And?"

"And he's closing the store. Said he's decided it'd be best to cut out early. He's giving me today to tell everybody, then in a month we're done."

"So what does that mean?"

"What it means is that you're out of a job, Bac."

"And you?"

"Me? I'm being posted out to the distribution warehouse in Seattle. He wants me packing plastic trays and straws. Can you imagine that?"

"Oh, fuck you, Leo. At least you'll still have a job."

"Yeah? You call that a fucking job? After all I've done to keep this place afloat, this is how he repays me. It isn't *fair*, man." He stood and kicked the crate, sending it clattering against a wall. "You know," he said, "it'd serve him right if someone showed up one day and robbed this place. He doesn't know how lucky he is it hasn't happened already."

Ordinarily, I'd have cut Leo off when he started in on one of his rants. This time I let him carry on to see where it was headed.

"Shit," he said. "I've even thought about it myself once or twice. Payback for being overlooked all the time."

I tore open a packet of paper napkins and handed him one.

"Yeah," I said, "I guess it really sticks in your gut to have your old man screw you over so much. If that was me? Hell, I wouldn't even hesitate."

He pressed the napkin against his face. Dark wet spots spread out from his eyes and nose.

"It's just a dream, Bac. Knowing how little Pops thinks of me, he'd probably pin it on me like a shot."

I shrugged nonchalantly, as though what I had to say next was just a thought out loud.

"Not if someone else did the robbing."

"Yeah, right. Like I'd trust anyone around here not to give me up. You might not have noticed this, Bac, but I don't have too many friends I can rely on."

"You don't always need friends, Leo," I said. "Just people desperate enough to help."


It took me and Leo less than an hour to plan a robbery right there in the storeroom. Leo said it would be better to rob the Barnaby's out on the interstate. Here, the takings were only collected by the security guys once a month. I guess Pops thought he could save them the trouble of coming every week to collect dollars and change. On the interstate, where the takings were good, they came every week. Leo was given the job of making sure the money was already bagged for when security arrived. There was a half hour window between the cash being taken out of the safe and transferred to the van. Tackling security was out of the question. Taking money off Leo, whether he was in on it or not, would be a cinch. I told him Morris was desperate enough to do anything as long as he got paid. I didn't mention anything about the Dice situation.

"So, what are we looking at here," Leo said, "a three-way split? Forget it, Bac. Me and Morris are taking all the risk."

"I never said anything about an even split, Leo. I just need enough to see me through until I get another job."

Leo chewed that one over. I let him think he was holding all the cards. Otherwise he would never have agreed to anything so dumb.

"But Morris?" he said. "The guy's gotten weirder since we left school. The last time I saw him, he was in here trying to get a free burger."

"Like I said, he's desperate."

Leo drew a long breath. "Okay. Call Morris, see if he's around. Pick up's Friday. Eleven a.m.. So we need to act fast. But listen, Bac? It might not be much, your split I mean."

"Leo," I said, "it's gonna be more than I've got now."


I drove over to Kim-So's, rapped three times on the wooden boarding and listened to Tim and Morris scuffling around. Morris, trying for some kind of voice I guessed was supposed to make him sound Black, said, "Who is it?"

"It's Dice," I said. "Who do you think it is?"

This sent them into a spin. I let them sweat for a while, then rapped again.

"It's me, you dummies. Bacuda."

There was some whispering while they decided who should go check. Eventually, Morris's grinning face peered out at me from between the boards.

"I knew it was you," he said. "You can't get anything over on old Morris."

He pulled the board free, and I climbed through the window. Inside, Tim was sitting on the floor. In the centre of the room was a small table with the remains of a night's fix on top of it. Scattered around the table were the empty packages from the food I'd bought them.

"Listen," I said, "I think I might have found us a way out of this."

"You have the money already?" Morris asked.

"No, Morris," I said, "I don't have the money, and there's no chance of an advance. I lost my job today."

Tim looked up at me. "Aw shit, Bac. I'm sorry, man."

"That sucks, Bac," Morris said. "You know, I never did like Leo. You want me to beat him up or something?"

"Nobody's going to be beating on anybody," I said. "And besides, Leo might be the last chance you've got."

"Leo?" Morris said. "Leo wouldn't even give me a free meal. I don't think he likes me. Why would he want to help us out?"

"Because he hates his Pops."

I went on to tell them the half-baked idea me and Leo had come up with. Well, to me it was half-baked, to them it was the crime of the century.

"But we don't have a car anymore," Morris said.

"Steal one," I said. "As long as you jack a car half an hour before, we should be able to get it done before someone raises the alarm."

"I know a guy lives across the street," Morris said. "He works nights and sleeps all day. I could have his car back before he knows what's happened. But what about a gun. I can't stick-up a place without a gun."

I said, "Try and remember this for more than thirty seconds, Morris: this isn't a stick-up. You don't need a gun for Leo to hand over the money, just give the impression you have one for anyone watching."

"Right," Morris said. "Like in that movie when the guy had a hard-on in his pants. Made everyone believe it was a gun. That was a funny movie."

"Exactly," I said.

Morris looked at Tim, who looked at me. "Okay," he said. "Let's do it."

"Alright then," I said. "I'll call Leo and let him know it's on."


*Friday*

I pulled into Barnaby's at 10:20am. Leo had told me he wanted me there in case anything went wrong. Said I'd be out of sight of the cameras and that he wouldn't go through with it if I didn't show. Tim sat low in the passenger seat, his head against the window. We watched the cars come and go, getting more anxious with every one that didn't have Morris inside. At 10:50 I was starting to think he'd been caught stealing the car, found somewhere to score, or overslept. There was always a myriad of possibilities when it came to Morris. Then, we saw him, driving a family saloon complete with one of those signs in the back that read 'Princess on Board'.

He parked at the foot of the steps to the entrance and shut off the engine. I could just make out his lips moving, probably psyching himself up. I checked the time on the dash. 10:53am.

"Come on Morris," I said, "what are you waiting for?"

As though he'd heard me, his door opened. He started to get out of the car, a plastic Trump mask in his hand. Then something happened that none of us, in a million years, could have seen coming. Walking down the steps and into the path of the car stepped Dice. Morris ducked back into the car as Dice planted himself in front of it, saying something we couldn't hear.

Why Morris decided at that moment to put the car in drive, I'll never know. Maybe he just panicked, or maybe he saw the man who'd took his thumb and saw red.

Now, Dice is a big guy. One of his legs is about the size of my waist. He has the bulk of a man who used to work out, got lazy, and let the muscle turn to fat, but not enough that it didn't lose its solidity. He was a fucking ogre dressed in sweatpants. So when the car lurched forward and connected with his knees, all it did was make him take a few steps back. The car stalled as Dice pulled out a gun. He levelled it at the windscreen and shouted for Morris to get the fuck out of the car. When the engine started up again, Dice fired, shattering the windscreen. A splash of red covered the driver's side window and the car shot forward, faster this time and with enough force to knock Dice to the ground. I turned my head fast enough that I didn't have to see his head disappear under the front wheel. Facing Tim, I focused on his eyes that were staring intently at the scene that was playing out in front of him.

Tim said, "Oh Jesus, thank God, Morris."

I turned my head back around and saw Morris falling out of the car. He was struggling to stand with a hand pressed against the spot where his right ear used to be. The car was up on an angle with Dice's head jammed under the wheel. His legs kicked for a minute then gave up the dance.

A group of people had gathered at the top of the steps, waiting to make sure the danger had passed before they thought about checking on Morris. The security truck pulled up then behind Morris's car and two guys climbed out. One ran to where Morris was collapsed on the concrete. The other stood by the truck making a call on his cell phone. Some of the braver people helped the security guy get Morris up the steps, at the top of which stood Leo, a bag of money in his hand and a look of confusion on his face. While the people hustled Morris inside, the security guy took the bag of money off Leo and threw it in the back of the truck. Left alone on the steps, Leo looked to where we were parked. Even with the distance between us, I could tell he was going to start crying again.


*Any Day Now*

The bloodbath outside of Barnaby's had jolted something in Tim. This time things had gotten too close.

I helped Tim through the worst of the withdrawal, letting him stay at my place so I could keep an eye on him. After, when he said he'd never ask me for anything ever again, I believed him. But when Morris, with one less ear to go with his thumb, shared with us his plans about taking Dice's place as the number one dealer in town, I knew it wouldn't be long before Tim was drawn back again. Seemed Tim knew it too. He called his dad, who told him about a treatment centre in Phoenix. Said he could look at selling the house, and how would Tim feel about that. His dad was more welcoming knowing his son had gotten over the worst of it, and Tim was more inclined to leave the worst behind. And me? I was going with him.

We drove the eighteen hours almost non-stop, taking turns behind the wheel and smoking up a chunk of hash on the way. We listened to the music that had sound-tracked our lives this far and talked about shit that didn't matter. Tim's hair had regained its former oily look and his eyes pierced clear and blue. Whenever I stole a look at him in the driver's seat, his eyes were fixed, like he could see exactly what lay at the other end of the road.

When we hit the desert, something bloomed inside of me. I looked towards the horizon. The sky seemed to hum with electric blue. I closed my eyes. Sunspots danced behind the lids, making their way to the peripheral edges before drifting back, as if drawn, always, to the same point.

# MASKED UP

**CHRISTOPHER OTT**

# 16

"So you just asked why am I a drunk? What happened? What's the story? I get it. People like you always ask. But let it go. Doesn't matter."

# METABOLIZE TO FREEDOM
Mike Zimmerman

It was so much better than I expected. I gave them the crap of it, and they still laughed. Now they were all warmed up and I would go in for the kill. I was killin' and that's all it was. Who knew I could do that, first time and everything? Now I used that Robin Williams bit, when he ranted about the cats outside his window screaming and keeping him awake while they fucked. "Name the kittens after MEEEEE!" Audience didn't know it wasn't mine and who the fuck cares anyway. Then I did my thing.

"You realize cats do it doggie style? Let that sink in." Crowd does and likes it. "Uh huh. Yeah. Yeah. Ain't no cat in the world ever been asked by press about that. 'Magine if cats were asked about doggie style. Fuckin' paparazzi runnin' around Hollywood screaming 'Hey, Morris, hey Garfield, hey Hobbes, how's you like . . . *doggie* style, kitties?' Cats have dignity *and* an agenda so they wouldn't put up with that shit if they knew what we hooomans were saying. *Hooomans.* That tabby'd be back there with his barbed dick all hard makin' it *kitty* style, totally taking that shit back and owning it. Right? Right?" Crowd said yes, right. "But we got it wrong about cats. We hoomans think, yeah, kitty's gonna do it sloooow. And sinuous. And be all kitty and lithe and sexy." And the audience says yeeeaah and I just can't believe that but I keep going and say, "but kitty . . . kitty ain't sexy like you think . . . kitty just a frat boy on a mission . . . kitty just want some pussssaaay," and now people are laugh-clapping, "and you know what it sounds like when frat boy kitty get some pussssaaay? It sounds like," and I jerked my hips while I sang that cat food commercial jingle, "meow-meow-meow-meow, meow-meow-meow-meow," hitting a meow on each hip thrust and singing singing singing, and just killing. I couldn't believe the laughter.

As I air-fucked my way across the tiny little stage in the tiny little club, I got within ten feet of a big fat dude sitting at a small thin table with another ugly dude. I saw him, I knew him, he knew me, and winked at me, and I almost shut it all down right then but instead kept giggling and meow-humping and did the thing that would define me forever: I pulled a locked-loaded semi-auto out from under the back flap of my Charlie Sheen-style bowling shirt and with my non-microphone hand aimed and unloaded four slugs into the big dude's chest, neck, and, I think, chin. Saw something in his lower face jerk open.

Oh, there's more. A bunch more. But you're gonna have to wait for the punchline.


Nobody likes a drunk. I figured that out over time. Aside from a shitty NFL tackle, who gets flagged more than the drunk? Bartenders: you're done, buddy, you can leave on your feet or head-first. Women: um no, I'm waiting for someone, seriously, no, I'm trying to be nice, like, no, fuck no, asshole fuck the fuck off. Strippers: sit on your hands, *I said sit on your hands.* Strip club bouncers: you think I don't remember you from last time? Hookers: don't even (calls for pimp). Pimps: see this, it's a taser, I'm doin' this to you so you remember. Diner hostesses: you can't eat here, leave or I call the cops. Bodega and liquor store clerks: can't serve you lookin' like this, leave or I call the cops. Cops: touch your nose, sir, hands behind your back, sir, watch your head, sir, oops guess you didn't watch your head you fuckin' turd. Doormen: you can't sleep here, lemme call you a cab. Cabbies: you puke in here, you fucking fuck and I'll . . ..

All of this pushed me to some self-reflection about my core skills. And I realized that while nobody likes a drunk, they will tolerate a funny one.

So I worked on my delivery. My last name is Farmer and the only first name I'd go by was Whup. Nobody gets mad at a Whup Farmer. I stole obscure material ("Fabricated half-inch pipe!"). Worked shit jobs for a while to get some cash, then quit for a while. Got eighty-sixed at a place or two. Found another shit job. When it's working you feel on top of the world. Okay, maybe not *the* world, but your world.

But everything changed five months ago when I changed

neighborhoods and walked into the Double Six.


So you just asked why am I a drunk? What happened? What's the story? I get it. People like you always ask. But let it go. Doesn't matter.

I said it doesn't matter. Know how I know? If I tell you my daddy was rich and we had millions and he abused me, you'd be like okay, I get it. If I tell you my daddy was poor and a drunk and beat me and my mother, you'd be like okay, I get it. If I tell you my daddy was a stand-up local middle-class businessman and a productive member of society and didn't approve of my lifestyle, you'd be like, okay, I get it. Maybe I wet my bed. Maybe I laughed at a kid in a wheelchair. Maybe a bored local housewife had me mow her lawn real hard when I was fourteen. Maybe I used God in a joke. Maybe I pissed on a baby. Maybe I killed kittens and disrespected Shemp.

If I tell you all the things about me, you'd be like okay, I get it. But do you?

You defend the stripper when I won't sit on my hands, but you keep asking me the one question I have no interest in answering and . . . well, I guess you don't like gettin' flagged any more than me.

'Cept you don't think you did anything wrong.

Lemme clue you: I don't think I did, either.


The Double Six was an old school city dive, about twenty feet wide and, shit, who knows how deep. It just kept going back there, you know? Bigga Duke used to say the joint was like a porn joint, meaning dick. You got the long bar on the right side, goes about halfway back. Booths on the left. Then the dartboards and pool table. Then the shitters. Then the back rooms behind folding wood and glass partitions. They were the mystery. Maybe tables back there for poker games or whatnot. Maybe who knows. I only got invited back there once and I didn't see shit.

So first time I go in, I'm fine. Hadn't even started drinking yet. I was cashed up from the last paycheck of the last job, so I went to work on light beer. This was my new place, had to start slow. And you know I actually wanted to go slow. I enjoyed it. Wasn't like I had the thirst and needed a bottle on the bar. That would come later.

Bartender was an Asian woman named Virginia. Dark hair back in a ponytail, T-shirt with short sleeves showing ink sleeves, bottle opener on a belt hook like Batman. Oh, I could talk to her. Drunks always know who they'll click with and who will stab them and Virginia, to her credit, would do one and then the other to me and it would be fun for both of us.

Funny drunk kicked in. I liked the Double Six right away and wanted to stay. Like forever. I got the first buzz, the pure one, and rattled off some shit to Virginia and she was okay with me for now. Ballgame on the TVs. Music would come up now and then, good shit, clientele had good taste in tunes. It got later and the place got tighter. I held court a bit. Surprised people let me.

A big hulk of a dude whumped on the barstool next to me and people around me cleared out. He needed the big and tall store. Had a receding hairline but grew the hair out the back in compensation and I would learn that some nights he preferred it in a ponytail and others he did not. He was probably sixty, but I dunno. His belt ran a pure circumference around him over his belly button, old school. And this was a *belt* because Bigga Duke ran about 450 pounds. Just my guess, I never asked. In fact, I never asked Bigga Duke anything, ever. This was our first back-n-forth:

"I notice you're a talker."

"'People smiling' is where it's at daddy-o."

"Yeah. No parent in the world would teach a kid that so where you come up with it?"

I paused. He was right. I had to tap dance without seeming like I had tap shoes on. It didn't help I was blinking through a good old drunk. "I got an imagination," was the best I came up with.

"Y'know, I always struggled with that. Virginia." He wiggled his finger at our glasses, and she nodded.

"You struggled with Virginia?"

"Imagination. I just see things as they are, I don't want them any way different. Things are and then things are. But I guess when people laugh, imagination is where they laugh from. And I like people laughing. Most people have a good laugh. Most people. That's kinda what I rely on."

"People laughing?" I was shitfaced now. Just flowing with the go.

Bigga Duke smiled at me and said, "Real laughter is real, and no one laughs around me. That tells me a lot."

Virginia put two fresh drinks in front of us and I said, "Hello, Virginia, would you like to laugh?"

She walked away and Bigga Duke just kept on talking. "I can tell when someone laughs fake. So I go out and I find real laughter. Sometimes I find a laugh here at this bar. Like tonight. From you. So I'll sit here and if you want to be funny, go ahead and be funny." And he pointed a kielbasa of a finger at me. "But don't be an asshole. I love everyone here. That's where your jokes need to come from now on."

"Wait what, from where?" I asked.

One hand grabbed my collar and pulled me close, the other cradled the side of my face. "From love, Shecky. From love."


Now I didn't expect that from any human, let alone Bigga Duke. And yeah, about that. I learned through various inquiries, discreetly and respectfully, that Bigga Duke was on the rolls as Mark Duke. Nothing fancier, no "Markus," no long-ass title. He was an angry, crooked fat guy with a jurisdiction. Bigga was short for "bigger." Bigga Duke's name was all about the optimism.

But that initial exchange stuck with me. In fact, it defined my existence at the Double Six. I took Bigga Duke's advice and no one ever told me to leave. I met some of Duke's other people. Guys like Bulsh, his bodyguard. But mostly I kept to the bar and the regulars and made my jokes. And maybe that was the difference this time. By following Duke's rule, I was a joker and not a wiseass. That felt okay.

Oh, and Duke wasn't kidding around when he said he sought out laughter. Because there was that one shitty night out of nowhere, he whumped down on that stool next to me and got his meaty paws on my shoulders and smiled at me.

"What'd I do?"

"No, what'd *I* do?" he said.

"What'd you do?"

"You ever heard of Boomba's?"

"Strip club?"

"Naw, comedy club. I'm goin' there on Friday night."

"Um . . . yay for you?"

Duke smiled and shook his head. "Yay for *you*."

"Not following."

"I'll be there at nine. You'll be there before me."

"I will?"

"Have to. To get ready. Yer performing at 9:20. I got you a slot."

I didn't say anything. I was drunk, of course, but I knew what he said.

Duke nodded at Virginia and pointed at me. "Lookit him. Speechless for once in his fucking life," and he and Virginia laughed. I kept 'em in stitches.

Duke stood up. "You'll do fine, funny guy. Don't be so uptight. Just remember the rule."

"What rule."

"Whatever you do on that stage," he said while walking to the back of the bar, "it's gotta come from love."


I never in my life had anyone looking out for me. And that's what Duke was doing in his way. Maybe he liked me, maybe he just wanted to see a guy take a step up. Maybe it came from love. The tubby bastard. Fuck do I know.

I do know I got no fucking material, let alone ten minutes. So I got drunker and thought about it and a few hours later I took a stroll around the block by the bar and pissed on some trash cans thinking it over. And drunk as I was, I still noticed the guy noticing me. It was warm enough but he wore a long coat. Hair cut close. Long face. He should've been smoking but wasn't.

"Watching me piss is five bucks," I muttered. "I'll take a dump for ten."

"Heard you're the funny guy," the man said. "The drunk."

"It comes from love."

"What?"

"Nothin'."

He let out some impatient air. "Let's talk, you'n me."

* * *

Here's what people don't get. Someone asks you to kill someone like Bigga Duke, life's done. You either kill Bigga Duke and disappear, or you don't and disappear. I'm a side of beef to him, this guy Slick. This side of beef is either gonna help Slick out or not, but either way Slick hacks the beef up into steaks.

The deal: Take out Bigga Duke, get $10K in cash later that night, disappear. Like, new city, whatever, I got the drill. The disappearing was the key part, Slick said. A public hit made a statement, and everyone will remember the funny guy. He promised me a gun the day of, and he would keep his word while reiterating the disappear part.

I knew a few things as a drunken idiot but not a stupid one.

If I said no, I was dead in my own piss puddle right there.

If I said yes, I wasn't gettin' no $10K. But I would disappear when I showed up to collect.

So there was no wrong answer. Just one answer.


Interesting thing about the comedy club when I pulled the gun. Bigga Duke had Bulsh along, like he always did. I never interacted with Bulsh so I can't vouch for his whatever, nor explain my indifference. But Bulsh fancied himself secret service, so while Bigga Duke faced me on the stage like everyone in the house, he sat cockeyed and faced the back of the house. 'Cause of course any threat wouldn't come from the stage.

Imagine your last moments are staring down comedy club drunks for danger and gettin' shot from the stage by the one guy in the building you trusted. You want a death? *That's* a death.

Bulsh did turn. Bulsh did see. It amounted to a holy shit moment, but also a deep moment of loss on his face, like he knew this moment was simultaneously his last and also a serious failure on his part. I put four in him, my muzzle trailing upwards as I fired, one in his lower spine, two in his shoulders, and one in the ear as he turned to me. His hand got close to his shoulder holster, but not that close.

Screams and chaos, ears ringing, sure as shit. Boomba's wasn't that big. I couldn't help saying, "Tip your servers," before I dropped the mike and the gun and walked offstage and out a back door without anyone coming near me.

So much for my comedy career. Really think I had something

there. And of course, you interpret that previous sentence as sarcasm. Douchebag.

I didn't show up at my $10K rendezvous. Fuck Slick. I went and got drunk. Roaring drunk. And I was no longer the funny drunk because I remember being tossed from two places on the far side of town, and then not much more.

The true drunk seeks oblivion even if he doesn't find it every night. Oh, I found it that night and then some.

Voices. Sort of registering them but barely.

"He was found down."

"No kidding. Smell that?"

A few moments of examination. I felt none of it.

I'd been here before, heard all this before.

"Acute, uncomplicated intoxication," the doctor said. "Fluids and vitamins and when he can walk to the bathroom, flag me down because then we discharge."

"Got it." A pause. "Doctor?"

"Yeah."

"I know he's just a drunk and we have to care. But this is what drinking yourself to death looks like, right?"

A pause. "Yeah. They get like this and become regulars here. They metabolize to freedom and we send them out. That's MTF, by the way, you'll get the lingo. One day who knows when, he'll come in and he won't MTF. And that'll be it."

Still not awake, but I hear. Could be a dream but the booze stomps dreams so . . . yeah.

Slick, at my bedside, in my ear: "How you doin', Whup? Ah. Lookitcha. Big Whup. Thought you'd want a drink after, so you weren't as hard to find as you thought you'd be, you fuck. But hey. It's tough, this life. Not everybody's up to it. Everyone's all talkin' about how you killed at the comedy club, Whup. How's about that? Wasn't sure you had it in ya. But you were supposed to disappear, kid, weren't ya? I got your money. That was the key part of the deal. Well, ya fucked that pooch, kid. Or maybe you only do cat material. Ah well. You get better kid. Soon you'll take that piss and they'll boot you outta here. We'll be waitin' for ya."


Ladies and gents, give it up for Whup Farmer, the Big Whup!

Never thought I'd hear those words. Or maybe that I would but I'd just bomb and never get on a stage again. C'mon, who would boo the Big Whup?

What I thought about in that hospital bed as I swam my way back up to the light, the fluorescent light: I couldn't believe how loud the laughter had been, or how I'd put home eight straight slugs one-handed. It was like no matter what I did in those minutes since I took the stage and left it, I couldn't miss. Gotta say, if you ever have a four-and-a-half minute stretch like that yourself, you'll know what I'm sayin'. I hope you do, just once.

Soon I gotta get up from this bed and take a leak and they'll kick me to the curb. Drunk's always get flagged, even in the ER. Then I'll be outside with all those waiting on me. And I'll just keep thinkin' about those four and a half minutes. And the laughter.

I promised you a punchline. Had a conversation in a bar a while back with some dude. This is long before the Double Six. Dude wore a suit and wasn't as drunk as I was and was a little judgey. Dude's all like, "You personify burning the candle at both ends." I thought that was a compliment. Kinda cool and badass, so I thanked him. And same dude's like, "You don't get it. What happens when the two ends meet and burn out?" And I laughed. Dude's like, "Why's that funny? You're burnin' out. Can't you *see* yourself?" I'm like, "Naw, naw, man, that's the wrong vantage point; that's not the info you need." Guy's like, "The fuck you mean? What info?" And I put my drunken hand on his shoulder and met his eyeballs man-to-man and said, "How long's the candle?"

Hey, I'm a pro drunk. I can hold my piss a loooong time, baby.

# 17

"Winter had returned, exactly as Jon knew it would. And, he, who knew better, fell victim to its tricks."

# OLD MAN RIVER
## Mark Rapacz

Jon was on his daily run, jogging across Marshall Bridge on a winter day that felt like spring. To his south, the Mississippi River was pristine with a fresh coat of powder from the night before. Not a track in sight. It was beautiful, almost too bright to look upon because of the whiteness. Despite the beauty, Jon knew the truth: the river was death. Especially on a day when a pristine layer of powder covered river ice, a mix of thin pancake sheets and slush. You couldn't trust it. Everybody knew this.

Except a young family walking across the Mississippi expanse with their dog and their kid. These people, enjoying pristine snow on a pristine day. Bright and clean.

Idiots.

Jon stopped in the middle of the trail, cupped his hands around his mouth and shouted, "Get off the ice!" Jon hated stopping during his runs. Messed up his pace.

The parents didn't look up, but the kid did and waved like a toddler. The dog looked, too, wagged its tail, danced upon snow hiding swift, cold death.

"Get off the ice!" Jon shouted again.

They didn't listen. The dog ran and leapt. The young parents laughed.

Jon bellowed this time with all the authority a man tights could manage. "Get. Off. The. Ice."

The father finally looked up.

"We're fine," he shouted back. "We do this all the time." Then he waved Jon off.

Jon was speechless and looked in both directions down the stretch of the bridge, trying to find anyone who could acknowledge the sheer insanity of these people.

There was no one. Just Jon, alone with the traffic whizzing by, witnessing certain death. He decided not to wait for it and jogged away.


Jon was out the door at 4 a.m., careful not to wake the kids or his wife. Valerie slept on the couch because Jon had kept her up talking about how irresponsible it was for those parents to bring their kid out on the ice like that. She understood. She agreed. After a while, though, she just needed to sleep.

Jon had a theory to test. He was convinced four frozen corpses were scraping the underside of river ice. He just needed proof. That's how that river worked. Nobody walked on it, especially in the winter. Especially when it looked safe. The river did that to people. Made people trust it. Monstrous in a way. People didn't understand the ice changed despite the weather. Open water when it was cold as hell. Frozen when it was warm as spring. There was no predicting it. This was the unknown quantity intermingling with the inherent treachery of river ice.

Shortly into his run, Jon slipped on a patch of ice as he rounded a turn onto Breadalbane Lane which led to the trails up to Marshall Bridge. He went down hard, but as graceful as his middle age allowed. It was a three-point landing: elbow, hip, knee. Perfect weight displacement to minimize the impact. He lay there for a moment, staring up at a streetlight and bare tree limbs above him, amazed he had not broken something. It felt heroic. Indestructible. The fall. The landing. The lack of pain on a frozen morning that most humans would avoid.

The temperature had dropped throughout the night so the melt from the unseasonable warmth of the day before left a thin sheen of ice across the path. Winter had returned, exactly as Jon knew it would. And, he, who knew better, fell victim to its tricks.

He fell many more times, with less grace. Fewer than three-point landings. Singular points. Solitary and angular. Direct on the elbow. Direct on the hip. A cartoonish backpedal that threw Jon onto his tailbone. These wounds would last. A lesser man would turn back and limp home. Cut his losses.

Jon planned to go under Marshall Bridge, where the lower trails would give a riverside vantage of where he last saw the family. To get there, Jon had to tromp through knee-deep snow and down a steep embankment. Wearing tights and running shoes, he soon slipped down the sandstone bank. He grasped at whatever shrubbery was within reach until his feet gave way and he slid for what must've been hundreds of feet. He landed hard on frozen sand. Again, he lay, assessing the damage. Total. He was a wreck. He pulled himself up and looked back up the cliff and found he stood taller than it. It was a three-foot drop at most, but in the dark, in the cold, with the snow crammed around his ankles, biting at his flesh—none of this was comfortable.

Jon stumbled to the shore where the river ice began. The city lights shone above and the cloud cover was low, so even in the dark of early morning, the bridge cast a shadow, but where the shadow did not reach, the snow glowed the dirty yellow of streetlights. Dark pools dotted the ice sheet like ink splotches across a sheet of paper. The river was devouring itself, just as Jon suspected. And, no, it was not reasonable. It was much colder than the day before and it was winter's dawn, when the coldest air settled at the lowest points.

That family was most certainly dead.

Idiots.

Just as Jon was deciding who he should call when he got home— emergency number, non-emergency number, some sort of frog team who took care of this sort of thing—he heard a booming voice.

"Hey, Asshole!" it shouted. "Get off the river."

Jon turned around and found he was many paces onto the ice, watching coal gray hunks tumble in one of the dark pools.

"Get off the river," the shadow on the shore shouted again.

Jon pranced back to shore, embarrassed.

The shadow was one of the homeless, Jon assumed, that maintained an encampment in the hidden ravines up and down this stretch of river.

This man carried a large, twisted stick, almost wizard-like. He was bundled in layers of clothing. Only his eyes and nose were exposed from under his bomber hat, fringed in wool that was once white, but now the same color of the dirty snow in the roadside gutters.

"River ice is never safe," the man said.

"I know," Jon said. "Saw a family out here yesterday. They had a kid, and a dog."

"Not smart," the man said.

"I yelled at them," Jon said. "They ignored me. I was seeing if they went under."

"Hmm," the man said and he walked to the river's edge, seemed to make a point of refusing to step foot upon the ice. "Old Man River, I suppose," the man said.

"Old Man what?" Jon asked.

"River."

"Huh," Jon said, quickly deciding this man was nuts. "Who's Old Man River?"

The man just nodded toward the ice.

"The Mississippi?" Jon asked.

To this, the man had no answer. Instead, he answered a question Jon never asked. "It takes the dumb, the lame, and the forgotten," he said.

The man with the stick was definitely insane. The wizard stick wasn't even some mysterious staff now that Jon got a better look at it. It was just an old hockey stick.

"Is it some kind of mystical thing?" Jon asked.

"No," the man said as he stared out at the river ice as the early morning traffic began to rumble on the bridge overhead. "It's just deeper and faster than people expect, and people are idiots."

"All people?"

"All," he said and then he continued on down the shore, letting that insult hang in the air like a frozen breath because Jon knew he himself was the "all" the man implied.


Jon tore a ligament in his ankle and the meniscus in his knee. His daily runs were now non-existent and with this came a kind of low-level insanity Jon had trouble controlling. He and Valerie argued more than usual, Jon was less talkative at work, and he let the kids cry before bed without bothering to check on them.

But, Jon was OK with letting things slip a little because he started creating something of a masterpiece—a spreadsheet that included all his death-by-river theories. All the obvious stuff was in there: missing persons records, murders, suicides, accidents. Anything water-related. Boat accidents north of the Metro Area or any incident upstream that could lead to bodies downstream, hung up on branches or in a dam or drifting cold and blue and flesh-ragged in river construction debris from eons ago.

It didn't take long for him to exhaust his local data sources, so he expanded beyond the Mississippi to other rivers around the world. He took his data and compared it to cities far more dense, towns that were far less dense. Rivers that were deeper, wider, narrower, shallower. Rivers known to be safer and those known to be more dangerous. He checked historical records in French cities, Argentinian cities. He found a trove of data from Seoul, all about the history of river death in and around the Han. He learned things about drug smuggling, murder, organized crime, all sorts of bad shit that seemed attracted to the rivers running through the hearts of cities. So many drownings around the gambling boats of Iowa.

This wasn't a passion that just came out of nowhere. Jon was known as the "Spreadsheets Guy" at work, but this current project was next level. Conditional formatting, auto-sorting, every shade of color available in the palette dropdown. And formulas. Hundreds, at least. All of which spat out tables and information, which led him to start incorporating real-time analytics of traffic patterns in places like Montreal around the St. Lawrence River and the Danube in Vienna. He compared the commuter behaviors of Sao Paulo to Kiev. He spent an entire week translating municipal data from Indonesia specifically in and near the floating markets of the Martapura Rivers. Traffic congestion in a river—that had to mean huge body counts.

Every variable Jon could think of, he put in the spreadsheet, tabulated the contingencies, followed the vectors, compared numbers, created pivot charts, and narrowed in on the finer details of local conditionals, such as the swimming habits of individuals native to tropical rivers to those of northern rivers. The size and flow rate around area dams. And, of course, ice floes. The entire field of research. Freezing patterns, lack of patterns. How pollution affects water temperature and rates of crystallization. He looked at vegetation and invasive species, which kind of underwater bramble could snag a body; hell, could trap a semi. There was a weekend where Jon looked at the erosion pattern of river valleys only in regions of mid-plate tectonic activity. Fascinating stuff. It all went in the spreadsheet.

His work began to suffer. Valerie became concerned. But this was just a phase, Jon reassured her and himself. Once he got his ankle and knee healed up, things would settle down. He'd be less into the flow pattern of glacial streams and whether this had any notable impact on the death rates of pre-Old Covenant people of Iceland (not much, it turned out, but Jon had to rely on Sagas that were not historically reliable).

Eventually, Jon's boss had a talk with him, and Jon understood very well that a leave of absence was probably a good idea. This just gave him more time to focus on his project because one thing was damn certain:

There was something going on here. The rate of death in and around Marshall Bridge was a few points higher than any other comparable city and river throughout the world. And this wasn't just calculating means and medians. He ran full correlational and regression analyses of every relevant variable and relationship within the spreadsheet and then ran further analyses of the relationships within his results. The coefficients were strong. Jon chi-squared the fuck out of his research.

So he began to make contact. He made the necessary phone calls, sent the necessary emails, cornered the necessary individuals at the Hennepin County Government Center, but no one would hear him out—despite his easy-to-understand visual aids. Even the forensic investigator Jon kept on the phone for nearly 11 minutes—a woman who was open to a few of his theories, including Satanic ritual and mystical elements—soon gently let him go and told him her personal cell phone was something he should never call again, but he could certainly leave a message at her office. Which Jon had done already, numerous times, but she seemed to miss that little detail.

Jon didn't take the dismissiveness and condescension by the "professionals" to heart. Rather, he used it as evidence for a new tab he started to populate on his spreadsheet, entitled:

The Old Man River Cover-Up.

* * *

Jon and Valerie had their first big fight in years. It was similar to their last big fight in nature—Jon's not there (psychologically), Jon's distant (emotionally), Jon doesn't talk when spoken to (vocally)—but this had nothing to do with any of his prior addictions and had everything to do with "all this murder talk."

The fight took place just before dawn when Valerie rolled over in bed and saw Jon was still on his computer responding to questions he'd been fielding from the social media group he started. Jon managed to keep his voice at a respectable level throughout their argument, but the moment Valerie suggested that his river killer theory might be a little far-fetched, Jon leapt from the bed and whispered, "I'm going for a run."

Jon hadn't run for weeks due to injury. He tried everything, but he could barely put his full weight on his left leg. Jon didn't care how slow he went or how gimped-up he trod. He was where he needed to be, in nature, along the lower trails, where the Mississippi waters lapped and the morning birds cooed.

It was true spring, now. The snow and ice were gone and he could feel the vernal equinox. The very idea of it. The air. The musk. The tilt of the Earth, the angle of the sun, and the faint sewage smell from the drainage channels leaking brown rivulets into the Mississippi.

Shit meant spring to Jon. It meant muddy trails and running through the nooks and crannies of the river shore very few but the drifters saw. The mud was black, the trees were budding, and Jon was doing everything he could to elevate himself beyond his knee and ankle pain. He winced. He yelped. More than once, he warbled a little like a dying bird.

Things were tearing. This was a fact. Very little healing had happened over the previous months and he began to wonder if scampering over stone and root was taking away whatever gains he'd made. This made him run all the faster. As he labored up and down the switchbacks, each lunge popped something. Each footfall enraged the mess in his ankle. Each swing of his leg gnashed at his knee.

But the pain became his partner. It brought him further up the river than he had been in a long time, five river miles from his house and on a trail to the old train bridge, but there he had to stop. Yellow tape stretched across the bridge and it was manned by a young cop—*Officer Carlson*, her nameplate said. She was clearly tired. Up all night dealing with whatever tragedy happened on the bridge. Jon was not tired, coming down from the adrenaline rush of running himself crippled. This made him bolder than usual. He didn't linger politely or pretend at indecisiveness. He dove right in.

"Was it a murder?" Jon said.

"Excuse me?"

"A murder. Was someone murdered on the bridge?"

"It's under investigation," Officer Carlson said.

"Or suicide?" Jon was trying to sound professional, like an investigative reporter who'd been researching these incidences for months—which he pretty much was.

Officer Carlson looked at him, had no words for a moment. "It's under investigation. Now, if you don't mind, please find another route." She gestured toward the way Jon came.

"There's a serial killer out here, you know. Been out here a long time. Likely, years," Jon found himself saying, leaning into some of the highlights from his spreadsheet. "I have the research. I've made the phone calls."

"What are you saying?" Officer Carlson asked. She widened her stance a little.

Jon mentioned everything he could remember off-hand. He felt the logical arguments flow through his head. The Old Covenant People of Iceland, the floating markets of Indonesia, the water hazard rate of Anoka, Minnesota. "Coefficients," he said, more than once, as if that was a magic word that tied it all together. She did not react how he expected. She seemed confused and possibly a little angry.

"Excuse me?"

"A dark force in the river," Jon said, concluding his case. "Killing people. The suicides aren't really suicides and the accidents only look like accidents."

"A dark force," she repeated. Then she radioed one of her colleagues and eyed Jon.

"Maybe I should talk to a detective or one of the higher-ups?" Jon suggested, a little irritated because why should he be doing her job for her?

A couple other cops exited their squad car parked across the pedestrian path and began approaching Jon and Officer Carlson.

"If I could only show you, or someone, my spreadsheet," Jon said. He searched for his phone. Nonexistent, of course. He had no pockets and was nearly naked in his short shorts.

"Sir, can you just wait here a minute?" and she crouched beneath the yellow tape and started walking toward her colleagues, shaking her head, making all the signs that she was in on it.

Jon had said far too much. He took off like he was being chased. Before long, he was tearing down the trail back the way he came, racing for the lower wooded trails, enduring the pain. So much pain. He let it consume him as the trees became a blur, and he struggled to breathe as his pace quickened regardless, the river itself sweeping him home.


Jon lost his job and Valerie left him. They didn't get a divorce, but Valerie insisted Jon live somewhere else until he dropped his "conspiracy theories." This, despite the proof upon his spreadsheet, now with accompanying multimedia clips of news conferences where the Governor spoke about "water quality of the Mississippi River Valley" and other coded messages. All of which Jon posted to his social media groups to the tune of many likes and much online chatter.

One of the positives now that he was not allowed to live in his house was that he could sublet a room just off Marshall Bridge. A perfect location for his daily patrols. Easy access to the lower trails where a municipal building of some suspicion rose along the shore and the entry point for ground zero of this Bermuda Triangle of the North.

Jon's patrols were not without difficulty. His injuries had become debilitating. Swelling turned to discoloration. Pain that used to come and go became ever-present. Jon's dreams of a swift recovery became the grim resignation that he would likely never walk properly again, let alone run. But the constant pain was something he was willing to bear for the good of the public, especially since he could never go to a doctor. Not now. Not when he was on the verge of breaking this thing wide open.

It was also the season of increasing incidents—the unreported kind. Jon's trend lines predicted a peak year. The timelines concurred, which meant a number of plausible outcomes. He knew winter was a high point and the killer (or killers) used the river ice as some kind of cover. Incidents spiked after a wet summer, which this last summer was. The killings also operated on a decade-long cycle according to the data that now stretched back 200 years to the time Fort Snelling was built as a frontier post for the unorganized territory of the Louisiana Purchase, which sat just a few miles south from Marshall Bridge.

Indeed, the conspiracy went back that far, which invited a number of possibilities such as a curse to the land or a yet-to-be discovered creature that held out since the prehistoric eras. Jon was learning Dakota to understand direct translations of native history that suggested such things, but so far he was months, if not years, from fluency.

Still, Jon kept the serial killer idea within the realm of possibility so long as it involved a touch of the mystical. His working theory was the spirit of some ancient killer (man or beast) that possessed the heart and mind of one of the locals to carry out what was clearly retribution for some trespass in ancient history. Jon knew there had to be a religious angle, just not any of the popular ones because one thing was clear: Old Man River was far more devious than evil incarnate.

These were all things Jon had to keep in mind as he hiked through the snow. He couldn't cover as much ground as he could back when he could run—not with his quad-cane—but Jon made up for it by optimizing his route, focusing on the hot zones under the Marshall overpass and sandstone ravine two klicks south.

The main thing was checking the ice floes. Those were his tea leaves. The river's hieroglyphs written in frozen script and erased from the day's sun.

He walked about twenty paces onto the river ice, but he was safe. He knew this. He could read the ice like a book. A shearwall marked where the shorefast ice had broken off at a freeze-up and continued downstream. Jon didn't go out further than that, beyond which the shore ice gave way to frazil and then frazil pans that were drifting downstream.

Still dangerous, but only for amateurs. Jon crept out further, reaching his cane out and testing each place he was about to walk until he made it to the ice ridge where he could stare directly into the murk. Here was Old Man River, an almost peaceful black with flecks of crystal that shone ghostly colors across the snow when they caught the rare light of sun. This was Jon's language now: black, gray, white, with brief explosions of ethereal color.

That's when a familiar voice called out from shore.

"Hey, Asshole! Get off the ice!"

Jon pulled his gaze from the water and saw the man with the hockey stick.

"It's fine," Jon said and he tamped his cane down a few times to prove how solid the ice was.

As if the man didn't hear, he said again, "Get off the ice."

The wind picked up, sweeping down from the northern bends of the river and howled under the Marshall Bridge.

Jon shook his head. "It's fine. I've been studying it for over a year. It's not just the ice," Jon said, as if that explained everything—every death that he tabulated, every data point, his theories and various hypotheticals coalescing like little frozen spears tumbling together on a river's surface before being dragged under.

The man didn't reply, so Jon said again. "It's not just the ice." He pounded his cane all around him. "See? It's fine," so long as you understood it.

The man stood silent upon the shore.

"Get. Off. The. Ice!" he shouted, almost desperate.

Jon stood defiant. The wind blew. The bridge howled. The water sounded like spring.

Clearly misunderstanding one another, Jon started toward shore to reason with this poor, insane fellow. He hobbled on his injured legs, minding the rough footing. He tested each step with his cane. He was careful. Precise. This was his spreadsheet now. All the data he needed. Foot falls like plot points. Plot points like suncups.

The ice cracked like midnight thunder and Jon went down. It happened so quickly, he lost his cane to the current. He managed two flailing strokes which was just enough to get him to the ice's edge, but the current had him by the waist and his grip was mittened. Loose and inadequate for the river's pull.

Lighted by the streetlights and darkened by winter's dawn, the man watched him. They were near enough to one another to speak without shouting.

"Help me," Jon said, but the man did not respond. He did not move.

Jon kicked his legs, but his injuries limited his range of motion and his winter patrol gear quickly began to weigh him down. He was only feet from shore, but above them rose a sheer sandstone bluff, which meant the same bluff stretched below the water. There was no touching bottom.

"Help," Jon said again.

The man just shook his head. "I can't," he said. "I'll go under, too."

Jon reached for purchase, found only ice as the cold shock dulled his limbs to numbness. His feeble, yet frantic, duck paddling soon ceased as well.

"Please," Jon said.

The man stood immobile. Jon wanted him to try something. A drastic measure maybe. A desperate lunge with the hockey stick. A cry for help up the embankment. An apology. Anything. Instead, Jon got his gaze, a shadowy witness, which was the same as nothing, Old Man River sharing his secret.

# CONTRIBUTORS' BIOGRAPHIES

***Editors' Note:*** *Where available, Twitter handles have been provided for each of our contributors so you can follow and engage with them on social media. Don't be weird about it.*

## EDITORS

ALBERT TUCHER (Contributing Editor; @AlbertTucher) is the creator of prostitute Diana Andrews, who has appeared in more than 100 hardboiled stories in venues including *The Best American Mystery Stories 2010*. Her first longer case, the novella *The Same Mistake Twice*, was published in 2013. In 2017 Albert Tucher launched a second series set on the Big Island of Hawaii, in which *Blood Like Rain* is the latest entry. He lives in New Jersey and loves NJ Turnpike jokes.

ROGER NOKES (Editor-in-Chief; @McCaffery_write) writes fiction under the pseudonym Stanton McCaffrey. His short stories have been featured in *Guilty, Mystery Tribune, Vautrin, Shotgun Honey, Yellow Mama, Out of the Gutter, Between Worlds*, and *Heater*. He has published two novels: *Into The Ocean*, and *Neighborhood of Dead Ends*. He works in communications with a UN agency.

JAY BUTKOWSKI (Managing Editor; @jtbutkowski) is a writer of crime fiction and an eater of tacos who lives in New Jersey. His short stories have appeared in various online and print publications, including *Shotgun Honey, Yellow Mama, All Due Respect* and *Vautrin*. He is the Managing Editor and one of the co-founders of **Rock and a Hard Place Press**, an independent publisher of noir chronicling "bad decisions and desperate people" in short and longer format fiction, as well as in the flagship ***Rock and a Hard Place Magazine***. He's also a father of twins, a doting fiancé, and a middling pancake chef.

LIBBY CUDMORE (Associate Editor; @LibbyCudmore) is the author of hipster mystery *The Big Rewind* (William Morrow, 2016) and "The Wade Agency" series in *Ellery Queen Mystery Magazine.* Her work has been published in *Tough, The Big Click, Hardboiled* and others, as well as the anthologies *Hanzai Japan, Welcome Home, Mixed Up* and *A Beast Without A Name: Stories Inspired By The Music of Steely Dan.* She is the hostess of the weekly #RecordSaturday live-tweet event on her Twitter account and the co-host of two podcasts, *The OST Party,* focusing on movie soundtracks and *The Shattered Shield,* where she discusses the FX cop drama *The Shield.*

PAUL J. GARTH (Associate Editor; @PauljGarth) is an editor for **Rock and a Hard Place Press**. His short fiction has been published in *Thuglit, Tough, Needle: A Magazine of Noir, Plots with Guns, Crime Factory,* **Rock and a Hard Place Magazine**, and several other anthologies and web magazines. He lives and writes in Nebraska, where he lives with his family.

R.D. SULLIVAN (Associate Editor; @_TheRussian) is a writer of fiction, comedy, and letters to the editor. She lives in Northern California with her family and three solidly mediocre dogs, where she runs, in no particular order, a corporate office, a winery, a subcontracting business, and herself ragged. Her own writing has been featured at *Fireside Fiction Magazine, Shotgun Honey,* and *Tough,* as well as in the *Killing Malmon* and *Murder-A-Go-Go's* anthologies. You can track her down over at govneh.com.

## CONTRIBUTING WRITERS
### (In order of appearance of work)

Bronx-born and raised, JASON ALLISON (@jasontallison) spent twenty years with the New York City Police Department; twelve as a detective, four as part of a Federal task force. Since retiring in 2018, he has presented to members of the Mystery Writers of America and attendees of Thrillerfest. His short story "Anosmia" was shortlisted for the 2020 Al Blanchard Award.

RUSTY BARNES (@rustybarnes23) is a writer, poet, and editor living in Revere MA but hailing from the foothills of the Appalachian Mountains. He's published 14 books including his latest, a collection of linked stories titled *Kraj the Enforcer.*

JIM GUIGLI began writing after retirement when he entered and won the 2006 Bulwer-Lytton Fiction Contest. That one sentence began an ongoing series of stories about a private detective, Bart Lasiter. Jim lives near Sacramento, California with his wife and two Labrador Retrievers.

ESTELLE PHILLIPS (@legalimportant) is a U.K. writer and poet whose work is published in magazines and newspapers, and performed at theatres and festivals.

JAMES McCRONE (@jamesmccrone4) is the author of the Imogen Trager novels—*Faithless Elector, Dark Network,* and the new *Emergency Powers*—"taut" and "gripping" political thrillers about a stolen presidency. His story "Numbers Don't Lie" also recently appeared in the 2020 short-story anthology *Low Down Dirty Vote, vol. 2.* James has an MFA from the University of Washington. A Pacific Northwest native, he lives in South Philadelphia with his wife and three children. He's a member of MWA, Int'l Assoc. of Crime Writers, Int'l Thriller Writers, Phila. Dramatists Center and the Sisters in Crime. You can learn more at http://jamesmccrone.com/

NILS GILBERTSON (@NilsGilbertson) is a crime and mystery fiction writer and practicing attorney. A San Francisco Bay Area native, Nils currently lives in Washington, D.C. with his wife. His short stories have appeared in *Mystery Weekly Magazine,* **Rock and a Hard Place**, *Thriller Magazine, Pulp Modern,* and others.

BOBBY MATHEWS (@bamawriter) is a Derringer-nominated short story writer and journalist based in Birmingham, Alabama. His checkered past includes stints as a reporter, editor, PR flack, bartender, paralegal, and investigator. This is his first story in **Rock and a Hard Place**.

For the last 15+ years, ALI SEAY (@AliSeay11) has written professionally under a pen name. Now she's shaken off her disguise to write as herself in the genre she loves the most. Ali lives in Baltimore with her family. Her greatest desire is to own a vintage Airstream and hit the road. Her novella *Go Down Hard* was released in 2020 by Grindhouse Press. For more information visit aliseay.com or find her on Instagram @introvert_fitness

DANIEL VLASATY (@DanielVlasaty) lives outside of Chicago with his wife and daughter. He is the author of *Stay Ugly*, *A New and Different Kind of Pain*, *Only Bones*, *Amphetamine Psychosis*, and *The Church of TV as God*.

J. ROHR (@JackBlankHSH) is a Chicago native with a taste for history and wandering the city at odd hours. In order to deal with the more corrosive aspects of everyday life he runs the site www.honestyisnotcontagious.com and makes music in the band Beerfinger.

ROB D. SMITH (@RobSmith3) is a common man attempting to write uncommon fiction in Louisville, KY. His work has appeared in *Apex Magazine*, *Shotgun Honey*, *Thriller Magazine*, and other publications. He co-hosts *The Abysmal Brutes* podcast that explores pop culture storytelling at https://theabysmalbrutes.podbean.com/.

JAMES LILLEY (@jameslilley1411), 34, Father of three. Works as a Casino & Arcade Engineer, is a retired professional boxer and active MMA and Bareknuckle fighter. Has had works published in various publications since he started submitting in August 2020. Was named *Versification*'s Punk of the Year 2020 and secured a deal for his poetry collection *The Blue Hour*, which was published in November 2021.

CHRIS HARDING THORNTON (@chrishardingth1), a seventh-generation Nebraskan, holds an MFA from the University of Washington and a PhD from the University of Nebraska, where she has taught literature and writing. She has worked as a quality assurance overseer at a condom factory, a jar-lid screwer at a plastics plant, a closer at Burger King, a record store clerk, an all-ages club manager, and a PR writer. *Pickard County Atlas* is her first novel.

GREGORY WOLOS's (@GregoryWolos) work has been published in over one hundred journals and anthologies, such as *Glimmer Train, Georgia Review, descant, Florida Review, Michigan Quarterly Review, The Pinch, Southern Humanities Review, Nashville Review, Baltimore Review, Los Angeles Review, PANK,* and *Tahoma Literary Review.* His stories have earned numerous Pushcart Prize nominations and have won awards sponsored by *descant, Solstice,* the Rubery Book Awards, *Gulf Stream, New South, Emrys Journal,* and *Gambling the Aisle.* Gregory's full-length collections include *Women of Consequence* (Regal House Publishing, 2019), *Dear Everyone* (Duck Lake Books, 2020), and *The Thing About Men* (forthcoming, Cervena Barva Press). His debut novel, *Kika Kong vs. the Dead White Males,* will be published by Adelaide Books in 2022. For full lists of his publications and commendations, visit www.gregorywolos.com. Most of Gregory's stories reflect Kafka's assertion that a literary work "should be an ice ax to break up the frozen sea inside us."

CHRISTOPHER WITTY is a former used bookshop owner who devotes his time to family and writing. Since achieving an MA with distinction in Creative Writing at Manchester Metropolitan University, he takes on occasional proofreading and editing work whilst selling books online to make ends meet. Fearful/angry/disillusioned (delete as applicable) of social media, talentless pop stars and governmental control, he escapes into books, comics and magazines as often as possible, often finding clarity in the words of Kurt Vonnegut, Cormac McCarthy and Bill Hicks. His stories have been published or will be appearing in Northodox Press and *Confingo.*

MIKE ZIMMERMAN (@zimwrites) has been a writer for 30 years, nonfiction and fiction, averaging about a book a year, most recently the crime novel *A Mosquito Over Sunset.* You can find him at www.zimwrites.com.

MARK RAPACZ's (@MarkRapacz) stories have appeared in a number of publications, including *Plots with Guns, Thuglit, Martian Lit, Tough, Water-Stone Review, East Bay Review,* the *Hawaii Review* and *The Best American Nonrequired Reading*. He has a few crime novels out there from some small presses, but those are likely difficult to track down. He lives in Minneapolis with his wife and two boys.

## CONTRIBUTING VISUAL ARTISTS
### (In order of appearance of work)

RICHIE NARVAEZ (@richie_narvaez) is the award-winning author of
*Roachkiller & Other Stories, Hipster Death Rattle, Holly Hernandez
and the Death of Disco,* and *Noiryorican.* He lives in the Bronx.

REGAN McGRORY is a second-year MFA candidate in Socially
Engaged Studio Art at Moore College of Art and Design in
Philadelphia.

ALFRED KENNEALLY is an amateur photographer residing in
Hampshire England. Check out his portfolio at
https://www.alfredphoto.org.

*Additional photos used through Creative Commons licensing from
Unsplash.com. Please support these talented creators:*

| | |
|---|---|
| René Böhmer | @qrenep on IG |
| Ian Usher | @iusher on Twitter |
| Christopher Ott | @notsogoodchris on Twitter |
| Vasily Ledovsky | @vledov on Twitter |